CLAIMED BY FLAMES

CLAIMED BY FLAMES
BOOK 1

LAUREN CROWNE

ENID BOOKS

He was in love with fire; she was destined to burn.

1

LILLY

You know those nights when nothing goes your way? This was one of those nights.

Who was I kidding? This was one of those *years*.

Given my luck, I certainly wasn't surprised when the guest I was currently trying to scam—no, not scam. The women who had trained me at the club had reminded me multiple times that I was simply *talking* to guests, not scamming them—didn't seem to be willing to budge from where he'd parked himself by the bar all night.

Red lights illuminated row after row of liquor bottles behind the aging, wrinkly, yet hopefully rich Mr. Anderson—my target of the evening—casting a soft glow over us both as well as the bartenders who darted back and forth behind him on this busy night. Mr. Anderson was like many of the guests who frequented the Red Rose: he was a demon, still had most of his gray hair—*most*, but not all— and had to be at least twenty years older than me and every other girl working that night. His black wings were thin from age, almost transparent between the edges, and they hung down loosely against his dark suit jacket. A long black tail draped limply behind him, and I had to smile and pretend to not notice how its tip constantly kept trying to slither around my ankles.

Whatever. I didn't need Mr. Anderson to be good-looking. I just needed him to have money to spend. As the only hostess at the Red Rose who wasn't a demon, my job was to encourage the wealthy demon men who came here to buy more drinks and spend some time with me. The guest got to experience a few hours of conversation and attention; I got a great tip at the end of it. Hopefully.

Sure, there were other girls working each night—demon girls with their pretty, dainty wings and easy smiles—but they didn't hold the allure to these men that I had, that of a poor, pitiful, helpless, innocent human.

Well, mostly human.

Half human.

Not that I was going to tell any of them that.

If I did my job well each night, I would end up with a nice tip for my time. If I'd been allowed to keep most of the money I made, I could have quit this place a long time ago, but unfortunately that was not how my life had turned out.

I'd already had a sneak peek at Mr. Anderson's wallet when he paid the bartender for our drinks, and if my quick glimpse was any indication, I might be able to call it quits for the night if he tipped me well enough.

I was so close to paying off my debt. A few more weeks, a few more rich demons like Mr. Anderson, and by my calculations, I would soon be free of this club, these heels, this too-small uniform dress that barely covered anything at all, the whole damn thing.

And free of Jae.

From behind the bar, Gwen caught my eye and held up two shot glasses in my direction. "Here you go, Lilly," she said, smiling behind bright pink lips that matched her equally bright pink hair. One red glass, one green, both filled with a clear liquid. She was my favorite bartender for a reason.

"Still avoiding Mr. Handsome?" Gwen whispered as I leaned over the bar to take them. Her eyes flicked to a table in the corner, and then she went back to making drinks, not needing an answer. I didn't have to look to know who she meant.

Mr. Handsome?

No. More like Mr. Hot as Fuck.

For the past month, a dark-haired demon had been a regular guest at the club, and as usual, he sat at the corner table by himself. He was probably in his late twenties with messy black hair that somehow still seemed effortlessly perfect, broad shoulders, and thick, leathery black wings and tail. Unlike his tousled hair, this demon's clothes were tailored to perfection. Without question, they were designer and of the latest style, fitting him as if they were made for him and him alone. Like all demons, Mr. Handsome's eyes were silver, and his shone like bright ice crystals even in the dim lighting of the club. More than once those eyes made me shiver when one of the overhead lights happened to reflect off his eyes just right.

By all objective standards, Mr. Handsome was gorgeous, hence the nickname, and it seemed like he knew it, an air of confidence surrounding him at all times as he sipped his drink and enjoyed how every single girl in the club came by to talk to him. From the way he constantly bought rounds of drinks for the other guests, he had to be rich as hell, a noble if the gossip was to be believed, and he definitely made no effort to hide his wealth.

Turning around to hand a shot glass to my guest, I glanced over Mr. Handsome's way to see him leaning back with one arm thrown over the chair next to him, his other hand on his drink. I would have loved to saunter over to his table and see if I could convince him to spend some money on me, but I already knew there was no point in even trying when he was constantly surrounded by girls all the time. I could hear them when I had to go by his table, complimenting his clothes, subtly and not so subtly flirting with giggles and stomach-churning bats of their eyelashes.

He caught me looking at him and I flinched, quickly turning back to my guest.

To old Mr. Anderson with the droopy wings and gray hair.

No. Mr. Anderson with the fat wallet.

I handed him the green shot glass with a smile. "To tonight."

"To tonight," he repeated, both of us holding up our drinks. "And to many more nights, I hope."

We clinked glasses and downed our drinks before sending them back to Gwen, and Mr. Anderson was none the wiser that I'd only had water.

"It's so crowded here," I said, leaning close to the old demon as if he couldn't have heard me from where I was before. Maybe he couldn't. I had no idea how old the guy was.

Catching his arm, I pretended to fall against him, pressing my body against his arm just enough that he'd think I was tipsy. Staring up at him, eyes wide, lips parted, pulling out all the tricks that usually worked on horny old demons like him, I gestured to the comfortable booths that lined the back wall, with their plush velvet seats and romantic lighting. "We could get to know each other better over there."

I only needed a couple more minutes, that was all, a couple more minutes to convince him to spend some time alone with me. I only needed him to say the word that he wanted a table with me. Tables meant alone time, and alone time meant money. Yet for the past thirty minutes, I'd been drinking shots of water and hoping this rich asshole would follow me to a table.

With no luck so far.

Go figure.

But now, with me pressed close against him, I could see it in his silver eyes, in the way the old demon couldn't focus on my face and how his eyes kept trailing down my neck to my chest. Maybe he was finally drunk enough to take me up on my offer. Maybe my time with him hadn't been in vain. Maybe I might be able to actually make some money off this guy, and maybe—

A hand slapped the bar top next to us. I flinched, as did my guest, the noise breaking the spell of the moment. I turned my head to see what jerk had decided to interrupt me just when I was about to close the deal.

Oh.

Him.

Mr. Handsome.

Of course.

Did he want to talk to me? No, why would he? That didn't make any sense.

"Gwen!" he shouted.

Then Mr. Handsome snapped his fingers. *Snapped. His. Freaking. Fingers.* I was used to demons treating me like their dog, but for a guest to treat Gwen, a fellow demon even if she was a bartender, like that? Here? At this club? No.

"She's busy at the moment, as you can see," I said to the newly named Mr. Annoying, my voice dripping with mock sweetness.

As if he hadn't seen me standing there, the black-haired demon turned to face both me and the old demon beside me. After taking a second to glance at him, then at me again, Mr. Annoying suddenly smiled and shook his head. "Oh! Sorry to interrupt! It's so crowded here tonight, you know? Maybe if I just... Excuse me, let me just..."

And then the jerk proceeded to try to squeeze between me and Mr. Anderson, forcing his way closer to the bar but at the same time putting distance between me and my money. I mean my *guest*.

While I started imagining every curse word I could think of but would never say to his face, Mr. Anderson maneuvered around him and put his hand on my waist protectively. "Maybe you're right and we should go someplace where we can be alone."

Jackpot!

I gave him the sultriest smile I could muster. "I completely agree. Let me lead the way."

On second thought, maybe I should be thanking Mr. Handsome instead of cursing him.

I turned around to head toward the table, but Mr. Handsome, or Annoying or whatever he was, somehow managed to position himself right in front of me, blocking the two of us.

"It doesn't normally take me this long to get a drink here. Think you could help me out?"

It took every ounce of everything I'd learned in the year I'd worked at the Red Rose to keep my face from expressing what I thought about his question.

"I apologize, but I'm busy at the moment," I said through clenched teeth. "I'm sure one of the bartenders would be happy to assist you. Now if you'll excuse me—"

"Yeah, but I already tried that."

I was about to tell him exactly what he should do with his drink and where he should shove it when I heard a loud crash over the music of the club. The interruption was probably a good thing because if I'd had to talk to Mr. Annoying for one more second, I wouldn't have been able to promise that my responses would be very polite.

Mr. Anderson had already dropped his hand from my waist, and then I saw the issue. A crowd of demons had gathered, their black wings blocking my view, but from the noise it was obvious that someone was fighting.

"Fucking perfect," I groaned as I rushed over, threading carefully around the tables and hoping to get there before someone broke something or someone.

Mr. Anderson and my eventual tips would have to wait.

"Hey!" I shouted, pushing my way through a group of demons who stood watching the spectacle. Once I cleared them, I saw what they were staring at. One demon was holding another by his neck, slamming his face into a table that threatened to break under the pressure. Lizzie, one of the girls working that night, was sitting on the floor nearby, crying. I grabbed her hand, pulling her to her feet.

"You okay?" I asked, doing a quick evaluation as she wiped away her tears and pushed back her blond hair. She seemed shaken, her wings quivering behind her, but overall physically fine.

"Lilly, I'm... He... It's my fault," she mumbled behind her tears, her fingers touching her face where I saw a slash that looked it had been made by something sharp. It didn't look too deep, but I could feel my own blood boiling at the sight of dots of blood starting to appear on her skin.

Some bastard had cut her? What the fuck?

I reached out and touched the wound, then took a deep breath to calm myself and focus. If I could focus for a second, I could...

"What are you doing?"

"You have to put pressure on it," I told her, hoping she believed that excuse, "so the bleeding stops."

"I didn't even realize it was bleeding," she said, more tears falling. "Thanks, Lilly. That feels... better."

I took my hand away, and as I'd hoped, the bleeding had stopped and the cut was barely visible. It wasn't perfectly healed, but she'd be able to hide it behind makeup now. My fingers still tingled from where I'd touched her.

"Who did this?" I asked her. "One of those guys?"

"Alec's ring," she said. "When his hand... It just... He said it was my fault, but it wasn't, and then Evan saw and... I tried to tell him it was my fault, but..."

I didn't need to hear any more.

"Go get security," I told her, and she nodded before rushing off. I didn't know an Alec or an Evan, and I didn't care. I wasn't about to let someone hurt one of my friends and get away with it. As lazy as our security team was when it came to us girls, there was no way of knowing how quickly they'd break this thing up. As Lizzie's blond hair disappeared into the crowd of black-winged demons, I realized I'd have to handle this myself.

"Hey!" I shouted at the two demons responsible, one still punching the other. "Stop it!"

Not that I really expected them to listen. As usual, no one was paying attention to me, or they simply didn't care that a human was yelling at them. All of the crowd's attention was on the large demon with black hair holding the smaller demon by the shirt and smashing in his face repeatedly.

As my mind raced to figure out what the hell to do next, the light hit the smaller demon's hand and I saw a big sparkling diamond surrounded by tiny emeralds and dots of red. So that was Alec, the demon who had hit Lizzie, cutting her face with that obnoxiously large diamond wedding ring of his.

Of course the bastard was married.

And now Alec's face was being smashed into the table by the one

Lizzie had called Evan. Alec was still conscious from what I could tell, but judging by the look in the bigger demon's eyes, I wasn't sure if Evan would stop until Alec was dead.

You know what? Good.

Wait, no, not good.

If a demon died in this club, we'd have to close, at least for a few nights. I couldn't risk letting that happen, not if I wanted to pay off this debt to Jae as fast as possible.

And I guess I didn't want a demon to die either.

I guess.

Screaming at them wasn't working, so my eyes darted around to look for another idea. We were on the side of the club where several games were set up for demons to play while they drank and watched the girls. There had to be something I could use.

I had an idea. Not a great one, but an idea nonetheless.

I snatched up a pool cue from a nearby billiard table and rushed forward, slamming it as hard as I could against the back of the larger demon. It hit him with a loud thunk, and then he paused and dropped Alec unceremoniously on the ground, his body hitting the floor.

From the sound of Alec's snorts as he tried to breathe through his bloody nose, I knew he wasn't dead at least, but my relief didn't last very long because once he was on his feet and standing next to the big guy, the whole room seemed to freeze. As if in slow motion, both demons turned their heads to stare at me, their silver eyes big and wild, their wings spreading behind them to create a terrifying curtain of black.

Shit.

Adrenaline pumping, I tried to make my voice sound as commanding as possible. "You and you," I said, pointing the stick at the two demons. "Get out of here. Don't ever come back. And the rest of you"—I swung the stick around to the crowd behind me, and everyone took a step back and out of the way—"go back to your tables. Buy the girls some drinks or you can get out too."

But no one moved. Instead, the crowd of silver-eyed demons

watched me with stunned faces. I held my position and waited out the silence, wondering if these men could hear the way my heart thrashed against my chest, threatening to jump out at any second. What were they going to do? Would they listen? Or would all these demons come after *me* now?

Blood was still pouring out of Alec's nose, dripping all over the floor. What could I, a sort-of human, possibly do if a crowd of demons—hell, if even *one* demon—suddenly decided to turn on me?

Nothing.

A human like me could do absolutely nothing. Jae had taught me that much.

But that was no excuse for not trying, so I knew I couldn't let myself shrink under their glares. All I could do was stay calm. I would be the epitome of calm energy in a black minidress and heels, threatening a roomful of demons with a pool cue.

I could handle them. Right? These demons were simply guests of the club after all, demons who spent their money on girls and booze, who came to the club to escape their boring lives. I'd spent time with many of the ones staring at me; I'd heard them whine and complain about their jobs and families, listened to their troubles, and then walked away with the money to show for it.

It was true that these demons could overpower a small human like me easily, but at the end of the day, they were men looking for attention, nothing more.

They were the pitiful ones, not me.

I was the hostess. I was in charge.

"Start moving," I ordered, "or I'm kicking all of you out too."

I held my breath, not sure if a single one of them would actually listen to my blatant lie because seriously, did they think I actually had the power to kick anyone out? Thankfully, mercifully, they seemed to buy it, and the crowd started to move, the men slowly lumbering away, back to their tables. Even the two fighters stormed away, albeit one slower and dripping blood as he staggered through the club, right into the security guard who had finally decided to show up and intercept them.

It was over.

I closed my eyes and let out a deep breath, trying to calm my heart so it didn't explode right then and there.

Shouting orders at the group of demons had felt...

Hitting that demon had felt...

Having that kind of power for once had felt...

Fantastic.

When I opened my eyes, my smile quickly faded as reality crashed around me at the sight of the floor. Broken glasses scattered around the table, a plate smashed to pieces, food and alcohol everywhere. The fabric of one chair had been ripped in a few places. Not to mention the blood on the table and floor. This was going to be a pain in the ass to clean up.

"Nice work," a voice said behind me.

I spun around, stick in hand, ready to threaten someone else, when I realized who had spoken.

Mr. Handsome.

No, Mr. Annoying.

But also Handsome.

Annoyingly Handsome.

His silver eyes flicked from the stick in my hand back up to mine.

"I was waiting on that drink," he said, leaning against the wall casually, his long tail lazily tapping the floor like nothing had just happened. He adjusted the cuffs on his white button-down shirt, rolling his sleeves up his arms. As if I weren't standing there with a six-foot-long stick in my hand. As if there weren't still blood spattered all over the table where the demon's face had been bashed against the hard wood of the tabletop.

He's a guest, I reminded myself as I seethed. It was possible he hadn't seen the fight. It was possible he didn't know what had just happened. It was possible he wasn't a total dick who was completely ignoring the fact that I'd just hit a demon with a stick and now had an entire corner of the club to clean up.

"I usually get better service here, you know."

On second thought, maybe he was a dick after all.

"Normally it's already at my table before I even have to ask, but for some reason, tonight it was delayed."

I didn't even know what to say. He was really asking about his drink? Right now? The demon didn't seem at all bothered by the mess in front of me; no, he only seemed a little irritated that I was taking so long to answer him.

"For some reason?" I blurted out. "Well... I was a little busy. In case you didn't see the fight just now."

"Didn't look like a fight."

"Then you need glasses."

"Would you like me better if I wore glasses?"

"What kind of question is that? No, I'm kind of busy. Actually, I'm—"

"I don't think I need glasses because I could see well enough to notice that ugly ring on the little guy's hand. If that one-sided beat-down started when that ring collided with the pretty girl's face, I think he probably deserved whatever he got, don't you?"

He had seen the ring too? And he knew what had happened to Lizzie. When I'd rushed over to the fight, I hadn't paid attention to where he'd gone, but he must have been right behind me to see it all unfold.

"So?" he asked.

"So?"

"So are you going to get my drink?"

My fingers gripping the stick tighter, I took another deep breath and let it out slowly. Very slowly. The adrenaline I'd felt earlier now veered sharply in the direction of frustration and annoyance. He might be the hottest demon I'd ever seen—I wasn't too proud to admit that—but maybe it had been for the best that we'd never talked this much before if he was this obnoxious.

"Go to the bar," I said behind clenched teeth. "I'm busy." I threw the stick on the ground and went over to the table to start cleaning up, hoping he would go away. Crouching down as best I could in this stupidly small dress and heels, I rolled up my sleeves and started to gather some of the larger pieces of the broken glasses.

"Isn't there someone else who could do the cleanup?"

So he was still standing behind me, watching me. Awesome.

"You're looking at her."

I hadn't even picked up the first piece of glass before he was next to me, squatting down and picking up a couple of pieces of broken plates. I had to scoot over to make room for him—he was so much bigger than me, but he moved easily, and together we were able to pick all of it up quickly.

He stood up first, dumping out the pieces he'd collected on the table, and then held out a hand to help me up.

I wasn't completely ready to give him back the title of Mr. Handsome, but after he'd helped me, I was willing to concede that he wasn't so annoying after all. This small act of kindness was certainly more than anyone else had offered to do even though the whole club had seen the fight and the ensuing chaos.

I took his hand and stood. It was surprisingly warm, engulfing my own and covering it like a heating pad.

He tilted his head toward me as if confused. "I meant for you to hand me the pieces of glass."

Oh.

Oh.

What had I been thinking?

"But this works too," he said, grinning a grin that made me want to melt into the floor from embarrassment. "I'm Max."

"Max."

"Yes."

Not Mr. Handsome or Mr. Annoying. Just... Max.

"I'm Lilly."

As he continued to hold my hand, the heat from his palm seemed to travel through my entire body, right up to my face, and my cheeks suddenly felt like they were on fire.

My hand still in his, I blinked, trying to think of what to say. I should have spent less time thinking because one of the pieces of broken glass I was holding in my other hand scraped against my palm.

"Shit," I said, wincing from the pain. Instantly I dropped his hand and put the glass pieces down on the table. When I held my palm out in front of me to examine the cut, I saw that it wasn't too bad, just a small scrape. Nothing I hadn't felt before.

"You shouldn't be helping me," I told him.

"Your hands are okay?"

"I'm fine. Really though, I got this. I'll be in trouble if a guest is hurt."

"It's not like you hit me with a pool cue."

I winced at the reminder, but he only smiled.

"You don't have to worry about me," he said. "I'm used to it."

When I looked over to see what he meant, he was holding up his hands. In all the times he'd come to the club, I'd never noticed his hands, never really been close enough to pay attention. But now that he was right here beside me, I could see them clearly.

Burns, the scars faded with the passage of time, and pink and white jagged lines, some larger than others, covered the tops of his hands and fingers, zigzagging up his wrist where they disappeared under the cuffs of his shirt. Some looked like deep cuts, while most of the burns maintained a rough texture.

"I'm not afraid of a few pieces of glass. Besides, what's a few more scars to add to my collection?" He bent down to pick up another piece of glass and put it on the table. "Looks like you have a few of your own," he said, nodding at my arm.

Instinctively, I crossed my arms, my hand running over the small scars on my arms that demons rarely noticed. The long sleeves of my uniform normally covered them well. "Who doesn't?"

"Probably a lot of people."

For a moment we stared at each other, and I wasn't sure what to say to him. I didn't want to talk about my scars or his drink or anything at all really. It was only a matter of time before word of this fight spread to my boss, and then... I didn't want to think about what happened next.

"I can do this on my own," I told him. "Really."

"I know," Max said, "but you don't have to. If it means I get my drink faster, I might as well help."

"Oh. So that's why—"

"Hey! Lilly!" I heard my name called out and turned to see Gwen running up to us. "Jae needs you. Oh shit—" Gwen stopped short, her eyes surveying the mess on the table and floor. "I didn't realize it was that bad. The bar has been crazy busy since you sent them all over there. I'm not complaining about the tips, but Jae's pissed, especially since you—"

"Gwen," I said, interrupting her, nodding toward Max.

The red-haired demon's head whipped to the side as if she was just then realizing that Max was standing there too. "Um, sorry to interrupt! I was just... um... Lilly? He asked me to get you, so..."

I glanced up at the second floor of the club, the balcony where I knew Jae would be. I had no doubt the demon was sitting up there, on that big couch where he liked to watch the floor below, all sprawled out with his whole entourage around him.

"I'll clean this up and then go talk to him," I told her.

She grimaced and shook her head. "No. I think you should go now."

There was no need to say anything else.

"Gwen can help you at the bar," I told Max as I walked past him. I think he might have said something back, but I wasn't listening. I needed to focus on what was going to happen next, what my boss was going to say to me when I got up there.

I could do this, I could totally do this, I repeated to myself as I headed for the stairs, one foot in front of the other, one step at a time. I tried to remember that feeling of cracking the stick down on that big demon earlier, hoping I could channel that same energy for this meeting.

When I got to the bottom of the stairs, I smoothed down my short dress and held my shoulders back. I'd faced down a whole crowd of demons tonight.

What was one more?

2

MAX

Her name was Lilly.

Like a pretty flower, not that I'd seen a flower outside the palace gardens in years. I'd lived in Vestia my entire life, and the air was always thick and humid, the days scorching hot, the nights bringing little relief. The heat of the demon kingdom of Vestia didn't allow for delicate plants to survive here long, that I knew. Trees, grass, flowers—none of it stood a chance here, all of them too delicate to survive, their beauty stripped away by the oppressive heat.

Yet there she was.

Lilly.

Of course I already knew her name—I'd heard other demons at the club where she worked say it many, many times—but that was the first time I'd heard Lilly say it herself. To me. The first time this mysterious human that I'd been watching for weeks, this beautiful woman who had seemed to be avoiding me, had held my hand and said her name.

And said my own.

Fuck, it had sounded nice.

The club's music seemed to fade into the background, leaving only a heavy silence as I watched Lilly's figure ascend the stairs, her silhouette outlined by the lights of the club, creating a glow around her long dark hair. It made her look ethereal and otherworldly, kind of ironic since she was the only human working at the Red Rose.

Why was someone like her working in a nightclub like this? It didn't add up. Unlike what my research had turned up about the rest of the demons working in this club, I'd been able to find almost nothing about Lilly's background. I'd researched her name, had my associates try to dig up some kind of background details, but all of it led to dead ends.

What if... A fleeting thought crossed my mind: maybe she was undercover like me. No. No way. I'd watched her long enough to know that something was different about her. But the way she held herself, the way she'd spoken earlier with a few of the disgusting demons who frequented this place... None of it added up.

There was something about her.

There were many things about her, this human who didn't seem to belong.

It was the mystery that surrounded her, like a captivating book I hadn't yet opened.

I'd have to approach her again, but not now.

Shit. What was I doing, standing there at the bottom of the staircase, my hands sweating like a teenager who'd never spoken to a girl before?

Several demons shuffled down the stairs, their wings brushing past me, and a few moments later, the two hulking security guards who were normally stationed upstairs, each with bulging weapons barely concealed under their jackets. Jae kept four additional guards in the club, but those were the two he kept closest.

From my research, I knew that Jae Balakir, twenty-nine years old, ruled Vestia's underground with an iron fist. Though he owned multiple nightclubs in downtown Vestia as a front, his real business was running a ruthless criminal empire dealing with drugs, extortion, and much, much more. Prior to the coronation of our new king, he frequently traveled to Eden to seek out corrupt human investors for his illicit enterprises. While he had never been arrested, I'd already uncovered records of his trips to Eden, not to mention numerous large cash deposits and withdrawals that didn't seem to match up to any legitimate business that I could find.

In short, Jae was dangerous.

And he was my assigned target.

Was Lilly alone up there right now with him, at the mercy of that monster?

But so what if she was? The human who had done her damnedest to avoid me each night when I came to the club, the human who would hardly look my way no matter how much I bothered her, the human I hadn't been able to dig up any information on, had been brave enough to intimidate a room full of demons, and they'd actually listened to her.

It had been so... hot.

That little human had somehow wormed her way under my skin, and my instincts screamed at me to rush up those stairs after her, but... if Jae knew I was connected somehow to her, if he already suspected he was being investigated, if I wasn't careful... I knew what the consequences could be for her.

I felt a tug on my wing. When I turned around, it was the pink-haired demon Lilly talked to each night, the bartender. Gwen Rhodes. Resident of Vestia her entire life; oldest of three siblings, two of whom had moved to the outskirts of town; owner of two bank accounts, one in the siblings' names.

"You're not thinking of flying up there, are you?" she asked, her eyes flicking to the stairs.

I shrugged, keeping my face neutral. "Just wanted to talk to her some more. She's... intriguing."

She crossed her arms over her chest, studying me. "I've worked here long enough to recognize that look in a man's eyes. Do Lilly a favor—don't make any trouble for her. More trouble is the last thing she needs."

My watch pulsed, and when I looked down at my wrist, I saw the code on the screen.

The king's code.

At this hour? Rand really had a knack for having the worst timing.

"Here, take this." Reaching into my jacket pocket, I pulled out a card and a pen. I scribbled on it and handed it to Gwen. "Give that to the girl who was hurt in the fight earlier. He's a great doctor, and he knows to send any medical bills to my address."

The bartender's eyebrows shot up in surprise as she read the card. "That's... very kind of you. Thank you."

I gave her a small nod, and my watch pulsed again.

I turned to go, but I heard Gwen's voice.

"Do you want me to give Lilly a message?" she called out after me.

I smiled back at her. "No, thanks. I'll come back tomorrow."

Outside the club, under the cover of night, I unfurled my wings and propelled myself into the air with a powerful downward thrust. Riding the updrafts high above the roads, I flew between the buildings that lined the busy streets below, the neon screens barking out loud advertisements lighting my way. On any given day, Vestia was hot on the ground, the heat from the pavement smothering the city like a thick blanket in the middle of summer, but this high up, the air was even hotter, the scorching temperature only eased by the wind rushing past me.

Apartment buildings surrounded the nightlife district. Rising up, I flew past a dozen or more tall brick tenements with rickety fire escapes zigzagging down their sides, each one looking like the whole building could crumble at any moment. A flicker of movement caught my eye, and I circled lower to see a group of demons lingering in an alley between apartments. Teenagers probably, out after curfew. On a normal night, I would have intervened or at least investigated, but right now I had an appointment to keep.

That didn't mean I couldn't scare them a little bit.

As I flew past the group, one of the demons looked up, maybe catching a glimpse of me. I pressed a button on the gauntlet I wore underneath my shirt opposite my watch, and, with an almost silent hiss, a narrow jet of flame shot from the gauntlet.

Bingo.

The fire struck a metal trash can in the alley below. In less than a second, the can exploded into flames, the demons scattering away.

The sounds and smells of the fire faded while I flew away, so I checked my hand around the cooling gauntlet. A minor burn, nothing I wasn't used to.

I'd have to come back to this area sometime soon and keep an eye on it.

Past the outer ring of the city, the skyscrapers disappeared in favor of smaller buildings, still multiple stories high but nowhere near the height of those downtown. Here I could glide easily, angling my way toward the palace, its parapets and towers silhouetted against the night sky. I flew a wide arc around the turrets to avoid being detected by the guards below. Swooping low, I alighted on top of a secluded section of battlements and folded my wings against my back before stealing across the empty tower to Rand's private chambers.

I knew exactly where Rand would be—the same place we'd been meeting for the past year since his coronation. I still had trouble believing my childhood friend was the king of all Vestia, but here we were. At an unremarkable patch of wall, I traced an intricate fiery sigil that glowed briefly before the hidden passageway opened. I slipped inside, the entrance sealing shut behind me.

The steam of his bathing room hit me immediately, a thick, humid mist rising from the perfectly clear water of the pool.

The twenty-seven-year-old king of Vestia reclined against the edge of the tub with his head on the marble behind him, a half-empty glass of wine next to him. Rand hadn't changed at all.

"A hot bath on a hot night. Sounds miserable, Your Majesty."

Rand looked over his shoulder at me as I walked across the marble floor. "Max. Took you long enough."

"I was working. For you."

"Which means you were hanging out at a club somewhere. What a life. You know I'm the king now, right? When I send you that code, you're supposed to drop everything and come to me. That's your job."

Scanning the room, I saw where servants had set up a small table with a robe, towels, and a few bottles of wine. I snagged a towel and tossed it at his face, but Rand caught it.

"Because you're obviously in the middle of an emergency right now, huh?"

Rand shot me a glare instead of answering and climbed out of the bath. After grabbing a robe, he threaded his wings through the openings in the back before tying it at his waist. Side by side, we might be mistaken for siblings, and we acted like it too. With our similar heights and black hair, we had grown up used to being confused with each other by those who didn't know us well. But our paths in life had been very different.

Rand's father was the major general for the previous king, commanding the royal Vestian armies in the war against the fae with honor. My own father had also served the king, though in a much more unofficial capacity as his royal assassin, a title no one knew even existed. Essentially, my father handled the dirty work no soldier would touch. To the outside world, my father was a simple soldier who had grown wealthy from several strategic investments. I'd inherited that wealth, but like all things, it had come at a cost.

Since the first time we met, Rand and I bonded in the way of two boys who both have demanding fathers. There were more nights we couldn't remember and inside jokes we'd never forget than I could count. It was a brief time where we were simply boys free to make our own choices, our own mistakes.

Then everything changed.

As the previous king became increasingly more unhinged and ruthless, Rand aligned himself with the crown prince and left Vestia. I stayed with my father until his death, spending my early twenties learning to be the silent shadow of the king, training relentlessly in weaponry and espionage. When the crown prince took the throne and then abruptly abdicated a little over a year ago, he supported Rand for king and suddenly we found ourselves aligned again, like two classmates coming back together for a reunion.

Except one of us was now the king and the other was his anonymous hit man.

Rand poured more wine for himself before holding out the bottle to me. "Drink with me, Max."

"I don't drink on the job," I said with mock innocence.

"Bullshit." Rand laughed. "As if that's ever stopped you. Or me for that matter. Come on, I can smell the booze on you from here. Hate to disappoint, but this wine isn't any of that sweet shit you like." He took a sip of it himself and eyed me up and down. "That suit looks good on you. I told you to trust me when it comes to your wardrobe."

"I appreciate you sending several of these over. I'm not sure why I need twenty different suits, but I'm not complaining."

"If you're going to live the life of a rich playboy, you have to look the part. You're lucky I happen to be the expert at that role."

"In other words, you're living vicariously through me?"

"Seriously? I'm the king. I have servants who leave me expensive bottles of wine. Even my servants have servants. My life is so controlled and observed by these damn servants that the only place we can actually talk in private is in my bathroom. Of course I'm living vicariously through you! I'm fucking miserable. Just one drink, Max. Please."

He shoved the bottle at me again, and this time I grabbed it and took a long swig.

"All this royal pampering must be rough, huh?" I chuckled, handing the bottle back. "Next thing I know, you'll have those same servants feeding you grapes and fanning you with big leaves."

"The thing is, I think they'd actually do it if I asked." Rand smoothed back his wet hair and shook out his wings, droplets of water falling on the stone floor behind him. He shot me a playful grin, and for a second it felt like we were both teenagers again, hiding stolen booze from our fathers, not two men in their late twenties with more responsibilities than we wanted to admit.

"You jealous?"

"Absolutely not," I insisted. "If anything, I'd prefer a little less pampering than what I have currently. Not that I'm complaining about what you pay me, but..."

"What?" Rand's eyebrow quirked up in surprise. "You better not complain because you and that damn meathead—"

"You mean Blaise?"

"Yes, of course I mean Blaise. I need his weapons and your expertise if we're ever going to get this kingdom headed in the right direction. You both have to be undercover so no one suspects you work for me. And I know it's tough, but this is what you were born for, Max. It's not like you were ever destined to lead a normal life. I mean, can you even imagine it," he said with a wave of his hand. "You? Me? Normal? No way."

"I don't know about that. I could picture you, the former king, now just a lowly commoner, working in some factory somewhere."

Rand shivered, his wings sending more water droplets onto the floor. "No, thanks. Although I'd probably look good in the uniform."

I snorted. "You're such a narcissist."

"I don't deny it. Enough chitchat. Let's get to it," Rand said. "I need updates from you. I need progress."

"You couldn't wait until a more normal hour?"

"There are no normal hours when my neck is on the line. When someone is plotting your murder, you can worry about it during whatever hours you want. Tell me you have at least some news for me and not that you've just been hanging out in a club for weeks doing nothing."

I frowned. "I've made progress with a few of the key players, but these things take time."

"Time is a luxury we don't have." Rand put down his wineglass, all traces of levity gone. "That I don't have. I've got these nobles hating everything I do, and if I give them much more time, they're going to have my head and put their own choice on the throne."

"Their own choice? And who would that be?"

"Do you want a list of names?"

My thumb touched the gauntlet underneath my sleeve. "If you give me one, you know exactly what I'll do with it."

Rand laughed. "That I do. I'd prefer to keep them alive for now, I suppose, but I'll keep you in mind. There are plenty of demon nobles who want a return to the days where they could own fae slaves and take Dust whenever they wanted. They think I'm all that stands in the way of returning Vestia to the way things used to be."

"No noble is going to get his hands dirty trying to assassinate the king."

"You are correct. They're going to pay someone else to do it for them, just like I pay you. And just like me, they'll find someone to do it whose interests closely align with their own."

"Dust dealers."

"Exactly."

Until recently, Vestian nobles were allowed to keep fae as slaves, and fae blood was drained, dehydrated, and sold in little vials under the brand name Dust. Once the pink powder was snorted, the user felt an instant high followed by a boost of energy and strength, like a shot of aphrodisiacs and endorphins all mixed together to deliver one powerful punch to the system.

Dust was outlawed when Rand took the Hellfire throne and all of the fae were freed. The former crown prince had developed a synthetic, lab-created version called Syn to be sold in Vestia, but it wasn't as popular as the original. Syn was by all accounts more potent, but purists—especially the rich demons who prided themselves on once owning the fae slaves—still sought the real thing and saw it as a status symbol that they had access to the illegal drug.

"Now is where I need you to tell me that you've made contacts with some of these Dust dealers so we can find out who is paying who. What's the status with the owner of that club you've been hanging around?"

"Jae Balakir. He keeps a tight circle. Gaining access isn't easy."

"Then work harder. What does he like? Does he have a weakness we can exploit? Figure it out and use it. This isn't just about me trying to save my own neck. You're on the line here too."

My thoughts turned to Lilly despite myself. Her connection to Jae could be valuable, but the idea of using her left a bad taste in my mouth. Still... she could be a way in.

"I've met someone on the inside... one of Jae's hostesses at the Red Rose," I admitted. "She seems like a favorite of his."

"There we go."

"She's human."

"Oh really? Fascinating. Not many of those live in Vestia these days. Leverage her access to him to find out if any nobles have made contact with her boss or his contacts. Use the girl as much as necessary."

"Lilly."

"What?"

"Her name is Lilly."

Rand tilted his head, watching me. "I see. Max," he said, his tone softer. "The relationship between the crown and your father was unique, and I'm glad we get to continue it. You've known from the beginning that your name will never appear in history books, that Vestia will never know everything your father, and now you, have done for this kingdom, the sacrifices you've made so that all of us living here can be at peace. So for that, thank you. I'm not saying thank you as the king either—I'm saying thank you as me, as Rand."

Rand was the king, and I? I was his friend, but I was also a killer. His killer.

"We both have a role to play," he said.

I tilted my glass to my lips, the wine tasting more bitter than it had moments before.

"I know," I said. "I know what this life means. I'll take care of it."

"Good." Rand finished his drink. "Don't forget what's at stake here."

A clear warning. I nodded. I knew I had a job to do.

3

LILLY

It wasn't hard to find Jae.

As the owner of the Red Rose, that arrogant demon made sure everyone knew who and where he was, always lounging on the biggest couch in the entire club so his fans could come pay homage before being whisked away by security.

The Red Rose was his flagship venue, but it wasn't his only club. Jae wasn't even thirty, but he already owned multiple clubs in Vestia. He wasn't at the Red Rose every night, but when he *was* in attendance, he had a presence that made him impossible to miss. Jae was easily over six foot tall, meticulous with his appearance with not one strand of his bleached-blond hair ever daring to move out of place. His suits were expensive, the fabrics vibrant blues and deep purples, whatever was trendy at the moment, his outfits dripping with silver chains and diamonds he wore around his neck and fingers.

All Jae had to do was stand up and go near the railing, letting his big black wings spread out wide behind him, and everyone and everything in the club would come to a screeching halt, normally followed by a loud cheer in his direction. He'd shout down that he was buying a round for everyone, and the entire club would go fucking wild.

Jae loved it.

When I was with guests, I'd occasionally see him stand up there and grin that damned grin down at all of us like he was the emperor of the universe, basking in the attention and soaking in the praise. The bastard had a wild edge that drew you in fast; his grins were captivating, drawing in men and women alike but hiding the quick, calculating mind that had led him to become one of Vestia's most powerful demons at a young age.

Tonight Jae was right where I knew he would be, with his flock of women surrounding him. Even though he could see the main floor below, Jae didn't seem to be paying much attention to anything other than the pretty eye candy on the couch with him. He had women—demons, just like him, of course—on either side, tucked under his wings, their tails tangling around his legs. I didn't recognize any of them, but that wasn't surprising. Over the past year, I'd grown used to the steady stream of women who threw themselves at him only to be replaced a day or two later by someone else.

Just like these groupies, the girls who worked at the Red Rose also seemed to appear and vanish as if they'd never existed in the first place. Yet I was still here. And we both knew why.

When I got closer to him, Jae's bodyguards allowed me to move past with a silent nod. Jae looked up when he heard my heels clicking on the floor. His deep purple suit jacket was strewn over the back of the big couch, and he'd rolled up the sleeves on his white dress shirt, revealing the numerous tattoos that snaked up his arms.

"Glad you finally decided to show up." He smirked as I walked over, not even bothering to hide the way his eyes trailed up and down my body. "I was starting to think I was going to have to fly down there and get you myself."

As if he'd made a joke, the ladies on either side giggled and curled into him even more.

Gross.

Staying on the other side of the low table in front of him, I pushed my shoulders back, keeping my posture stiff and confident to let him know I wasn't scared of him.

"I was working," I said, making sure to keep my voice calm and level even as he stared me down with his ice-cold silver eyes. "As you know."

"Always a perfect employee, aren't you, Lilly?"

I didn't respond since he knew damn well that I *was* a perfect employee, his best employee in fact. He loved showing off his only human hostess.

"But how perfect are you if you don't come when your owner calls?"

My owner. As if. Jae wasn't just a rich demon who had manipulated me into working off a ridiculous debt. A debt that would soon be paid off no matter what I had to do.

"And," he said, drawing out the word, "it seems you caused an issue in the club tonight as well."

I needed to choose my words carefully. "No, I didn't. I... I was stopping an issue actually. I—"

I hated how my voice was starting to tremble. I hated it so much.

I wasn't scared of Jae. I *wasn't*.

I forced myself to take a step toward him.

"Stop," he said, holding up a hand. Then with one finger, one finger wearing a gold ring covered in diamonds, he pointed to the ground. "Pets crawl."

"Jae, really? You seriously want me to—"

He tilted his head to the side, examining me. "Crawl."

The sounds of the ladies' giggles made my face start to heat up again. Even though I hadn't taken my eyes off Jae, I instinctively knew all of them were staring at me now, waiting to see what I would do. When I still hadn't moved, Jae took his arms out from around the ladies and leaned forward on the couch, elbows on his knees, huge wings on display.

"Everyone. Leave us."

With no hesitation, the women scattered away, their heels clacking and wings shuffling as they obeyed in an instant. Jae broke eye contact with me to nod to his bodyguards, and then, surprisingly, they left too and we really were alone.

Shit.

This was bad.

He turned his silver eyes back to me and licked his lips, the ghost of a smirk playing at the corners of his mouth. "Well? You know I don't repeat myself."

What choice did I have? Truthfully, none. Even if Jae knew what I'd done downstairs, it didn't seem like he was going to kill me, but I'd already pissed him off by not listening. I didn't need to make this any harder than it had to be.

Saying a silent prayer of thanks because I knew our floors were clean, I slowly lowered myself to my knees without a word.

Jae leaned back on the couch and spread his legs wide, a grin breaking out across his face. His tail twisted and tapped lazily against the floor.

"There we go. Come on," he said, patting his leg. "Come closer. Show me that the pet I bought can listen."

You didn't buy me. I came here willingly.

But there was no point in correcting him right then. If he was about to reprimand me for what happened downstairs, I needed to listen to him and behave just enough to hopefully earn a lesser punishment.

Placing one hand in front of the other and swallowing my pride with a gigantic gulp, I crawled across the floor to him. That didn't mean I had to grovel. If Jae wanted me to slink across the floor like a damned pet, I'd be the most confident pet he'd ever seen. There wasn't much dignity to be had when crawling, but I was not going to let him see me sweat, so I locked my eyes with his and never looked away.

"Good. Very good," he said when I finally sat back on my heels at his big black boots. "I knew you could listen."

What would he do this time? Would he yell at me? Hit me? There was no way to know.

"Do you know who the two demons were, the men you... interrupted... earlier?"

Jae's voice was rough, a deep and raspy rumble, but he softly ran his hand down the back of my head, smoothing down my hair. I stayed still, letting him, even though everything inside me told me to run away as fast as I could. Not that I would get very far with his guards posted on the stairs somewhere.

"No," I told him.

Jae stared into my eyes as he continued petting me. "One was Alec Alexandros. One of my best customers."

"Jae, let me explain. The smaller guy started it. He hit Lizzie and then—"

"Pets," he said, drawing out the word as he kept stroking my hair, "do not address their masters so informally. Especially when they've been disobedient."

Shit. I didn't at all like the way this was going. I needed to think fast.

"I was trying to protect your business," I insisted. "How would it look if your club became known for fighting?"

"My business, hmm?" No longer petting my hair, Jae leaned forward and brought his hand around to lift my chin up, his silver eyes examining my face. His wings cast a dark shadow over me. "Should I kill him then, to protect my business? Rip his wings off first and then his tail, all to protect my business? What do you think that would do for my business?"

"I... I don't know... I didn't think..."

"Exactly," he said, letting go of my chin and sitting back against the couch, his wings folding behind him. "Of course you didn't. But I can't let our guests think my girls could attack them at any moment. It's necessary to *protect my business* as you put it. Someone must be held accountable. They will demand blood, as they should. If someone should bleed, should that someone be you?"

"No," I insisted. "I didn't do anything."

"You hit a demon."

"Because one of them hit Lizzie. She was bleeding."

"So? You already took care of her, didn't you?"

He'd seen it. He'd seen that bastard hit Lizzie and didn't care. He'd sat back after it happened and watched me heal her cut. Jae was the only demon in Vestia who knew what I could do, who knew about my past, who knew... everything.

"You thought no one would see your little trick, hmm? What if someone had seen the way her face healed when you touched it? What if someone suspected what you really are? What would I do with you then, Lilly?"

"I don't know."

"Exactly. You dared to use your pathetic little ability to help some whore instead of the demon who was truly injured. If Alec realized what you'd done, what then? He would have demanded retribution, and I would have been obliged to agree. Your punishment would have been severe and violent. I know you're part human, but surely your brain can comprehend at least that much."

This bastard. I needed a different tactic before I ended up with even more scars than I already had.

"If I can't work, you won't have a human hostess in your club."

"Ah." He nodded as if I'd somehow gotten the right answer on a quiz. "There you go. We can start there. Let's begin with you telling me how grateful you are to me for everything I've done for you. For rescuing you from Eden, for allowing you to work in my club."

As if being able to advertise a human hostess wasn't bringing demons to his club in the first place.

Jae and I had played this game many, many times before, so I knew exactly the words he wanted to hear. It didn't matter that all of them were lies; I could say this speech in my sleep and not miss a word. By the gods, I was going to recite every single one of them right now if it meant avoiding whatever devious shit he had planned for me.

"Jae, I will always be grateful to you for bringing me to Vestia. I don't know what I would have done without your help."

"You would still be in Eden. Sold off to some rich buyer, I'm sure, by that family of yours."

I didn't need to be reminded, my whole body tensing at the memory. Once I was done with Jae and this debt, I was going to do whatever I wanted, go wherever I wanted, be whoever I wanted. I just had to bide my time, put up with his crazy for a little while longer, and then I'd be free.

Jae went back to petting my hair. "That's why I offered to help you escape and come here. I flew you across an ocean at great cost. Hired you. Allowed you to become my favorite pet. Keep going. And what else?"

And I hate you.

"And I am grateful that you're giving me time to pay off my debt."

"It was a huge expense to get you out of Eden. I gave you a job, found you housing, and who do you have to thank for saving you? Who are you loyal to for all he's done for you?"

Kneeling there on the floor at this monster's feet, there was only one right answer.

"You, Jae. Only you."

Jae smiled, smug and victorious. He reached over to a shelf and took out two glass vials; one vial was filled with liquid, one with powder, both cotton candy pink. I knew immediately what it was: Dust, the most potent illegal drug in all of Vestia. Jae tilted the vial with the powder back, pouring the pink contents into his mouth. Within seconds his pupils were blown wide, his breathing quickened, all telltale signs of someone who had taken Dust.

"Do you want this one?" he asked, holding up the remaining vial.

I shook my head.

"Stand up," he said. Beads of sweat were already forming on his forehead. Jae took off the lid and handed it to me. "Now pour it down my throat."

He smirked and then opened wide, waiting for me. As disgusted as I was by a drug made from the blood of fae, at least I wasn't the one taking it. I watched as the pink liquid dripped into his mouth and Jae wiped his face with the back of his hand.

Jae threw his head back against the couch and groaned. "Fuck."

At his words, his breathing increased. It was as if the pink Dust had suddenly filled his lungs, flooding him with a feeling of euphoria. His eyes glowed a brilliant silver, and a thin sheen of sweat covered his forehead. His breathing became deeper and sharper, and the effects of the drug began to take hold. I could feel the energy radiating off him.

"It was made in Eden," he said between breaths. "The user will think it really is Dust, at first, when he feels the highest high, but then..."

"Then what?"

The drug now coursed through his veins like wildfire; I could tell by the way his eyes darted around and his breathing increased. He grabbed my arm with a fierce grip, pulling me onto the couch with him.

"Then it goes to his heart," he said, his voice low. "And he dies."

My own eyes flew wide with terror and I tried to pull away, but Jae wouldn't let me. "It's poison? What the hell? Did I just give you poison?"

Jae grinned. "You sure did. You better suck it out of me quickly, Lilly."

What the fuck?

This crazy bastard wanted me to do what?

"Hurry," he said, his chest rising and falling, the grin never leaving his face. "This feels so good, but the clock is ticking..."

A thought occurred to me: what if I just... didn't? What if it really was poison and this sicko was finally the cause of his own death? There was no one but us up here on the second floor, no one to see what was happening...

But also no one to say that I wasn't the one who poisoned him. My fingerprints were on the vial. There was no one to vouch for me. I knew no one would.

So I did it.

He let go of my arms, and I grabbed at this fucking insane demon's shirt, fumbling with the buttons to get my hands closer to his skin. If the poison was going to his heart, I needed to start there. When I reached his skin, I pressed hard, forcing myself to concentrate despite this ridiculous situation. I had no idea how long it would take or if I'd even be able to do this, but I kept going, my palms applying pressure.

I was so focused on his chest that I yelped in surprise when Jae grabbed my face and slammed his lips against mine. It wasn't a kiss, not that it would have made it better if it was; this was a show of dominance meant to prove something. I tried to pull away, but his hands were like shackles, refusing to let go. His lips were urgent and unyielding, but there was no passion or warmth between us as his tongue slithered into my mouth, only the cold realization that he saw me as something to be possessed and used.

But the knowledge that he was still poisoned, still in need of my healing touch, kept me in place for a moment longer. It was a battle between my innate sense of duty to heal and the sheer revulsion I felt for the demon in front of me. I forced myself to continue despite his sloppy kiss, keeping my hands pressed to his chest, focusing on drawing the poison out of him even as I fought the bile rising in my throat.

I sure as hell wasn't going to go to jail because this asshole died.

With one final surge of effort, I felt the poison give way, its hold on him broken. His pupils began to contract, and his tight grip on me relaxed. As his breathing returned to normal, I ripped my hands away from him, backing away as if he were a venomous snake.

"Is it done?" he asked, his voice slurred, his eyes glazed with a mixture of relief and lingering pleasure from the drugs.

"It's done," I snapped.

Jae let out a breathy laugh and released me.

I wanted a shower, I wanted to go home, I wanted to be literally anywhere other than right there right then.

"That was fucking awesome." He chuckled, buttoning his shirt. "Now get your ass back out on the floor. Oh, and fix your makeup—you look like hell."

4

LILLY

I was late for work the next night.

But I felt like I deserved it after what had happened with Jae.

Slipping through the back door of the club to get ready for my shift, I heard the sound of Jae's voice.

Speak of the devil, and he shall appear.

If I could sneak around behind the stairs, I knew I could avoid him and get to the dressing room in time to change before he ever saw me. After last night, I preferred to avoid him as much as possible or else risk his wrath again.

I stopped short. There, coming down the stairs, was Jae and... Max?

What the hell?

Ducking behind the stairs so they wouldn't see me, I peeked around to see Max say something that made Jae let out a bellowing laugh as he clapped Max on the back.

So they were buddies now?

Jae guided Max over to Holly, a blond demon who possessed what I had to assume was the highest-pitched voice in the Red Rose, maybe in all of Vestia. If Holly hadn't always been so incredibly sweet and kind to me, I would have hated working with her for the noise alone. Even on a busy night, you could hear her shrieks and giggles from across the room, so it wasn't surprising that she squealed just as loudly when Jae practically pushed Max toward her.

Max flashed her a grin, said something I couldn't hear, and Holly twirled a lock of her pretty blond hair around her finger and giggled. Her wings fluttered behind her as I watched her place a hand lightly on his arm. Seriously, could she be more cliché?

Not that I didn't do the same thing with my own guests.

I was such a hypocrite.

Irritated with myself more than anyone else, I pulled the hood of my sweatshirt tighter over my head. So what if Max talked to her? If anything, I hoped Max was as wealthy as he appeared and that Holly made a lot of money from him. There would be plenty of demons in the club, and I could focus on them instead.

I'd just stepped out from behind the stairs when a hand latched onto my shoulder.

"We still need to discuss your punishment for last night," Jae whispered into my ear.

I turned around and tried to give him my most innocent look. "Um... shouldn't I go change and get on the floor?"

"You do look ridiculous in those clothes." Jae flicked back my hood and eyed me up and down. "You know I prefer you in much less."

"Right, then I'll go change and—"

His hand clamped down on my shoulder again. "No. Upstairs. Now."

As Jae guided me up the stairs, I glanced behind me. Max and Holly were still down there talking, but Max caught my eye. For the briefest of seconds, he seemed confused, probably because he didn't recognize me dressed in jeans and a sweatshirt and not my normal uniform, but then he smiled and held up a hand to wave.

Jae's grip on my shoulder grew tighter as we walked up the stairs. I couldn't think about Max right then anyway. I had to figure out what Jae was planning and how to survive it.

Once we were in the upstairs lounge, he flopped down on the couch and pointed to the floor. "Kneel."

This again?

At least this time I was wearing jeans. Wanting to make this go as fast as possible, I knelt on the floor beside him.

"Good girl. And because you're being so good"—Jae smirked down at me—"I've decided I won't punish you for last night after all."

Relieved but not wanting him to know it, I resisted the urge to touch the small scars on my arms, evidence left behind from previous punishments.

"In fact, I have a job for my pet. You have been requested by one of the regulars."

"Who?"

Not that there was any point in asking for more information. Jae would tell me exactly what he wanted me to know—no more, no less. All I could do was wait until he decided to grace me with more intel.

"A potential investor," Jae said as he twirled a strand of my hair in his hand. "He's someone who, if he isn't treated well, could end up being a pain in my ass and harmful to this business that you're so concerned about protecting, pet."

This wasn't completely out of the ordinary. I was used to being Jae's eyes and ears in the club. Demons spilled their secrets without hesitation to a pretty human hostess. Jae knew that all too well and took full advantage of the novelty of my being the only human in a demon club.

I didn't mind sharing bits and pieces of conversations I had out on the floor, but I was also very aware of the consequences for whatever special guest this might be. If he said the wrong thing in Jae's eyes, or if something in whatever deal they had didn't go Jae's way, I knew how it would all end.

"You're going to kill this guy anyway, aren't you?" I asked. "So what's the point of me talking to him?"

Jae's hand stopped, no longer stroking my hair as he glared down at me, his silver eyes cold like ice. "I forget how dumb my little pet can be. There's not a single thought in that brain of yours, is there?

Ah well. Can't be helped I suppose. Let me teach you something tonight, Lilly. Give me your hands."

I held out both hands, palm up.

Smirking at how quickly I obeyed, Jae pushed back my sleeves and cupped both my wrists with one hand, bringing them together. Then with his other hand, he reached into his pocket and took out a small device. At the sight of the weapon, my whole body went stiff and I jerked back, but Jae kept a firm grip on my wrists.

No. Not this again.

My breath caught in my throat when he pushed the button on the side and that familiar metal blade snapped into place. I didn't dare move as he brought it near my bare arms, letting the sharp side rest against my skin.

Don't panic.

But how could I not when the memories of other cuts he'd left on my arms were still fresh in my mind? I knew from experience that he would only get a sick pleasure out of seeing me struggle, so I needed to calm the fuck down, *but how*? I could feel my arms starting to tremble, and that only scared me more now that the blade was pressing into the soft underside of my arms.

"Could I take this knife and slice off pieces of the demon's wings, one by one, until he was nothing more than a pile of parts?" he asked, pressing the knife in. I felt the initial sting of a cut, but Jae still didn't let go even as a dot of blood appeared on the surface. A sick smile spread across his face. "Of course I could. I still might. But then what am I left with?"

"I don't know, Jae. I don't know. Please—"

"Here's your lesson tonight," he said, slowly dragging the knife down, opening up a small cut on my skin. "Sometimes it's better to keep a pawn alive, especially if that pawn could end up being useful later. You understand, don't you?"

I did. Too well.

With an amused laugh, Jae released my wrists and I instantly jerked away, putting pressure on the cut with my hand as he snapped the blade closed and put it back in his pocket.

"I knew you would, darling," he said, going back to stroking my hair. "This particular pawn is very, very wealthy. He's requested time with you. Keep him happy and report back to me with what you find out about him."

"Is this for free or can I keep whatever he tips me?" I asked, pulling down my sleeves to cover the cut now that it had stopped bleeding. "I think I could have my debt paid off in a few more months, depending on—"

I gasped as Jae clenched his fingers around my hair, yanking my head back. "It is always about money for you, isn't it? No loyalty at all, after all that I've done for you?"

"Jae—"

"Shut up," he snarled. "You're lucky I haven't whored you out yet, you ungrateful bitch." With a shove he released my hair, allowing my head to fall forward.

"I'm sorry," I muttered, staring at the floor, trying to catch my breath.

"I don't give a shit about your tips. This pawn, with his connections, could be a powerful business ally," Jae continued. "When we discussed him investing, he said he wanted a dance from you first. I need you to show him the possible value here. Don't disappoint me."

Now that I could breathe again, my mind was reeling. The rooms in the back of the club were reserved for private one-on-one dances, but everyone knew that nothing was off the table once the door closed, including sex if the guest was willing to pay. It was true that I'd enjoyed the privilege of never having to work private rooms before, which made me wonder why this guest was different. Reporting back to Jae on gossip I'd learned wasn't anything out of the ordinary, but being alone with a strange demon in a private room? Feeling a little bolder now that he'd put away his knife, I had to ask.

"But if I'm alone with him, what if he wants to...? Do you really want me to...?" I let the sentence trail off, searching his eyes for the answer.

Jae's eye twitched, and I had to stop myself from recoiling in shock. Jae typically maintained the epitome of control and confidence, not letting even the smallest hint of irritation break through until he erupted in anger. Jae's explosive moods were that much scarier because you didn't see them coming; most of the time he was cool and suave. Until he snapped, and then the moment could end with more than one dead demon at his feet.

I'd seen it happen before, which was why I'd become a master at reading Jae's moods over the past year. I'd paid close enough attention to know when to stay the fuck away from him or when to smile and say nothing. But if something this small, a simple eye twitch, was breaking through his facade, it meant Jae was more concerned about this demon than he was letting on.

Interesting.

Jae stared at me for a moment before leaning back on the couch. He patted his thigh, and I shuffled up from the floor and into his lap, grateful to be off my knees. With me straddling his waist, Jae's hands went to my hips, squeezing and holding me in place.

Jae grinned, a lazy grin that hung on his face like rotting meat. "Is my pet that desperate for attention? You should have said something sooner."

"That's not what I meant."

"It wasn't?" he asked, using his grip on my waist to rock me in his lap.

"No, it's just that... I don't want to do something to upset you."

"Such a considerate pet. I expect you to behave as I've taught you." He pulled me against his chest, his hold growing tighter as his fingers dug in. "Don't disappoint me," Jae whispered into my ear. "Show him a good time. A very good time, just like I know you can, but do not step outside my boundaries. Meet the manager on duty in the back and he'll take you to the room."

"Yes, sir."

At my words, his arms relaxed, allowing me sit back and put a few inches of distance between our chests. The mask was back, his features again calm and collected. When we'd first met, I thought Jae was capable of anything. I hated how right I had been.

Whatever. I'd do what he asked, keep my head down, and soon I would be gone and never have to see this bastard again.

Then Jae waved a hand in the air to indicate that he was done with me, the rings on his fingers reflecting the dancing lights of the club. Not wasting a second, I hopped off his lap, ready to get the hell away from him.

I hadn't made it five steps away before I heard Jae say my name.

Damn it. I had been so close. I stopped, took a breath, and steeled myself with a smile as I turned around.

"Yes, sir?"

"Come back here for a moment."

At least I didn't have to crawl this time. Instead, Jae stood up when I came near him, his sheer height and size making me momentarily forget my earlier bravery. How could I even pretend to feel brave when this monster, both literal and figurative, was towering over me?

Slowly, definitely deliberately, Jae's wings extended out at his sides. Once fully expanded, they were as long as he was tall, thick and dark and blocking out any light around him. As I stood in his shadow, Jae reached up to hold my chin, squeezing it between his fingers. He tilted my head one way and then the other.

I dropped my eyes to the floor to avoid his, hoping he would interpret it as a sign of submission and let me go. What I didn't expect to see was the way the tip of his tail started to sharply tap-tap-tap against the floor, a telltale sign of irritation.

"No matter what he asks you to do, you're still my pet. Do you understand?"

Until my debt is paid. Then I'm never going to see you again.

Waiting on my answer, Jae gripped my chin harder until my eyes shot up to meet his as I tried not to wince.

"I don't have any use for a pet who can't listen," he said. "Back in Eden, a half-blood like you would have been sold to someone much worse than me, and in an instant I can make that happen. You know I can."

"Yes, sir. I understand."

"And one other thing." He released my chin and took a step back, his wings furling back against him. "I'm driving you home tonight."

My heart sank. I knew full well what that meant for me, what Jae would expect from me later for the "favor" of driving me from the club to my shitty apartment.

All I could do was face it, and him, like I did everything else: head-on.

5

———

LILLY

"You okay?" Gwen slid a shot glass across the bar top to me.

I caught it, downing whatever mystery liquid was inside immediately. It wasn't water this time and it burned, but I didn't care. If anything, I was grateful.

"Yeah, I'm fine."

A hand touched my arm, and when I turned around, I saw Lizzie, the mark on her face from the other night almost unnoticeable.

"I wanted to thank you," she said, "for helping." Her black wings fluttered behind her. "You didn't have to do that."

"I did what anyone would have done. I'm just glad you're okay."

She touched her face. "Yeah, I'm actually great. I still had the doctor Max recommended look at it just to make sure I didn't need stitches."

Wait... what?

My heart skipped a beat at the mention of Max, a weird feeling striking me before I could suppress it. Max had spoken to Lizzie? He'd recommended a doctor? It must have happened after I went upstairs to talk to Jae.

Lizzie continued, her voice full of genuine appreciation. "The doctor said everything was fine, that it was like I never had a cut at all."

I forced a smile, my mind whirling. "That's great. You must heal fast."

"I guess. Or maybe you're my good luck charm."

"I don't know about that..."

"Heads up," Gwen called out to the two of us before shuffling away and busying herself at the other end of the bar.

"Lilly." I heard Jae say my name, and when I looked over, he was standing at the bottom of the stairs.

Lizzie shot me an apologetic smile, and I smiled back. We both knew the sound of that voice.

"Thank you," she whispered before disappearing into the club.

Much of the night's crowd was already around Jae. Several demons must have seen Jae come downstairs and were trying to get his attention, but he ignored them.

"Five minutes," he called over to me, nodding toward the hallway that led to the private rooms. "Get ready." Without waiting for a response, he turned and headed down the hall.

As soon as he was gone, Gwen reappeared, holding up a bottle of clear liquor.

"Do you want another one?"

"Yes. Immediately."

"What gives? What does that bastard have you doing tonight?" she asked as she refilled the shot glass.

"Some VIP has requested me for a private dance tonight."

She slammed the bottle down. "I thought he didn't let you do those since you're his favorite."

"Must be my lucky night."

"That bastard. I mean, it will probably be good money, but... are you okay with this?"

Without hesitation, I tipped the shot glass back, drinking it all in one gulp.

"I guess that answers that," she said, grimacing. "Come on, let's get you changed out of your uniform. I have some stuff in my locker you can wear."

Within a few minutes, I was back out in the club, my makeup touched up, my clothes changed, two glasses of champagne in my hands.

I was dressed the part at least. Gwen had loaned me a strappy red bralette and matching thong—only after she cursed a few times about the new cut on my arm—and I kept the outfit covered under a black silk robe.

How hard could a lap dance be really? I could do this. Of course I could do this. It was just one dance, and there were cameras in the rooms in case this guest tried anything I wasn't comfortable doing. As the only human girl working at this club, it was common for guys to seek out the fantasy of the big bad demon who wanted to boss around the poor little human, so I knew I could play into that. Demons like this guy probably wanted to feel the power that came with control, the rush from making a human feel like she was beneath him.

If that was what he wanted, I could give it to him. If I piled on the flattery, threw in a few well-placed sirs, and flashed some big doe eyes at him, after a few songs I'd end up with a nice pile of cash for my efforts. The club had a three-song limit, so all I had to do was dance around for a while, get back in Jae's good graces, and be done with it.

Champagne in hand, I had just turned down the hall to head to the private rooms when I heard footsteps following me. Glancing over my shoulder, I was surprised to see Max. There was no reason for him to be back there; in all the nights I'd seen him at the club, I'd never seen him get a private dance.

Had Holly made him change his mind? Or Lizzie? Maybe he liked blondes.

Not that I cared.

I shook my head. I had no right to feel jealous, no claim to his attention. He was just a regular at the club; I was just a hostess.

I pivoted on my heel to face him, and he stopped. "Are you lost?"

"Nope."

"Okay." I started back down the hall, but his footsteps continued to get closer. I slowed down a bit, but then he slowed down too; I sped up and so did he. What the hell? He was obviously trying to stay behind me, but why? The only things at the end of this hallway were the private rooms.

I'd had enough. "Are you following me?"

"I'm simply walking in the same direction as you."

"Then stop."

"Stop what?"

"Stop, you know, walking."

"Would you prefer that I fly?"

"I don't care what you do."

"You seem to care a lot about whether or not I'm walking behind you."

I took a breath. What he did was none of my business after all. I needed to focus on what I was about to do.

"What's the rush?" Max asked, walking faster and getting in front of me.

I had to take a step back, holding the two champagne glasses tight to keep them from spilling, when he spread out a wing and leaned one arm against the wall to stop me from going farther.

"I'm working," I told him. "What are you even doing back here? It's not like you ever get private dances."

"And how would you know that?"

"I... I just know. I work all the time. I see things."

"So you do pay attention to me."

I was just about to tell him that was completely and utterly false when I heard someone clear their throat, and when Max finally moved out of the way, there was Alister, the host who was in charge of the private rooms. Alister wasn't much taller than me, both of us at least a foot shorter than Max, and he squinted down at his tablet, the light from the device reflecting on his glasses.

"Lilly," Alister said, looking up to see me before his eyes flicked to Max. "I see you're both—"

"What room am I going to?" I interrupted.

"Mr. Ivanore, you're here too," Alister continued, bowing slightly at the waist.

I sighed. Of course Alister would defer to a guest like him over me. At least I'd get to find out which girl Max was meeting. However, instead of leading Max to his room, Alister turned to me.

"Right this way, Lilly," he said, turning to go down the hall.

I took a deep breath and stepped forward. But then Max bumped into me.

"What are you doing?" I asked him.

"Now I really am following you."

"Please don't. I'm meeting someone."

"I know."

"You do?"

"I do." He nodded, a grin spreading across his face. "You're meeting *me*."

Wait... what?

"You...? I'm...?" My brain seemed to be malfunctioning; words were no longer working. Max was the one investing with Jae? All of my assumptions about Max, for better or worse, were suddenly thrown out the window.

Alister unlocked the door and held it open. "Room three was already paid for, sir. On the house. I think you'll find it very comfortable."

Max looked as if he was deep in thought. "Three, hmm? Don't you have one that is more... private?"

As my brain tried to process what was happening, Alister didn't miss a beat, closing the door and immediately typing something else into his tablet. When Alister held up the device to show the new pricing, I fully expected Max's eyes to pop out of his head at the cost, but he didn't, instead agreeing immediately.

Other than Jae's office, room seven was the one room in the entire club without cameras. It was saved for rare occasions where the utmost privacy was required, and the price was so insane that it was hardly ever used. Since Jae had picked room three, I'd assumed he would be watching the cameras. But if we went to room seven, we'd be completely alone. If he was the type of demon who was working with Jae... I had no idea what to expect.

"Will this be acceptable, sir?" Alister asked, gesturing to the price list again.

"I'm sure it's too much," I tried to say, but neither of them were paying attention to me.

Max glanced over to me and raised an eyebrow, the light reflecting off his silver eyes, making them sparkle even more than normal. "It's fine. I expect you'll be worth it?"

I had no choice but to roll with it at that point. I plastered on a smile. "Of course."

"Then please follow Lilly. Right this way." Alister held out a hand, indicating for us to head down the hall.

To room seven.

Who *was* Max?

Just like before, I could sense Max's presence behind me as we walked down the dark hallway, only this time he was physically closer. It wasn't just that he was so much taller than me, though that was part of it. There was something different in the air, a tension that hadn't been there before, and I could feel the pounding of my heart matching each step that took us closer to room seven.

When the door clicked shut behind me, I froze, the reality of what I was about to do sinking in. I was alone in a small, dark room with a male demon I hardly knew. There were no cameras here, and I wasn't sure if anyone could even hear me out in the club over the music. Jae had said that Max had connections, which wasn't surprising since the Red Rose was one of the most exclusive clubs in Vestia, but what kind of connections were those really? Max had never given me any hint that he might be dangerous, but there was something about him that had even Jae on edge.

But when I looked at Max's face grinning back at me from where he sat on the couch, I was reminded of how he'd helped me clean up after the fight. How he'd been the only one to offer to help actually. Right then, with his foot tapping along to the music of the club, his knee bouncing in anticipation, Max seemed more excited than anything else, like an eager puppy who couldn't wait to play with a new toy.

It was... cute.

No. I shook my head to clear that thought away. It wasn't cute at all. It couldn't be cute, not when many demons had looked at me like that in this club. Max wasn't the first, and he wouldn't be the last. I wasn't there to think about how cute he was anyway.

I placed the two glasses of champagne down on the small side table.

"Are there any refreshments?" he asked.

"Other than champagne?"

"Sure."

Ah. Of course.

I instantly knew what he was really asking for. *Refreshments* was code for Dust. Max was asking if I had access to Dust.

Could I get Dust? Sure. Any girl at the club could. Did I want to get it for him though? Not at all. The mere idea of snorting a powder made from someone's blood was repulsive. It wasn't used out on the floor of the club, and since I didn't work the rooms, I never had to deal with it.

Not to mention that I had to be careful. Jae wanted to use Max as a potential business partner, but if this guy ended up being a Knight of the Flame or if he was tempted to rat me out after I got the Dust for him, I would be the one in trouble.

But I also didn't want to make him mad.

"Am I not enough for you?" I asked.

As if on cue, a new song started on the speakers, and I let the silk robe fall to the floor behind me.

All of Max's foot tapping ceased.

I could see his silver eyes trained right on me even in the darkness. Forcing myself to ignore the way my heart was fluttering in my chest, I stepped closer to him, moving to occupy the space between his legs. Why was I so nervous? It wasn't anything out of the ordinary to sit in a man's lap for a song or two. Why did this feel so different?

Standing there between his legs while he stared up at me, I had to remind myself I was in charge. Shoving my nerves down, I tried to focus on the moment. The room wasn't very large, the small table and couch serving as the only pieces of furniture, and with his big frame and wings, Max seemed to take up all the remaining space. It wasn't like I could look away; no matter where I looked, there he was, this incredibly handsome demon whose eyes trailed up and down slowly until they met my own. His mouth opened as if he was about to say something, but then he didn't, and the mere hint that I might have made a demon like Max speechless gave me enough confidence to take the next step.

I bent over at the waist, invading his space slightly to gently push on his shoulders, and Max took the cue immediately. He leaned back on the couch to give me room to climb into his lap, my knees resting on either side of his thighs.

It was an amazing thing to have this huge demon watching me so intensely, to be so close to him, to feel his powerful thighs under my own. I stayed like that for a moment before reaching behind him to touch the edges of his wings. They were so *soft*, like the most supple leather I'd ever felt, velvety and smooth and seeming to melt under my touch. I could have stayed like that for hours, rubbing the tips between my fingers and just enjoying the sensation, but then he shivered.

Oh.

I wasn't the only one enjoying the sensation it seemed.

Not bothering to hide my smile, I sat back in Max's lap. Even in the dark I could see a glimmer of surprise sparkling in his silver eyes, but that look shifted quickly as his eyes narrowed, and instead of surprise, Max's eyes were full of desire. The beat of the song had picked up, and with new adrenaline pumping through my veins, my hands gripped his shoulders and I let my body grind down against his.

He swallowed. "H-hold... on..."

"Hmm?" I continued to dance against him. It was so hard to imagine him stumbling over words that I had to tease him a little.

"W-wait. Wait a sec. What are the rules here?"

While I was getting dressed, Gwen had given me a quick rundown on what to expect, including a list of how I should answer questions like this. Ordinarily the answer was that guests were not supposed to touch the girls when we were alone like this. But Max was no ordinary guest, and there were no cameras watching us back here.

"You're thinking of investing in this club?"

He nodded. "Yes."

"If you're an owner," I said, leaning close, whispering in his ear, "you'll make the rules."

Immediately one of his hands slid up to cup the back of my neck, pulling me back to meet his gaze.

"Is that how it works here?"

My breath caught as I met his stare, his silver eyes seeming to glow in the dim light of the room. There was something different there; gone was his usual playfulness and in its place was something dark. Something angry.

Panic spiked through me, and I faltered, losing the rhythm of my movements.

Max seemed to notice my hesitation, the anger in his eyes vanishing, and he frowned. "What's wrong?"

"N-nothing," I stammered, scrambling to regain my composure. "You just surprised me. That's all."

Max's eyes narrowed, searching my face. I plastered on a sultry smile and rolled my hips to distract him, leaning in close again. "But I love surprises," I purred, hoping I sounded more confident than I felt. "Don't you?"

Max's grip on my neck tightened for a moment, then relaxed. "I do enjoy surprises," he allowed with a slow smile, apparently accepting my excuse. His hands slid down to grip my hips, guiding my movements. "You're becoming one yourself, Lilly."

My fingers trailed down his chest, popping open the top button of his shirt and then the one below it.

"Flattery will get you everywhere." I grinned.

His breath hitched as I swept my fingers down his chest, my fingernails lightly scratching at his skin.

"What exactly will it get me?" he asked. "Tell me."

Instead of answering, I stood up and spun around, and I heard him huff a complaint. I felt the same, even that quick separation made me miss the warmth of his touch.

Sitting back down, I perched myself on one of his thighs, and within seconds his hand crept around and gripped my hip, keeping me in place. Following the beat of the music, I started to grind back and forth against his leg, and I let my hand wander up over my head, my fingertips dancing along the skin of his neck until I was able to tangle them in his hair. Running my hand up the back of his head, I heard him gasp when I dug my nails in a little bit.

So he liked that too.

With new confidence, I started to roll my body back into his chest, continuing to lightly scratch against his scalp. I felt a finger slowly trail down the middle of my back. Just the tip of his finger, with the smallest hint of his nail barely touching my skin.

His finger kept moving lower, making me shiver, until it hit the clasp of my bralette. Max hooked his finger underneath it, tugging a little. "May I?"

I tried to turn around, but he held me there, the hand on my waist firm.

"Yes."

As a new song started, Max unlatched my bralette easily, and I shrugged it off and tossed it on the couch beside us. I thought he would immediately touch my breasts, but he didn't. Instead, Max trailed his finger down my bare spine again, this time at an even slower pace, drawing little circles on my skin so slowly that it felt he was setting fire to every individual nerve ending.

"Beautiful," he murmured in my ear. "Without wings, your skin is so... bare."

"Have you ever touched a human before?"

"No."

I felt a strange surge of pride at his confession. Some distant part of me knew I was supposed to be the one entertaining him and not the other way around, but I couldn't help but enjoy the feeling of his warm hand on my hip. Arching into his touch, I let my head fall back against his chest. The touch of his hands was addictive, and I wanted more, everywhere. If we kept this up, I wasn't sure I'd want to stop him.

His fingertip continued down before sliding around my belly to hold me at my waist.

"Why are you here?" he asked, his voice low in my ear.

"To dance for you. You're the one who requested me."

"That's not what I meant. Why do you work here?"

"And what about you?" I changed the subject. "Why are you back here tonight? You never get private dances. Why tonight?"

"I wasn't sure if you'd agree."

As if I'd had a choice.

"If you invest in this place, you'd be able to summon me back here anytime you wanted."

Max's hands dropped to his sides, and I instantly felt like I'd said the wrong thing again. "Is that really how he runs this place?"

"Well..." I needed to choose my words carefully. If this entire dance was to entice him to invest in this club, I certainly didn't want to be the reason he didn't. "I suppose you'll find out about all the perks once you become Jae's partner."

"What kind of perks does he offer exactly?"

I pulled back slightly, smiling and keeping my tone light. "He makes sure that important guests like you get the absolute best service."

"If that's true, why are you always avoiding me?"

"I'm not avoiding you right now," I said, letting my body rock against his chest.

"Mmm," he said, his hands rubbing against my bare stomach. "No, you're definitely not."

His lips brushed against the back of my neck, and his warm breath made me shiver in anticipation, a pulse of electricity seeming to course through my body. His mouth moved slowly across to the other side of my neck before he nipped at my skin gently.

"This okay?" he breathed more than said.

I nodded.

"I want to touch more of you," he said. "Tell me I can."

It was an easy decision. We'd long moved past me wanting him to simply enjoy the time with me. I didn't care whether he invested in the club. No, this was something else entirely. Something selfish. I wanted his touch for myself.

"You... *you* can."

I gasped when his hands slid up my bare stomach to cup my breasts. His touch was so warm, gentle yet firm, exploring every inch he could with an almost reverent touch. His head was crooked over my shoulder, watching, I knew, so I arched my back more, letting him see all of me.

"You're so beautiful," he murmured.

But then our time was over, the last song ending and the lights in the room coming on.

Of all the fucking times.

Neither of us moved from the couch at first, but then finally I stood up. I grabbed for my robe on the floor, but Max caught my wrist, pulling me back to him. We stayed like that, face-to-face, my bare chest against his unbuttoned shirt, the lights now on.

"Stay right here." His voice dropped to a husky whisper. "Just a little longer."

"Okay." I nodded.

He took my robe from my hand and looped it behind me, helping me thread my arms through it and then fastening it in the front under my chest.

"Lilly, have you ever thought of quitting here?"

Huh?

"I'm just saying maybe you should quit."

Holy shit. Had the dance been that bad? I tried to replay it in my head, but there was no way I'd misread everything that had happened. His touches, his mouth on my skin... Gods, had I been that awful? My own mortification aside, Jae was going to be pissed.

Bristling, I stood up off his lap.

"I appreciate the feedback," I said stiffly. "But I am happy with my job." I forced a smile. "It allows me to spend time with men like you, after all."

Arrogant, annoying demons like you who have no business being this attractive.

Max shrugged his suit jacket back on, his wings gliding through the expensive fabric easily. Then he took out an envelope from his pocket, placing it between the long-forgotten champagne glasses. My tip. I had no idea how much was in there, but I felt like I'd earned it at this point.

"Then tell me something," he said.

I froze. What if he asked me about Jae? What if he wanted information that I couldn't give? I braced myself, hoping he wasn't about to ask me anything that might reveal too much about what Jae did behind the scenes.

"If you could go anywhere, where would you go?"

I laughed. I couldn't help it; it just bubbled out of me. His question was so unexpected and absurd that I stared at him in disbelief. Go somewhere? The only places I went were home and work.

"I... I don't know?"

"Really? You've never thought about it? Let's say you did quit this place. Other than this fine kingdom of Vestia, of course, surely there's somewhere you'd like to see one day."

"Well, yes, that's true." I thought of the postcard I had safely stashed away in my apartment, one I'd made sure to bring with me across the ocean. "One day I'd like to see the coast. There's a port kind of far away from Vestia that I'd like to see."

"Cambria?"

"You've been?"

He nodded. "Once when I was a child. My father had business there, and I tagged along."

Max's expression changed, and I didn't want to ask why. I knew from experience that asking about a man's family wasn't always the smartest way to earn a higher tip, and we'd had such a good time together so far, I didn't want to end on a sad note. But when else would I have an opportunity like this, without cameras, without Jae's watchful eyes, to ask Max questions about himself and solve some of the mysteries surrounded him?

"Since you asked me a question, I have one for you."

"Go for it. Ask away."

"Why do you want to invest here?"

"Let's just say that I know a good opportunity when I see one." He smirked, seemingly content to keep me guessing. He went to open the door but stopped. "Can I ask one more question?"

"Sure."

"Why do you keep working here?"

"I apologize, but that's not really any of your business."

"I suppose that's true." Max kept his hand on the doorknob, but he looked over his shoulder at me, smirking. "But I was never good at minding my own business."

Max opened the door, and there, looming in the doorway as if he'd been about to burst in, was Jae. My heart dropped into my stomach at the way I could see the barely contained rage simmering behind Jae's silver eyes.

Almost immediately, Jae's expression shifted as he looked to Max, and his mouth curled into a stiff smile that didn't seem to reach his eyes.

"So how'd my girl do?"

6

LILLY

Jae snatched up the envelope of money Max had left on the table, pocketing it inside his jacket before snapping his fingers at me. As much as I wanted to say something about the tip, I knew better than to hesitate, especially with that look on his face. I rushed off the couch to Jae's side, and he draped one arm around my shoulder, extending his wing to wrap around me. Jae looked Max up and down. Max, who was still standing there watching us. Max, whose typical smile was replaced by a blank expression.

"Didn't realize you two were hiding back here. Was there a problem? If you'd like a different girl tomorrow—" Jae started to say, but Max interrupted him.

"No."

For the briefest of seconds, I saw Jae's eyes narrow as he sized up the other demon. Then he chuckled.

"Glad to hear it. Let's talk business tomorrow, okay? We're closing up, and I have to take this one home. You. Get your shit," he said to me. "We're leaving."

Max took a step forward, and I immediately turned toward Jae, placing my hands on his jacket, adjusting the lapels. It was better to distract than try to correct him, especially since I'd recognized the look in Jae's eyes instantly, the storm brewing, his anger threatening to unleash. The touch of my hands seemed to be enough to draw Jae's attention down to me.

"I need to change," I told him.

Jae dipped his head down to my ear, his voice thick and husky and not at all quiet. He was so close that I could smell the alcohol on his breath. "On second thought, get your stuff tomorrow. I need you now."

He spun us around, guiding me down the hall toward the club's back exit, but he glanced over his shoulder at Max. "This one will be back tomorrow if you're wanting more time with her. If she has the energy to work, that is."

Jae winked, and then the club door slammed shut behind us as if sealing my fate.

"Don't bother getting in the car. Wait right there," Jae said, pointing to the front of his black sedan.

I had seen Jae's black sedan parked outside the club many times, but that night, as I stepped out into the humid evening air, it seemed to exude an almost ominous aura. Sleek and powerful, it was an embodiment of Jae's personality. The polished black paint absorbed the streetlights, giving it a lustrous sheen that reflected nothing but cold luxury. Every line, every curve, was engineered to perfection, designed to both allure and intimidate. The tinted windows were like darkened mirrors, hiding secrets I couldn't begin to fathom and didn't want to. Even the tires were art—broad and assertive, gripping the road as if they owned it. To Jae's admirers, of which there were many, that car represented wealth and status, an object of desire. But to me it was a symbol of something darker, something sinister lurking beneath the opulence. The price tag might have been extravagant, but the cost, I knew, was something far more profound.

Jae gave a signal to his driver, who took the hint, leaving us alone.

In the blink of an eye, Jae was in front of me. He pushed me back, and I fell onto the hood of his car. Jae leaned over me on his elbows, pinning me in place. His mouth was on mine, messy and dominating, and even though I didn't want to kiss him, even as I pulled back, it didn't matter.

As his mouth moved off mine and onto my neck, he reached down with one hand, running it up my thigh and under the hem of my dress.

"Jae, stop."

"What did you just say?"

Just as suddenly as he had pushed himself on top of me, Jae backed off, standing at the front of his car and staring down at me. His hand was at his side, and then I saw it, the metal shining in his hand.

A knife.

"It's just... I... I thought you were taking me home."

He came closer, and with one hand he pushed my shoulder back, pinning me against the car.

"Eventually. First I want to watch you touch yourself."

"What? Here? No. Jae. I can't," I said, but then I felt something cool and metallic against my leg.

"Say that again," he said, and I felt the metal turn, a sharpness sliding on my skin.

"I was just... I was worried that..." I needed to think fast unless I wanted to end up with more scars than I already had. "Jae, someone might see."

"Then you better hurry up."

Jae took a step back, and his black wings spread out wide behind him, shielding me at least a little. The end of his tail tapped the asphalt in irritation. Working for him this past year, I'd learned that when Jae said to do something, you did it.

His silver eyes stared at me, my knees still spread from where he'd stood between them only moments before while he kissed me, my robe scrunched up around my hips.

"Jae..." I glanced around and licked my lips, which were still puffy from the way he had attacked my mouth the second we'd left his club and he'd shoved me onto his car.

The demon raised an eyebrow as if daring me to question him

again. "Get on with it. Or do you need help?"

He came closer, leaning over me, and for the briefest of seconds, I hoped that meant he would pick me up off the car, but instead, he reached under my dress and hooked his fingers under my panties, pulling them off in one rough yank.

He smirked and brought my thong to his nose, inhaling deeply. "You smell fucking delicious. And you were wearing this?" Jae asked, twirling the thong around one finger. "Such a slut, aren't you?"

"You didn't let me change."

"Ah, so you do know how to be obedient, but you choose not to be? Because right now you're being a little bitch." He shoved my thong into the back pocket of his pants and then grabbed my ankles with each hand. He pulled my feet to the edge of the hood, and I fell back, flat against the hood of his car.

"I told you to get on with it, but I don't see you touching yourself yet. Don't you know how?"

"Mm-hmm."

"Use your words."

I propped myself up on my elbows and hesitantly reached one hand down. "I know how."

"How to what?"

"How to touch myself."

"Doesn't fucking seem like it." Jae crouched in front of the hood of his car, still holding on to my ankles, but he kept his eyes focused between my legs as my hand wandered lower.

"Let's go to your apartment first." My voice warbled under his intense scrutiny. "Or mine."

"Shut the fuck up and touch your cunt."

Taking a deep breath, I slid my fingers lower.

"That's no good." He leaned in closer, his mouth only inches away from my flesh. "Needs to be messier. Move your hand more."

The second my fingers left, he made a face and then spat right onto my pussy. I gasped as his thick saliva hit my clit, and I could feel it running down between my folds.

"That's fucking better," he said, and I could feel his hot breath on my skin. "Now make yourself come."

"Jae. I can't," I whined, my face wrinkling up as I tried to hold back the tears that threatened to spill down my cheeks.

My pitiful complaint only seemed to make him madder. Jae's grip on my ankles tightened, his fingers digging into my skin. "You will. You will or you will regret it. It's now or never, sweetheart."

Despite the nickname, there wasn't an ounce of sweetness in his voice. I let my head fall back against the hood, my hair pooling behind me and serving as the only barrier between me and the cold metal of his car. It was better to do what Jae said, get it over with as quickly as possible, and then he'd let me go home.

Squeezing my eyes shut to block out the fact that I was mostly naked in the parking lot, I took a deep breath and let my index finger start to rub small circles.

Instead of Jae, I thought of a different pair of silver eyes. I thought of an easy smile and eyes that danced with mischief; I thought of the way his fingers had trailed down my back. I thought of... Max.

Mercifully, Jae let go of my ankles and I heard him stand, the sound of a zipper following. I could hear the thwap of him stroking his cock while he watched me.

"Look at you, getting off on the hood of my fucking car in the middle of a parking lot, you stupid human slut."

"Jae..."

"That's right. Say my name, bitch. Scream it. Let everyone hear you touching that stupid cunt and calling for me."

My fingers worked furiously, the slick from my cunt only making it harder to find just the right amount of friction. I worked harder, rubbing faster.

"I own this club, this car, and this cunt."

No sooner than the last gasp left my mouth, Jae was on the hood of his car, one knee on either side of my head. He furiously stroked his cock over my head.

"Lick my balls while I come all over your face."

I tried to lift my head to get my tongue to his heavy balls, but with his body over mine, I could hardly move.

"Can't even do that right. Fuck it. Lie back so I can paint your face."

Jae grunted once, twice, his hand moving up and down on his dick until finally his hips shot forward, sticky hot cum squirting onto my face.

I stared up at him, still trying to catch my breath, but Jae snorted and slid back off his car, zipping up his pants.

"You look like a fucking mess."

"Wonder why," I muttered as I sat up and scooted back on the hood, my legs aching from being held apart for so long in one position.

"Are you talking shit? Really? A face covered in cum and you're still mouthing off?" Jae was right in front of me, looming over me. He reached out his hand, wiping some of his cum off my cheek and nose with two of his fingers.

"Open up." He stuffed those fingers into my mouth, and obediently I parted my lips to let his fingers in. He jammed them toward the back of my throat, sneering. "Maybe I should have fucked your mouth instead. Sucking dick is at least something I know you can do right."

Forcing back the urge to gag, I did my best use my tongue to clean his fingers, swallowing the salty cum without needing to be told.

"That's it," he said when he was satisfied, then took his fingers out of my mouth. He walked around to the driver's side, opening the door. "You gonna sit there all night? You want someone to see you like that? You really are a slut. Get in the car, idiot."

Not even waiting for me to get off the hood, Jae was already starting the car. I hurried to get down, scrambling to grab my robe and running in my heels to the passenger door.

"Get in the fucking car," Jae barked.

"Should I go get the driver?" I asked, thinking of the alcohol I'd smelled on him. The owner drinks for free after all. He didn't seem drunk, but it was hard to tell with him.

Instead of answering, Jae gave me a sideways glance. It wasn't like I had a driver's license anyway—no human in Vestia did. I normally walked home, and with each second that passed, walking seemed like a better idea.

Once we were in the car, Jae dug in the center console until he found what he was looking for: a tiny glass vial containing pink powder.

Dust. The real thing this time, I assumed.

The clubs had always made Jae money, but now not only did he have his income from the clubs, he also had a very profitable, though illegal, side business dealing Dust.

"Open it for me," he commanded.

I twisted off the top and Jae took his hand back, holding up the glass vial and pouring the pink powder into his mouth. He tossed the vial in the back seat and put that hand on my thigh.

As we drove, Jae's phone buzzed, and he took his hand off my leg to take the call, holding the phone to his ear.

"What do you mean, the delivery didn't go through?" he shouted into the phone. "An hour ago everything was fine, and now you're telling me that it's fucked?"

I could hear a male's voice on the other end, but not what they were saying; it was all too garbled.

"I don't care if the entire dock catches on fire. Get the shit or I'm holding you responsible."

A few more words were exchanged, something about an unexpected fire, and then Jae hung up, flinging the phone down onto the center console with a grunt. Instead of returning his hand to my thigh, his fingers gripped the steering wheel.

He was mad. And I was stuck in his car with him.

"You're going to pass it," I said, pointing to my high-rise building when it looked like he wasn't slowing down.

His head jerked my way at the sound of my voice, as if he'd forgotten that I was even in the car. The Dust he'd taken had made his pupils wide and black, the silver of his eyes barely visible.

Instead of answering, Jae reached over to put one hand behind my neck, the tips of his fingers digging into my throat. With his other hand, he spun the steering wheel, tires screeching as we turned in to the parking lot. He gave my neck a squeeze, hard enough that I flinched, before removing his hand.

"I'd had other plans for us tonight, but it seems like we just got interrupted. Stupid fucking idiots can't handle a small fire."

If I could have personally thanked whomever or whatever had caused a fire to interrupt us, I would have.

It had only taken a few minutes to drive to my apartment, and we'd barely even approached the building when Jae slammed on the brakes, my body lurching forward from the sudden shift.

"Since you seemed to please your guest tonight, I'm going to use you again," he said. "We're going somewhere."

"What? Where?"

He turned to me sharply. "Gods, do I have to spell everything out for you? You're coming with me. That's all you need to know. I thought you'd be grateful for less work."

Jae then nodded to my door, my indicator to get out. It wasn't like I needed to be told twice.

After I watched his car tear off into the distance, I did a quick check of my surroundings. Grimacing as I stared at the cracking concrete walls of my own building, I realized that Jae's car probably cost more than the entire building was worth. Just another high-rise apartment building crammed between the rest, like all the other slums in Vestia. The city of progress and innovation, my ass.

Since it was so late at night, there was no one else anywhere around, the whole street dark and empty. Most of the streetlights around my building were broken, the remaining few casting a yellowish tint on the brick walls of the building and the pavement below.

Alone out there still seemed safer than being in the car with Jae.

What else should I expect from a demon like him? When he first offered to get me out of Eden, it had seemed like I hit the jackpot. A fully paid ticket across the ocean, an escape from everything back home. A rich demon willing to give even someone like me a job. A demon willing to keep my secret.

I'd been so naive.

"How much for a date?" a man's deep voice asked.

Nope. Not dealing with that tonight.

Cursing Jae for dropping me off in the middle of the night and not even having the decency to make sure I got up to my apartment okay, I ignored the voice, tightened my robe, and hurried toward the stairs that ran up the side of my building.

"Hey," the guy called out. "I was talking to you."

No shit. And I was ignoring you.

I'd only made it up a few stairs when something wrapped around my ankle and I fell forward, my hand grabbing the railing to keep from crashing onto the metal stairs below me.

What the hell?

I looked down, and even in this barely lit stairwell, I could see a black tail looped around my ankle.

Damn it.

Suddenly a hand snuck around my waist, pulling me up and off the stairs as the tail released my leg. I started to kick as my attacker set me on the ground and pushed me forward, my palms scraping against the brick of the building's wall as I caught myself. I spun around, face-to-face with a dark-haired demon who was at least six foot tall with broad shoulders that easily dwarfed my size. He shoved an arm against my chest to keep me in place as he leaned down to look at me, and he smelled like sweat and alcohol and everything gross in the world.

"Jumpy little human, aren't you?"

I grabbed at his hand, trying to pry it off me, but he only pushed me back against the wall harder.

"Get your hands off me," I told him. "Now."

I weighed my options. I could scream and maybe someone would come out to see what was going on, but in the middle of the night? Unlikely. And even if they did come out, knowing the type of scumbags that lived in this dump, I doubted any of them would lift a wing at the sight of a demon messing with a human.

I tried to wiggle to the side to put some space between us, but his hand stayed firm.

"I said, take your hands off me." I stayed as calm as I could at the moment, my heart beating against my chest. Of course this jerk did the opposite and wrapped his other hand around my waist, pulling me closer to him. His fingers dug into my hip, no doubt leaving bruises for me to find tomorrow.

"What's the rush?" the demon asked, his voice low. "It's been a while since I got to play with a human, especially one as cute as you. I wouldn't mind taking my time tonight."

Oh hell no.

I swung at him with my hand that was holding my phone, but he knocked me away easily, the phone clattering down the stairs while he backed me against the brick wall of the building, pressing his large body against mine.

"You really thought that would do something to a demon like me?"

He slammed a hand over my mouth as I screamed, and he leered down at me, spreading his wings out wide at his sides.

"Come on," he sneered. "Don't be such a little tease. Coming home this late, dressed like that? I saw you getting out of that fancy car. What's one more date for a girl like you?"

"Fuck you!" I yelled, my voice muffled by the palm of his hand. I kept pushing back against him, but the asshole wouldn't budge.

He only laughed. "I just want to have a little fun, that's all. What else are you humans good for anyway? You're so small and helpless. It's cute really."

His wings curled even more inward, completing the cage to block me in place. Keeping his hand tight over my mouth, he dipped down, his face coming toward my neck. I shrank back against the wall, anything to put some small measure of distance between us, but then I felt the warm, wet press of his tongue and—

"Hey, pal."

A voice. Male. I couldn't see him, but it sounded slightly familiar, and for just a second I thought it might be Jae, back to make sure I got home all right. But no. Of course it wasn't Jae. Under other circumstances I might have laughed at how absurd it was to even consider that the demon come to save me might actually be Jae.

Thankfully the sound of someone else's voice was enough to get this asshole to stop licking my neck. It was too dark in the alley to see who was speaking, but I felt a surge of relief that now at least someone was there. Someone would see what this asshole demon was doing. Someone would stop him even if I couldn't. I shouted behind his hand, hoping that thrashing around would be enough of a clue to this stranger that I was in trouble.

"Quit it," the demon growled at me. "And you, get lost," he said over his shoulder to the demon watching us. "This is none of your business."

"I suppose you're right," the stranger said.

Seriously?

I slumped back against the wall at the realization that he wasn't going to be helping me. Was that it? So much for having a savior, but really, what else should I have expected from a demon? I was on my own. Nothing new there.

The demon's silver eyes were big and wild as he stared down at me. I had to do something, and quickly. Taking advantage of how close his face was to mine, I slid my hand up behind his head, my fingers finding his hair.

"Especially since"—I heard the voice again, so he *was* still there?—"from where I'm standing, it looks like she's got it handled herself. But I was never good at minding my own business."

The demon's forehead wrinkled in confusion, and that tiny moment gave me the opening I was waiting for. I reared back and spit in his face, and when he pulled away, I dug my fingers into the back of his head and pushed it forward. As I dodged, his forehead slammed right into the wall behind me.

There was a flash of light—or was it fire? I wasn't sure, but whatever it was gave me enough time to grab my attacker's head again, and

I rammed my knee into his crotch as hard as I could. When he hunched over in pain, I wrenched away from him. I needed to run, fast, up the stairs and to my apartment.

There wasn't time to think or breathe or even question the distinct, loud thud I heard at the bottom of the stairs or the smell of smoke in the air. There wasn't time to do anything other than race up the stairs as fast as my heels could take me, and there was no way in hell I was even going to look back.

Once inside my apartment, I slammed the door shut and threw every single lock. Pressing an ear against my door, I listened, waiting to hear something. Anything. But I didn't hear a thing. There was no sound of footsteps or wings or anything at all actually. Had he not followed me up the stairs? If either demon had flown up the staircase, I might not have heard him, but then he should have been able to catch me before I made it to my apartment.

I didn't wait even a minute before turning on my shower, cranking up the water temperature as hot as it would go.

I was alive and alone.

Like always.

7

MAX

"You should have seen her, Blaise. I was about to step in and help when she spit right in the guy's face. This girl *spit*, Blaise. No, not a girl. I take that back. This *woman*. She spit. In the guy's face. It was beautiful."

I heard a clang behind me, loud enough for me to turn around and see what had drawn Blaise's attention away from the weapons he loved so much. The tall demon was still standing behind the table where he had been sharpening a large collection of silver knives and swords, their metals shining in the low light of Blaise's workshop. But instead of continuing to sharpen them, Blaise's silver eyes were staring at me, his mouth open, the demon blacksmith not even bothering to pick up the sword he'd dropped on the table.

"Did you just say her spit was beautiful?"

"The *moment*, Blaise. I'm talking about the moment that was beautiful. Her anger and her spirit, and just *her*."

I flopped into a chair across the table from Blaise, my friend and the best damn weapons specialist I knew. I took out the knife I'd used earlier on that drunk asshole, and Blaise handed me a rag when he saw it. As I absentmindedly cleaned off the blood, I leaned back in my chair and thought about the way Lilly had looked running up those stairs to her apartment. The way her long hair had swished behind her as she ran. She'd been terrified, and I would have gone to her, but by the time I'd taken care of things downstairs, she was long gone.

"You should have seen her, Blaise. No, on second thought, I don't want you to see her because then you might fall in love with her. She has this brown hair that's not curly but it's not straight, and it feels so... *soft*."

"Did you kill the demon?"

I looked down at the knife in my hand, its color once again a shining silver. "Yeah, but anyway, I was talking about her hair."

"Did she see you?"

"Of course not."

"Weren't you supposed to be following your target and not some girl?"

"Not a girl. A *woman*."

"Whatever. Was that club owner the guy she spit on or not?"

"Jae Balakir? No. Although I would have paid good money to see that. I had two of my guys set one of his trucks on fire though. I got caught up at the club and had to use that tracker you installed on Jae's vehicle to find out where he went. Turns out it was to drop her off, and then this other scumbag thought he could touch a lady with no consequences. You should be congratulating me, you know, for making Vestia a safer place for women."

"You did your job," Blaise deadpanned. "Don't expect a high five."

"I never do."

Blaise and I stared at each other for a moment and then he nodded, both of us understanding. He picked up the sword he'd dropped earlier, taking a long look at it.

Seemingly satisfied, he held it out to me to take. "And now you need a new weapon?"

"No," I said, weighing the sword in my hand before placing it on the table with the others. "All of mine are fine. In perfect condition actually."

"Because I made them. Then is there a new mission I need to know about?"

"A small one coming up. We're still following the Dust. I really want to nail this one down before we make a move."

I picked up one of the freshly sharpened knives from the table, twirling it in my hand. Blaise was meticulous and analytical, cautious and reserved; likewise, each weapon was just like him: nothing flashy but deadly all the same. Blaise and I had always been opposites in terms of personality, but we had one major trait in common—the love of a good weapon. And these—*these* were good. The best.

We had worked together for years, and he knew exactly what I liked, and this—this knife—was exactly what I liked. The perfect weight. The perfect shape. The perfect hilt and grip that felt like it was made for my hand. Blaise's craftsmanship was second to none, one of the many reasons why he was my sole weapons supplier.

Even if he was a grumpy asshole.

Maybe it was from all the time he spent down in his sweaty workshop.

I spun around and faced a paper silhouette of a demon on the opposite wall. The demon who had attacked Lilly on the staircase was about the same size as the outline, more or less. He'd seemed bigger with his wings out, a classic tactic used to intimidate that hadn't seemed to work with her.

Blaise said something but I ignored him, focusing instead on that familiar tug I felt in the back of my mind whenever I held a weapon, those feelings that only seemed to take shape when I let the darkness invade my thoughts. Those same feelings that had been loud last night when I saw the demon approach her.

If Lilly hadn't acted, I would have torn his throat out. I would have carved out his tongue and sliced off his lips for coming near her. I would have severed each of his fingers for daring to touch her.

With a quick flick of my wrist, I released the knife, letting it dart across the room toward the silhouette, hitting with a soft *thunk*.

Bull's-eye. Right between the eyes.

To my surprise, the knife started to crackle, and I could smell the sharp scent of paper burning before I saw the start of the flame. Then the knife darkened, and the paper around the knife started to blacken as well, the silhouette curling in on itself as I finally saw the barest hint of orange.

Fire.

It wasn't a big flame, hardly even a flame at all, as if the knife had served as a tiny lighter. That had to be it. What started as a flicker of light quickly spread out from the knife, forming a black ring around it, and in a matter of seconds the circle of flame expanded to engulf the entire piece of paper. The silhouette and, to my surprise, even the knife itself were gone, and in their place was nothing more than a pile of black ash on the floor.

I whistled. "That's new."

"It is."

When I turned around to look at Blaise, he crossed his arms over his chest, and since I'd known him so long, I could see the smallest hint of self-satisfaction at his creation.

"Self-combusting. Ignites on impact. Minimal flame for decreased visibility."

It was so rare to see anything even sort of resembling emotion from Blaise, so I couldn't resist teasing him a little. "Aw, is papa proud of his baby?"

"Damn right I am. That's an S-class weapon. There's nothing like it in the world."

"You did your job then," I said. "Don't expect a high five."

"Fuck you."

"Seriously though, it's both deadly and discreet, just like you." I grinned. "Well done. And it looks like it leaves very little trace," I said, pointing to the ash.

"The knife is made of a blend of metals that burn up with the intended target, so there are no fingerprints or weapon left behind."

"Should I worry about the ash containing some kind of chemical signature that could be traced back to us?"

Blaise scoffed. "As if I'd be that clumsy."

"Perfect. Then I want six dozen. Can you send them over tomorrow?"

"What?" Blaise pointed the knife in his hand at me. "No. I only made three prototypes, and you just burned one of them. You're going to have to give me a month or two at least to get that many of these knives ready. Have you already gone through all the flame darts I sent you?"

"Darts are boring." Before he could stop me, I leaned over the table and grabbed the knife from his hands. Blaise was smart, but he was too slow. I slid the knife into my pocket. "Seven dozen, and I'm giving you two weeks. That's the final deal."

"I haven't even told you the price."

"I don't care about the price. You know that."

"You rich bastard. You still have a blank check from the royal family?"

I smiled. "More than ever with all these new missions from the king. I even hired a new driver. Got to keep up appearances, you know."

"You live like a prince in that huge penthouse with your personal chauffeur while I suffer in this hot basement."

"You love your basement."

"You're a lazy, spoiled asshole, you know that? I can get the knives for you in four weeks. Six dozen knives. That's all you're getting. And now I need you to leave so I can get to work."

"Deal, but I'm not leaving. We haven't finished our earlier conversation."

"About what?"

"I already told you," I said, gesturing to my mouth. "The spit."

Blaise stared at me.

I stared back at him.

How did he not get it? Maybe he had spent too many hours down in his workshop. Maybe the heat from his exploding knives was getting to him.

Blaise closed his eyes and sighed. "You're telling me that you came here to talk about a girl."

"A *woman*, Blaise. Keep up. She has these green eyes, and her back, it's so... so bare and—"

He slammed his hands down on the table in front of him, the swords and knives rattling. "Hold the fuck up."

"What?"

"Green eyes? You mean she isn't a demon?"

"No, she's human. They're bright green and—"

"You didn't say that before. All you talked about was her spitting."

"Yeah." I sighed and leaned my face into the palm of my hand as I imagined the events of a few hours ago playing out again. "Spitting."

"Max. Listen to yourself. I've known you for a long time, but I don't like this at all."

"What do humans like?"

"No. We're not having this conversation. You can't get involved with a human. Not now."

"That's the thing. I didn't have to get involved. I was going to do something, but then she spit on the guy. I thought I already said that?"

"Max."

I held up my hands in surrender. "I know, I know. But after I bring down this target, I'm going to rethink my life. They say the new king is ushering in an era of peace. If Vestia is at peace, he won't need me anymore."

"You're talking about Rand, right? The same demon who used to lie and say he was training with you and your father when he was actually out drinking who knows what who knows where but now gets to play at being king? It's all lies and bullshit. Whatever kind of peace your friend—"

"Our friend."

"Our *king* is promising is the same bullshit the nobles always say."

"But what if he's right? I like peace. Peace sounds nice."

"You don't know the first thing about peace. You know about weapons and death, and that's all you're paid to know."

"Then maybe it's time I change that. You know, quit the game, settle down. Get married, have a couple of little me's running around."

"Are you serious right now? You watched one girl—a human no less—spit on a guy, and now you want to get married?"

"I saw a lot more than that."

"How much more exactly? No. I don't want to know. Don't tell me."

Sighing, I leaned back against the wall. "You're right. Who am I kidding? There's still a lot of illegal Dust to clean up in this city or Rand's going to have my head. Or someone will have his head. Or both our heads. Speaking of our great, wise king—"

Blaise grunted.

"He's asked to see both of us."

Blaise didn't even stop sharpening the sword in front of him. "I'm not going."

"Nu-uh. You know that's not how this works. If His Majesty asks—"

"No. I have work to do. Now more than ever if we have another job coming up. I don't need to waste my time with that obnoxious prick."

I put my hand to my heart in mock surprise. "Blaise. You should know better than to talk like that about our great king."

"Our great king who has been on the throne for less than a year but still acts like he's a teenager. Our great king who used to pretend you'd done something when it was really him so he wouldn't get in trouble with the general."

"We were kids then, and his father was scary. Is still scary. But Rand's changed."

Blaise grunted again, obviously not convinced.

"Well, somewhat changed," I admitted. "There are even rumors that Rand's fallen in love."

"If the past is any predictor, I give it two weeks."

"The rumor is that he got matching tattoos with his new love."

Blaise could not have looked less impressed. "So regal."

"Could it be that you're jealous? I can see why; you spend all day down in this dark basement with only your tools to warm your cold, dead heart."

"First, there's no way my heart is cold when it's hot as shit down here, and second, you spend all your time acting like some rich prince, pretending you're not the king's faithful dog."

"It's not like I have a choice, Blaise. This is the life I was born into. It's not like you'd ever be able to find someone who could put up with your attitude anyway."

"Are you challenging me?"

"Me?" I grinned. "Never. I'd tell you to lighten up, but there's no point in wasting my breath." I dug into my pocket and pulled out the letter. "Here," I said, smacking it against his chest with a hard thud. Damn, it was like the guy was made of metal himself.

Blaise took the letter from me, his eyes widening as he read it over.

"Is this a joke? A masquerade ball? And that bastard wants us in uniform?"

"That bastard is our king, and we are both Knights of the Flame—in name at least. The masquerade ball isn't for a few weeks, so that gives you time to get adjusted to the idea."

While Blaise read over the letter again, I pocketed the other knives from the table.

"Now let's talk about this next job. Looks like it's time to gamble."

8

LILLY

The televisions behind the bar could barely be heard over the music in the club.

"*Crime has reached new peaks in Vestia recently,*" droned a demon in a red suit behind a big wooden desk, "*and our new king...*"

"I've heard quite enough of that," I said to no one in particular as I reached over the bar, found the remote, and changed the channel. No one in this club needed to be reminded of the chaos that was happening all around us, me included.

The Red Rose was supposed to be a break from life, a fantasyland of booze and women, a place where demons could talk to a pretty girl and enjoy a drink in peace. It was one of the most exclusive clubs in the capital, catering only to the very wealthy and their friends. It was an escape for me too in a way. Working here was so completely divorced from the life I'd lived in Eden that some days it was hard to believe my other life had ever happened at all.

When outsiders saw the demon kingdom, they saw Vestia as the place where science and engineering had conquered the natural world, a wealthy kingdom where demons were using their hard work and intellect to shape the natural world to their desires. Anyone who saw the skyscrapers and bright lights would assume that a growing kingdom like Vestia would be full of new opportunities.

I'd thought that too. Until I actually set foot in Vestia five years ago and realized that those opportunities weren't open to everyone, that a human-looking girl was less than scum in the eyes of most demons outside the confines of the Red Rose. Inside the club, within the dimly lit walls adorned with red velvet, my worth was measured by my ability to allure and charm. My body, my smile, they were commodities, traded for the fleeting satisfaction of the demons who frequented this place. Outside the club's heavy doors, in the grand kingdom of Vestia, those very attributes that were so prized at the club meant little. They didn't define my intelligence or kindness; they didn't make me a better person or a valuable citizen. I was just Lilly, the hostess from the Red Rose, not a young woman with dreams, thoughts, and feelings. A commodity inside, an afterthought outside, trapped in a reality that seemed to undervalue my true essence. The irony was cruel, and the realization even more so.

"Hey, cutie."

I had dealt with my share of unpleasant guests at the club, but Dominic was in a league of his own. From the moment he slunk up to the bar, his confidence oozing like a poorly contained oil spill, I knew I was in for a long night. Tonight was no exception. He had parked himself at the bar, his beady eyes fixed on me, a grin revealing a set of teeth that looked like they hadn't seen a toothbrush in weeks.

"Evening, beautiful," he drawled, his voice dripping with a sleaze that made my skin crawl.

I forced a tight-lipped smile, reminding myself that I was at work. "What can I get you, sir?"

"A little friendliness wouldn't hurt," he replied, his gaze traveling up and down my body in a way that made me feel like I needed a shower. "Aren't you supposed to make the guests feel welcome?"

"I'm here to serve drinks, sir. If you need something else, I suggest you speak to Jae, my boss."

He chuckled, a sound that seemed to slither down my spine. "Jae?

I don't understand why a lovely creature like you would work for someone like him."

I clenched my jaw, anger bubbling within me. But I held it back, reminding myself that Dominic was a paying customer, however repulsive he might be. Not a well-paying customer; this demon was cheap as shit.

"Jae's a good boss, and this is a good job." A big, bald-faced lie. The biggest lie that had ever existed in the history of lies.

Dominic's smile widened, and he leaned closer, his breath hot. "Come now, don't be coy. You could do so much better. Let me take you to this card game I play. We'll go in style, and I'll even let you sit in my lap. Someone with your looks deserves to be treated like a queen."

He wasn't wrong, yet somehow when it came out of his disgusting mouth, it sounded like the opposite of what I wanted.

"Sir, I've told you what my job is. If you want to drink, drink. If you want to talk to someone, I'm sure there are other girls working tonight who'd be happy to oblige. I will go find you one myself."

For a moment, Dominic's silver eyes flashed with anger, but then he settled back, smirking. "Feisty, aren't you? I like that. Maybe you're just playing hard to get."

I wanted to scream, to tell him to leave me alone, but I knew I couldn't. Instead, I forced myself to stay calm, to keep my voice steady. "I'm not playing anything, sir. I'm just doing my job."

He seemed to finally get the message, his eyes narrowing as he took a swig of his drink. "Fine, be that way. But don't think you're too good for someone like me. You're just a waitress after all."

Keep your cool, keep your cool, I chanted in my head, letting it echo like a mantra. I knew I had to be professional, but I also knew that there was no way I could do that while standing anywhere near this ugly bastard, so I turned and headed straight for the bar.

"You look ready to break something," Gwen said when she saw me.

"Just this one demon's skull." I smiled back at her, and she nodded.

"I'm dying to hear about last night though. Can you tell me about it before you get sent to jail for killing a guest?"

"Last night?" My mind immediately went to everything that had happened at my apartment. I'd hoped that coming into work would take my mind off Jae and that crazy demon both, but instead, I'd felt anxious all evening. Each time someone's wing happened to brush against my arm or I smelled the scent of alcohol, my brain replayed the way I'd been shoved against the wall, the way that demon had licked my skin.

"I don't really want to talk about it."

"Oh no, was he that bad of a tipper?"

"Huh?"

"Mr. Handsome."

"Oh. Him."

I'd been so on edge since that attacker that I hadn't thought about Max at all. Now that she mentioned him, I suddenly remembered the way he had touched my bare back, reverently almost, and my face started to heat up when I remembered how he'd shivered when I touched his wings.

"Hello? Lilly, are you with me?" Gwen waved a hand in front of my face.

"Sorry! I think I blanked out there for a second."

"You definitely seem distracted tonight." Gwen smirked back at me as she filled two more shot glasses. "I'm not surprised he finally requested you. He never stays long if you're not here."

"Really?"

"You should have seen him last night after you left. As soon as the rumor got out that he'd agreed to a dance with you, the other girls practically surrounded him. They wouldn't let him leave."

I didn't like the way my gut twisted at the thought of my coworkers hounding Max.

"And? Then what happened?"

"Nothing. He left a little while after that. I was surprised Jae let you even do the private dance in the first place what with the way that asshole likes to flaunt you around here." Her eyes flicked up to the second-floor balcony where Jae was usually sitting. Watching. "He can't stand to have his cute little human hidden away, can he? Have you thought about getting a different job?" Gwen asked. "One where that bastard isn't your boss?"

Outside of this club, the demons of Vestia hardly gave humans a second glance. Especially demons in perfectly tailored suits with perfectly messy hair like Max. But here? In this club? At the Red Rose, a human girl was an exciting rarity, and the demons who came here were eager to see that rarity up close. It wouldn't have been surprising if he'd come here wanting to see a human in person.

Most demons I met got a sick thrill out of ordering me around, as if telling me to sit in their lap only further proved the dominance of their species in their mind. That was fine with me for now. I'd let them think they were in charge and bat my eyelashes and talk sweetly and take their money.

"I will one day."

"Very convincing."

I leaned over on the bar, resting my chin on my palm, and sighed. "I don't plan on working here forever. Jae helped me out once, and I'm paying him back."

"Jae doesn't 'help' anyone. You borrowed money from him?"

"Something like that."

"That was dumb.

"Tell me something I don't know."

"And how long is it going to take to repay him? Better to get out now if you can."

"There aren't a lot of places that will hire humans, and the other clubs that do want to hire a human girl... Well, I'm not interested in that."

"Other girls do it."

"And that's great for them. Just not for me."

"What about going back home? Surely you have a family that misses you back in Eden."

"Not an option. Really, Gwen, I'm fine. I appreciate that you're taking the time to care, but stop worrying about me. I have a job and a roof over my head. I can put up with—"

"—having to work for that flying disaster of a demon, but continue."

"So do you! I'm fine. Really."

"Saying you're fine doesn't make it true." She nodded toward the back corner table and smiled back at me. "I still think you should try to hit Mr. Handsome up for a private room again. Get him alone, make up a tragic backstory. Cry a little. What if he runs a company or something and can get you a new job?"

"If he does run a company, I doubt it's the kind that hires humans."

"You won't know unless you ask."

"No, thanks," I told her. "I'm going to act like normal."

"I'll gladly take over his table if you don't want to talk to him."

"No!" I said a bit too loudly. "No," I said again, this time keeping my voice hushed.

"Good. Then give me your tray and you bring him *this* instead."

This?

That?

I'd never seen a more ridiculous drink.

In fact, I could smell it before she even placed it on the bar in front of me, the sickeningly sweet aroma floating through the air like cotton candy.

"What is *that*?" I asked Gwen, pointing to the red monstrosity.

That was a martini glass, the rim absolutely smothered with pink sugar crystals, the glass itself filled with some kind of thick red liquor that looked like syrup. I watched as Gwen sprayed whipped cream over the liquor, and as if it needed even more sugar, she dropped a bright pink lollipop into the mix, resting it against the edge of the glass like a garnish.

"*That* is for him." She nodded behind me, and when I looked over my shoulder, there he was.

Max.

The low hum of conversation and the rhythmic beat of music

filled the club, but all of that seemed to fade into the background the moment I spotted Max. He was wearing a fitted gray dress shirt that he'd unbuttoned at the top, the sleeves slightly rolled up, exposing his muscled forearms. Scars like the ones he'd shown me before snaked up his arms, and I wondered again how he got them.

What kind of life had led to being covered in cuts and burns?

Did I want to know?

He waved, and I whipped back around to Gwen.

"Max ordered that?" I asked her.

"You're on a first-name basis now?" She picked up a bottle of hot sauce and shook it over the top of the drink, little splotches of red dotting the whipped cream. "He asked for something sweet and spicy, so that's what he's getting."

"Since when are you so accommodating to a guest?"

"Since now."

My stomach was churning at the sight of it. "I'm going to vomit."

"Do it later. Right now, can you bring this to him?" Gwen asked.

"I'm going to get a headache even looking at it."

"Like I said, I can get someone else, but—"

"No, I've got it."

I carefully picked up the glass by the stem and held it out in front of me, as far away as I could without spilling it. If any of this drink got on my clothes, I planned on blaming Max. I carried the drink across the club to Max's usual table in the back. He sat up straight when he saw me and smiled, but I forced myself to keep my eyes on the glass. Not because my insides seemed to twist inside when he smiled at me like that. No, not at all.

I just didn't want to spill anything.

"Perfect!" he exclaimed when I placed that disgusting mess of a beverage on the table.

"It's not what you normally order."

Whiskey neat was his regular drink, a second one ordered as soon as he finished the first. Sometimes he would order random sweet mixed drinks, like tonight, the sugar content high enough to give me a cavity on sight. Unlike the rest of this crowd, he never touched Dust that I saw, and he never came into the club with loud, aggressive energy like all the rest.

"So you do pay attention to me."

"I've told you before that it's my job to pay attention."

"And here I thought you were avoiding me tonight. Gwen told me she'd make me a surprise tonight, so this looks like it."

"I didn't realize that she would do that for you."

"Let's just say that we have mutual interests." He clapped his hands and looked up at me. "I like sweet things. Do you?"

"Not really."

"Good to know." His silver eyes flicked from me to the drink and back to me again. "Are you going to watch me drink it?"

"I'm having trouble believing that anyone would drink that."

"Share it with me."

"I'd rather not."

"Your loss," he said as he plucked the lollipop from the drink and popped it into his mouth. Max tilted his head to the side, obviously amused with how disgusted I was by the whole thing.

I had to hold back a laugh at how ridiculous this was and how pleased he seemed with himself the longer I stayed at his table. I couldn't look away as he held eye contact with me and twirled the candy around in his mouth, his silver eyes sparkling as if he was daring me to look away first.

"What are you doing?" I asked.

"I'm enjoying talking to you at the moment."

There it was again, that same queasy twist in my gut that I'd felt before. And I didn't like it. I knew he was simply flirting with me like he did with the other women who worked there. The worst thing I could do would be to assume it was anything else.

"If you don't need anything else...," I said, turning to go.

His smirk was gone in an instant. "You're not staying?"

"I have other things to do, like... work."

"Wouldn't that work include making your guests happy by joining them for a drink?"

That's right. The guests. I glanced around the club, but everything seemed normal, just busy. After what had happened last night, everything and everyone was making me jumpy. The demon who had attacked me last night was nowhere to be seen, and it's not like he knew where I worked anyway. I still couldn't shake the uneasiness I was feeling, and each time a demon passed me, I had to resist the urge to flinch.

"You're different tonight," he said.

"What?"

Max took the lollipop out of his mouth and twirled the stick between his thumb and index finger as he stared at me. "Yeah. Different. Like you're on edge."

"You're very observant."

"I pay attention to things too. Guess I'll just drink this thing alone. With all this sugar, I might die, you know. They say too much sugar is bad for your heart, and with the hot sauce, I might be a goner."

Watching him, I would have bet money on the fact that Max was fluttering his damn eyelashes at me, and for the first time I noticed how long his were. Why did guys always have the good eyelashes? It wasn't fair.

"Are you pouting?"

"Sort of," he admitted.

"I would hang out, but we're short-staffed tonight," I told him. "I can see if one of the—"

"No. I'm busy too."

"What? You just said—"

"I can't be busy?"

"Busy drinking"—I gestured to the thing in front of him, still undrunk—"that?"

"Sure. It's not bad really. I like sweet things."

"That sweet thing is going to have a little bite."

"Even better."

"You're different tonight too, I think," I said.

"Oh really? Am I more handsome than I normally am?"

My face went blank. Did he know about the nickname Mr. Handsome? Had we ever called him Mr. Handsome near him where he might have overheard?

Play it cool.

"I'll take your silence to mean yes. When can I see you alone again?"

"I'm sure Jae can work something out with you."

"That's not what I meant. When do you get off work?"

"Not until late." It wasn't entirely a lie. The club would be open for several more hours, but I had no intention of leaving with him, and I didn't need him hanging around while the club closed either.

"Is Jae taking you home again?"

"He's not here."

"I saw him earlier. He invited me to a card game actually."

"He did?" Jae played cards one night a week. He'd dragged me to these game nights more times than I could count, ruining my nights off by making me act as his arm candy while he cheated his way to wins.

"Yep. Should I go?" Max asked.

"If you feel like losing money."

"I don't know about that. How are you getting home tonight?"

For a second I thought about last night, when Jae hadn't bothered to make sure I got home safe, and how badly that had gone.

"I'll manage somehow," I said.

A brief moment of hurt flashed across Max's face, and I felt a twinge of guilt but shook it off. I didn't owe him any explanation, and I'd learned long ago not to trust anyone, especially not guests who wanted to see me outside of work.

I didn't have much time to think about him since the club was crowded with demons and we were understaffed. Without more girls to occupy their attention, our guests were getting louder and drunker by the hour. We were busy and Jae wasn't there, so when it came time to close, Gwen and I were able to lock up quickly.

Grateful to be done for the night, I changed out of my dress into dark jeans and an oversized black hoodie. Vestia stayed hot, so hot you could feel waves of heat rising from the pavement, but it was better to suffer the heat than the unwanted stares of demons after dark. Especially after what had happened last night, I knew it was better to disappear into the shadows and get home as quickly as possible.

After pulling the hood over my head and grabbing my backpack, I pushed open the back door. Even though I had to walk home, it was still better than having Jae drive me like last night. I'd only taken two steps when I heard a voice.

"Hey," I heard someone say behind me, and I stopped.

No, not again.

Ready to bolt back into the safety of the club, I twisted around, my eyes widening when I saw Max waving. He pushed off the wall of the club and came closer, his black wings folded behind him.

Why was Max out here? How long had he been waiting? Should I be creeped out by that?

"I'm hungry," he said.

"Um, okay? What are you—?"

He checked his watch. "Know anywhere around here that's still open this late?"

What was even happening? He could have just eaten at the club. I pointed down the street. "There's a twenty-four-hour diner two blocks over. Just turn left, go straight, and then you'll see it when you—"

"Care to join me?" he asked. "My treat."

It was around three in the morning, and after being on edge all night, all I wanted to do was go home, wash the smell of booze out of my hair, and crash.

"I need to get home."

"Are you walking home alone at three in the morning?"

I squinted up at him and took a step back. "Maybe..."

"That question came out wrong."

"Did it?"

"It did. But now that I know," he said, "I'll walk with you."

"You don't have to do that."

"I know."

It didn't seem like he was going anywhere, and I knew it wouldn't be terrible to have someone walk with me just in case.

"Fine," I said. "Do what you want."

He grinned. "I always do."

We fell into a rhythm with him by my side, and I was filled with a weird mix of feelings. On the one hand, having Max's towering presence beside me was reassuring, but with every step I still couldn't shake the sense of unease that kept gnawing at me. Was I being paranoid because of last night? Or was it Max, the way he carried himself with total confidence, the fact that I was letting a guest from the club walk me home, his connection with Jae?

But as we headed down the street, I could tell that something wasn't right. I had a bad feeling that was slowly sneaking up my spine the farther we got from the bar. A quick glance over my shoulder confirmed what I thought.

"Keep walking," I whispered to Max, "and don't look behind us."

What was the first thing he did? He looked behind us.

"I said don't look!" I hissed, nudging him in the side.

"Remind me why I'm not looking?"

Despite myself, I took a quick look myself. Yep. The black car was still there. "Because I think we're being followed."

I could tell he was about to look over his shoulder again, so I tugged on his arm, pulling him down an alley between the buildings before he had the chance.

"Don't be so obvious," I whispered, pushing him behind me and into the alley. I peeked around the corner and watched as the black car slowly pulled past us. "They're driving away, but I want to see if they stop up ahead or keep going before we go out there."

"Lilly...," Max whispered, and I realized he was right behind me, his head hooked over my own. With him this close, all thoughts of the car following us vanished, my mind inundated with the smell of his cologne and the closeness of his body. Memories of straddling his thighs, of leaning in close to his skin, of touching his wings, flashed through my brain.

I shook my head to clear those thoughts away.

"It's a black SUV," I said. "Tinted windows. Looks like it stopped up ahead." I didn't like this. Jae didn't own a black SUV—that I knew of at least—but I also wouldn't put it past him to have someone following me. If he saw me out with another demon, I didn't know what he would do.

I brought my bag around to the front and unzipped it, rummaging inside until I found what I needed.

Max whistled when he saw it in my hand. "You carry a knife?"

"I do now. Never know what kind of creeps are out there. That's why I dress like this, so no one will pay attention to me."

"That's so different from how you are at work."

"That's work, this is life. There's a difference."

"Lilly..."

"Stay back," I said, holding out my arm to block him from going past me. "I'm watching to see where this car goes."

"Lilly...," he said again. "We're safe, I promise."

"Yeah, of course we are. Now that we're hidden."

When I heard him laugh, I spun around. "What? Why are you laughing?"

"Because you are too cute."

"Excuse me?"

"Okay, first," he said, holding up his hands in defense, "let's put away the knife."

"But—"

Before I could say another word, the knife was already out of my hand and then it was in Max's, and with a quick move of his wrist, it was back in my backpack. I was going to ask him how he did that, but then I saw that he was laughing. At me?

"What's so funny?" I asked him.

"You were really concerned for me."

"Well, yeah! One of us needed to be concerned. You can't walk around this part of town looking like..." I gestured to his expensive jacket, his expensive watch. "Like *you* without drawing some kind of attention. Usually the bad kind. There are dangerous demons in this neighborhood, Max. This area is crawling with scum who won't hesitate to rob you. Are you even listening to me?"

It didn't seem like it. Max was staring down at me, an amused smirk on his face, his silver eyes dancing with mischief, which only made me feel even more flustered than normal when I looked at him.

"What?" I wondered if I had something on my face. Or my hoodie. Or something that was making him stare at me with that goofy grin.

"It's..." He chuckled and shook his head. "It's nothing."

Max took a step forward and then another, until he was right in front of me. Crooking one finger under my chin, he pushed up, tilting my face toward him. His silver eyes narrowed as he examined my face, focusing on one cheek and then the other. I forced myself to not look away even as he watched me like I was under a microscope.

"You really are cute," he finally said.

With him looking at me like that, I felt like I could melt into a puddle of mush right then and there. I gulped and forced myself to maintain eye contact, if for no other reason than it gave me an excuse to stare into his sparkling silver eyes. "And?"

He wrinkled his nose at my question but kept his finger under my chin, pressing up. "And?"

"That's all you're going to say? That I'm cute?"

"Is there something else you'd like me to say?"

"Cute is what you call a puppy or a child."

"Or a kitten," he offered. "Kittens are cute."

"I'm not a kitten."

He smirked and nodded to my backpack where I'd hidden the knife. "Maybe a kitten with claws."

"Maybe."

He laughed and took his hand away, stepping back from me. "I'd love to find out. You should go out with me sometime."

"Huh?" Had I heard him, right? Was this a joke? There he stood in clothes that most likely cost more than I made in an entire month, maybe two months, and he was asking *me*, a human, out on a date?

"Not to a diner. Like on a date. A real date. Go out with me," he repeated. "How about tomorrow?"

As much as my heart leaped into my throat at the idea of going on a date with him, there was no way I could say yes. If Jae found out that I was dating someone, a guest especially, he'd be furious. It seemed like he was already having someone follow me, so what would he do if I was dating someone for real?

Until I could pay off my debt and move far away from Jae's authority, it was better to not bring anyone into my crazy world, especially if that someone was aligning himself with Jae.

"Sorry, no."

"With your work schedule, lunch might make more sense, right? I can meet you for lunch most days, I think, depending on my meetings. My days are usually pretty open. Let me check my schedule," he said, taking out his phone. "Wait. What did you just say?"

"I said no."

"Why would you say no?"

Because my crazy boss will murder me if I date someone.

Because my crazy boss will probably murder you too.

"First, it's arrogant to assume I'd say yes, and second, because it's not a good idea for us to date."

"Do you have a boyfriend?"

My hand gripped the strap of my backpack tighter. "It's not that..."

"Oh. A girlfriend then?"

"No, no girlfriend."

He scrunched up his nose, tail tapping the ground behind him. "You're really saying no?"

"Yeah."

"Wow." He stared at me for a second and then let out a loud laugh. "Wow. Just... wow." He kept laughing to himself.

"Why are you laughing?"

"Because I don't remember the last time someone told me no."

"Seriously?"

"I'm just being honest." He shrugged before seeming to think for a minute. "I'm not sure, but I think I kind of like it."

"You like being told no?"

"I didn't think so. But when you do it, yeah. I have to say that it's sort of refreshing." He stepped out of the alley and back onto the sidewalk, looking both ways as if trying to find something. "I'll ask you again tomorrow."

"My answer will be the same."

"We'll see. Where'd that car go, the one that was following us?"

"Hopefully it's long gone."

"I hope not," he said, taking out his phone and dialing. "Since that's my ride."

"That... was your car? Following us?"

"Hey. Yeah, circle back around," he said into the phone before hanging up. "I'll have to say something to my driver about maintaining more distance to avoid being seen. He's new. You know how it is."

"No... I don't."

The same black car pulled up alongside the curb. "Get in. I'll drop you off at your building. It can't be too far if you were walking, right?"

"Not that it's your business, but yes. I can walk home on my own just fine."

"I know, little kitten, but I was never good at minding my own business."

There was something in the way Max spoke that made me want to trust him even though I was quickly realizing that I knew nothing about him. That same intangible quality that made it seem okay to get into the sleek black SUV with him and give the driver my address. So I did.

Max held open the door, and I slid into the back seat with Max following suit.

"Have you worked at that club for a long time?" he asked after a moment.

"A few years. Ever since I came to Vestia."

"You came here with your family?"

"No." It was better to leave it at that. Max didn't need to know about what my life had been like in Eden. No one did.

Thankfully, right then his phone buzzed; he glanced at it and pressed a button to silence it. "Anyway," he said. "What were we talking about? Your trip across the ocean to the lovely kingdom of Vestia?"

"Do you need to take that?" I asked, gesturing to his phone.

"No," he said. "It's fine. Just work."

At three in the morning?

"What kind of work do you do exactly?"

But the phone buzzed again.

"Answer it. It's okay," I insisted. "If they're calling at three in the morning, it's probably pretty important."

With a groan, Max signaled for his driver to pull over, and he got out to take the call.

Alone in the car, I started to wonder what I was doing, especially if he didn't want me to hear his phone call. I was letting a stranger drive me home in the middle of the night. How did I even know he was actually taking me home? How many other girls had he taken home in this same car? I was already mulling over excuses to get out when the door opened and Max slid back in.

"Work is the worst, am I right?" he asked, and I couldn't help but wonder what type of work called him at three in the morning.

He sighed and stared out the window, tapping his fingers aimlessly against the glass. "Don't you ever just feel like quitting and running away somewhere?"

He had no idea.

I stared out my own window, up at the tall buildings that loomed over the cars below; neon lights and 3D advertisements flickered in the darkness, their dazzling lights illuminating the chaos of the city. The restless energy of Vestia, even in the middle of the night, could feel claustrophobic and suffocating in its own way, but it was still nothing compared to the weight of what I'd felt in Eden.

"Trust me when I say that somewhere else isn't always better than where you are," I said.

"Where you are can be pretty great, huh?"

"I don't know about that."

"I do."

When I looked back at him, I realized he wasn't staring out the window anymore. Instead, he was looking right at me. I was about to ask him why when he pointed out my window. We were there. The car pulled up alongside my building, and when we got out, Max frowned and wrinkled his nose.

"You live here. Why?"

I rolled my eyes. "Thanks for the ride," I told him as I headed for the stairs.

"Hold on," he said, grabbing my wrist to stop me. "I didn't mean to offend you. I just want to understand."

I stopped, but he didn't let go of my wrist. "You might not realize this, but there aren't a lot of housing options for humans in Vestia. Not cheap ones at least, and my bastard landlord is raising my rent next month too."

"A bunch of criminals live here."

I raised an eyebrow. "How do you know that?"

"Oh. I saw it on the news, I think. Let's get you home safe," he said, spreading his black wings so that they formed a protective barrier around the two of us as we approached the building.

I thought of last night and what had happened. If that stranger hadn't distracted that demon long enough for me to get away, I didn't know what I would have done.

"You really don't have to do this," I said, patting my bag where I kept the knife. "I have claws, remember."

"I know I don't have to, Lilly, but I want to. What floor do you live on?"

"Seven."

"Where's the elevator?"

"You think this place has an elevator?"

Max grimaced. "You walk up seven flights of stairs every day? On purpose?"

"If I want to go home, yes." I noticed the displeased look on his face and gave him a pointed look. "Not all of us have wings. Or our own personal drivers to take us places."

His eyes looked sad for a moment, then they lit up. "I suppose that's true, but you know what? You have something even better."

I snorted. "Somehow I doubt that."

"You do," he insisted. "Me."

Before I knew what was happening, Max had scooped me into his arms, and we were flying. I wrapped my arms around his neck to hold on while his large black wings rhythmically pushed the air down and sent us higher. His strength was palpable; each powerful beat of his wings directly contrasted with the gentle way he held me. Max flew fast, incredibly fast, so fast that my insides felt jumbled around and my heart thumped against my chest. Max's own chest seemed to vibrate from the effort, but his grip on me was careful, reassuring.

When we reached the seventh floor, Max's wings folded gracefully, and he landed with agility despite his size. He placed me down gently on the walkway that ran along the seventh floor, but even once my feet were on the floor, his hand didn't leave my back.

"Next time warn me," I told him as I smoothed my clothes and steadied myself, my heart rate slowing. "But thanks."

"No need to thank me. You smelled—"

My eyes shot up to his. "I what?"

"Your hair—"

"Probably smells like a bar."

"—smelled sweet."

Why did he have to keep saying stuff like that? The more he said, the sweatier my hands felt and the more my stomach twisted, and when he was looking at me like that... What if I threw up right then and there?

There was no time for puking because Max held out a hand to signal me to keep walking past him. He stayed on the landing, and as I unlocked my door, I looked behind me and Max was still there, wings still folded behind him, his hands in his pockets, watching me.

He was making sure that I was going to get inside safely, I realized.

Was I being too cautious? After all, had he shown me anything other than kindness so far? He was maintaining a respectful distance, and he was waiting to see that I was safe in my apartment. He'd helped me clean up after the fight. Maybe it wouldn't hurt to get to know him outside the Red Rose. I hadn't taken a chance in years, not since the last time I did, and it had ended so, so badly.

"Um, Max?" I called out, turning to face him.

He looked up, his eyes wide, as if surprised that I was addressing him. "Yes?"

My hand gripping my doorknob, I shifted from one foot to the other, trying to find the right words. "I, uh, I have tomorrow off from work. I have some errands I need to do."

Max's brow furrowed, a confused look on his face. "Okay."

I sighed, feeling foolish. Why was this so hard? "I mean, if you wanted to... you know, tag along, I wouldn't mind."

Max's confusion vanished in an instant, a slow smile spreading across his face as his tail suddenly tapped against the floor. "Yes."

"Not as a date. Just two... I don't know... two friends. Doing errands."

Max's smile widened. "I'd like that, Lilly. I'd like that very much."

I nodded. "Good. I'll see you then." I turned to go inside but paused once more, looking back at Max. "And thank you. For tonight."

His eyes softened, and he gave me a small nod before I pushed my door open. And then he was gone, flying into the night, and I was alone in my apartment.

I leaned against the now-closed door, my heart still racing from the unexpected exchange with Max. I ran my fingers through my hair, a shaky laugh escaping my lips. A part of me couldn't quite believe what had just happened, and another part of me was relieved the awkward conversation was finally over.

Walking to my bedroom, I felt like something was different. The air held a scent that didn't belong—earthy, with a hint of cinnamon and smoke. I drew in a deep breath and pulled my sweatshirt up to my nose, inhaling the scent. There it was again, that strangely intoxicating aroma, clinging to the fabric. Then it hit me—this was Max's scent. I closed my eyes, the memory of him holding me and flying me to my apartment, the firmness of his chest against mine, his breath tickling my ear.

Opening my eyes, I shook my head and took my sweatshirt off. What was I doing, swooning over a shirt? It was silly. Creepy even. But as I got ready for bed, the rich, smoky aroma still lingered in the air as an ever-present reminder of Max. The apartment was empty, and even though I eventually put the sweatshirt back on—because it felt colder than normal in the apartment, no other reason—I somehow felt slightly less alone.

9

LILLY

I dreamed of ice.

The bone-chilling cold and the icy water that surrounded me as I fell into the depths of a frozen lake, its surface cracked open. Panic clawed at my chest as the frigid water filled my lungs, and I couldn't help but think that this was it—this was how I'd die. Alone, abandoned, and forgotten.

I tried to cry out, but there was no one to hear me. My voice drowned right along with me in the bitter darkness. In those final moments, I remembered the coldness of the world, how it had always been cruel to me. And I wondered if maybe, just maybe, I deserved it.

But then the dream shifted. No longer was I submerged in ice; instead, I was bundled in blankets beside a small, warm fire. It flickered in the fireplace, casting shadows upon the walls of the small room where I'd stayed while I healed. Flames crackled and popped, the only sounds in the empty room, and I imagined that I could see visions in the flames, happy people dancing and twirling in the orange and red.

But there were no happy people in that house, not in my dream or in my reality.

"Hey! Lilly!"

I jolted awake, gasping for air as I felt the remnants of my night-mare linger.

"Hey, hey, it's okay. You're safe." Charlee's voice broke through my panic.

Charlotte Pembroke, or Charlee as she'd insisted I call her within five seconds of us meeting, was one of the first humans I befriended in Vestia. The only human I'd befriended in Vestia. Living down the hall from me in an apartment just as small and run-down as my own, Charlee had quickly become someone I could complain to and commiserate with. With her blue eyes, shoulder-length black hair, and quick smile, Charlee was a bright spot in the gloomy world of Vestia, a friend in a place where trust was rare and friends were even rarer.

She was also... a thief.

A brilliant one actually. Her skill with locks was unmatched, her uncanny ability to dig up information unparalleled, both only rivaled by her talent at inventing new gadgets to help her with her crimes. Charlee was nothing short of a genius really. A mad genius, and her apartment matched the persona. The entire place looked like a war zone of tools and metal: bits and bolts strewn everywhere, electronics tossed carelessly on the couch, circuit boards and wire cutters filling her kitchen instead of plates or glassware.

It wasn't like I either approved or disapproved of how she made her money, because who was I to judge? I didn't ask about her exploits, but occasionally she'd fill me in, including the time she broke into Dominic's penthouse—the same ugly, gross demon who flirted with me at the club. Once when I'd complained to her about him, Charlee had found his address and broken in to steal his entire collection of self-portraits (of which he had many, which made carrying them out quite the feat since Charlee and I were about the same size), replacing them with caricatures of him she'd drawn herself from my description. I'd heard all about it from Dominic at the club the next day, but even I had to laugh at that one.

In a kingdom ruled by demons, where humans were often over-looked and dismissed, Charlee had found a way to make a living that suited her skills. She had a knack for slipping in and out of places unseen, her nimble fingers making short work of almost any lock. It was a dangerous game, one that could cost her dearly, but Charlee played it with a grace and confidence that I couldn't help but admire.

I blinked a few times, trying to focus on her pale face hovering above mine. She seemed worried, her blue eyes wide with concern.

"Char... Charlee?" I stammered, wiping the tears away with the back of my hand. "How did you get in? I know I locked the door."

"Remember who you're talking to, Lilly." She smirked, twirling a lockpick between her fingers. "Locks are child's play for me."

"Right." I chuckled, pushing myself up into a sitting position. "Sometimes I try to forget about your..."

"Talents?"

"Something like that."

I could see the worry etched on her face. It was clear my nightmare hadn't gone unnoticed.

"So what was the nightmare about this time?" Charlee asked, her playful demeanor shifting to one of genuine concern.

"Uh, you know..." I was barely awake and definitely didn't feel like delving into the details, mostly because I didn't want to have to think about it again. "The usual stuff."

"Come on, Lilly, I can tell when you're holding back." She crossed her arms over her chest. "You don't have to go through this alone."

"I know, but..." I sighed. "It's just... hard to talk about, you know?"

Charlee placed a reassuring hand on my arm. "Of course I know. But that doesn't mean you have to suffer in silence."

"Thanks. Maybe... maybe another time."

"All right. But remember I'm here for you—day or night. Even if I have to pick the lock every time."

"Please don't make a habit of that."

"Deal." Charlee's blue eyes, which normally twinkled with mischief, seemed more concerned than anything else. "Just promise me you'll reach out when you need to, okay? Us humans have to look after each other in this place."

"How's your shoulder feeling?" I asked her, happy to change the subject. She'd complained of a sprain a few days ago, and I'd healed it under the guise of showing her a massage technique.

She rolled her arm, testing it out. "Perfect thanks to you. You sure you don't want to quit that club and go work as a medic somewhere? I don't know what magic you did to it, but—"

"It wasn't magic." I tried to keep my expression neutral, but my heart was pounding in my chest. My healing ability, and the reason I had it, wasn't one I was ready to share with anyone yet.

"Uh, okay," she said, her smile faltering. "I didn't mean that literally. You just have a gift for it. Anyway, you told me you had today off, but then you weren't answering the door, so... Here I am. Looks like a good thing too since I found you like this."

"What time is it?" I glanced at the clock by my bed and gasped at how late it was. "Shit. I overslept, but it feels like I didn't sleep at all."

"Nightmares will do that to you."

A knock at the door made both of us jump.

"Expecting someone?" Charlee asked.

Max. I'd completely forgotten and slept later than I'd planned. The memory of telling him to come by today hit me like a brick. I must have been out of my mind to invite him back here. At least it was during the day; if the sun was up, I could almost count on the fact that Jae would still be asleep. His long nights at his clubs meant that he rarely ever did anything during the day.

"No. I mean yes. It's no one," I said, finding the hoodie I'd worn the night before and throwing on some jeans to go with it. "He's helping me run errands."

"*He?*" Charlee all but shrieked the word. "That crazy boss of yours is actually here in the daytime for once? I've got to see this demon with my own eyes because I have some choice words for him."

She practically leaped off my bed and headed for the door with me rushing after her.

"Charlee. No, not him. Definitely not him. Look, this is nothing, I swear. Just a friend. Please don't make this weird."

"Uh-huh. Okay, sure. Whatever you say. You forget that I'm a good judge of when someone is lying."

"I'm not lying," I insisted, pushing past her to open the door.

Max stood there, black sunglasses hiding his silver eyes, black wings folded elegantly against his back. He had on a white linen short-sleeved shirt that showed off the muscles of his forearms and the scars and burns I'd seen before. His fist was raised, poised to knock again.

"Hey." Max grinned, his fist turning into a wave, but I didn't have time to think about how unnecessarily cute that grin was because Charlee moved in front of me to get between us.

"How do you know Lilly?"

"Max," I said, stepping beside her, "this is Charlee. She lives down the hall."

He extended his hand. "It's a pleasure to meet you, Charlee from down the hall."

Charlee's eyes flicked from his hand to his face. "What kind of weapons do you use? Swords?"

Max took back his hand. "I'm sorry, what?"

"I can tell from your hands. Calluses on your fingers, the scarring pattern on your arms, those are typical of someone who's used to gripping sword hilts. Or daggers. What kind do you keep on you? Do you have favorites?"

"I'm so sorry," I interrupted her. "It's her thing; she's an inventor."

"And you invent weapons?" Max asked.

"Nope," I said, pushing on Charlee's back to get her the hell out of my apartment before she said something she shouldn't say. "She's never even considered something like that, not in a million years. Bye, Charlee, see you later."

She glanced over her shoulder at me as I forced her out the door. "I approve, by the way. Have fun on your date."

"I told you, it's not—"

"We will," Max said.

Charlee gave me a knowing smirk as she brushed past him, giving me a thumbs-up once she was outside. I closed the door, feeling a sudden surge of panic. Max was in my apartment. Alone in my apartment. We were alone. I'd been alone and mostly naked with him at work, so why did this feel so different?

And what on earth had possessed me to invite Max to my apartment?

"Stay here for a second," I told him before hurrying into my bedroom to finish getting ready and grabbing my bag. I contemplated changing out of the sweatshirt and jeans or putting on some makeup, but then thought better of it. I didn't need to impress him since this wasn't a date. The gods knew he'd already seen enough of me at the club. A few minutes later I reemerged into the living room where Max lounged on my faded couch, sunglasses resting in his hair, tail lazily tapping against the floor, looking completely at ease.

Max raised an eyebrow when he saw me come back into the room with my sweatshirt still on and a big bag slung over my shoulder. "You do know how hot it is outside, right?"

"I do." I pulled my hood over my head and tightened the strings as if to make my point.

"Are our errands today particularly dangerous then? I told my driver to wait around the corner, and I've got my sunglasses, but I wasn't aware that I needed to go completely incognito for... uh... whatever it is we're doing."

"We don't need to be undercover if that's what you're asking." Max seemed to stiffen, and I wondered if I'd said the wrong thing. "It's just helps to not draw attention," I explained. Although I wasn't sure how possible that was going to be with a demon over six feet tall following me around. "All right, let's get this over with." I grabbed my keys from the counter. "We've got errands to run."

Max nodded to my bag. "And are we burying a body?"

"Nope." I headed toward the door, and he was quick behind, taking the bag from me and slinging it over his shoulder. "It's laundry day."

And yet it felt like something totally different.

In all the times Max had come to the Red Rose, in all the nights I'd seen beautiful demon women surround him and fawn over him, in all those nights I'd never once seen Max look as bewildered and fascinated as he did staring at the room full of ancient washers and dryers in the basement of my apartment building. Lined up in a long row of beige metal, the old machines hummed and whirled and clicked and clacked, yet Max stood there smiling like he was staring at the most interesting pieces of art he'd ever seen.

The few other occupants of the laundry room stopped what they were doing and stared at Max. His appearance screamed wealth, and the suspicious looks they were giving him told me they were all thinking the same thing: What was someone like him doing in a place like this?

I couldn't blame them for their curiosity. Max seemed entirely out of place, yet his excitement was genuine, his eyes sparkling with anticipation. I caught a few raised eyebrows from my neighbors as they sized him up, but Max seemed oblivious to their scrutiny, his attention completely focused on the washing machines and dryers.

"Is this..." Max seemed to struggle for words, his voice filled with a strange sense of wonder and disbelief. "Is this where you wash your clothes?"

I didn't even bother hiding my laugh. "Yep. Superglamorous, huh?"

He moved forward, practically bouncing on his heels. "This is amazing. I've always wanted to do something like this."

"Like laundry?"

"You know what I mean."

"I really don't," I said. "Do you not wash your own clothes?"

"Of course I wash my clothes. That's why I smell so good."

I could feel my face heating up, remembering how Max's scent had lingered on my clothes last night.

"But I don't actually wash them," he continued. "Someone else does. I think? They're all dry-cleaned. Does that mean they're washed? I don't ask questions."

One of the dryers made a loud noise, and in an instant Max's wings were out at his sides, his body between me and whatever had startled him.

"At ease, soldier." I chuckled and placed a hand on his arm, and at the contact, Max visibly relaxed, his wings folding behind him again. "These machines are old and make all kinds of noises." Did he feel that uncomfortable? But no, that wasn't it, because in a flash he'd relaxed. He looked over his shoulder at me and smiled again, his earlier excitement back as if he hadn't just acted like he was about to fight a dryer.

He placed my bag on the floor and squatted down in front of one of the washers, taking off his sunglasses to get a better look, seemingly mesmerized by the way the clothes spun inside. "I don't know. I put them in the thing, and then they're back in my closet."

"The thing. Okay. That thing is probably your hamper."

"A hamper…"

I shook my head and reached for the bag, starting to take out my clothes. Max was suddenly right beside me, his head hooked over my shoulder. I glanced up at him—he looked eager to help but utterly clueless about what to do.

"Here, let me show you. It's easy." I explained the process, and Max listened intently, nodding along as if I were describing the most interesting thing in the world. We sorted clothes, set the machines, and through all of it, Max seemed genuinely delighted by the entire process. It was slightly unnerving, having this tall demon hovering right beside me, hanging on my every word, even if my every word was mostly just how to put in detergent and separate whites from colors.

"You're really enjoying this, aren't you?"

Max pulled back as if shocked by the question. "How could I not?"

"Because it's just laundry."

"To you maybe. But to me it's something I've never thought about before. My… uh… my servant, he buys my suits for me mostly."

"You let a servant buy your suits?"

"He has really good taste. And the clean clothes just appear like magic in my closet."

Magic?

It was better to change the subject.

"Have you always had servants to help you?" I asked him. "Your parents never showed you how to do things like this?"

Max ran a hand through his dark hair. "My mother died when I was just a kid, and my father was more focused on his job than anything around the house."

"I'm sorry to hear that." Maybe I'd chosen a bad topic after all. "But I understand. Business was all my father cared about too."

"What kind of business was he in?"

"Trade." It was better to keep it general and hope he didn't press for answers.

"So you learned from your mother?"

Definitely a bad topic.

"No." I went back to sorting my clothes. "I've just lived on my own long enough to pick up a few things. Basic survival things."

"I know basic survival things," he insisted.

I made a face. "Are you sure about that? Because ten minutes ago you didn't know what a hamper was."

"I knew what bleach was for without you telling me."

"You did, that's true," I admitted. "You have a surprising amount of knowledge about how to use bleach to clean things for someone who seems to have never actually cleaned something before."

"What can I say?" Max smiled, his silver eyes twinkling. "So does that mean you think I'm smarter than I look?"

I chuckled. "Maybe."

Once we set the timers on the machines, I turned to face him. If only Max knew what a strange sight he presented, this tall demon standing in the basement of my building in what was obviously expensive clothes, this same demon whose face had lit up at the mere idea of doing laundry.

As we stepped outside, Max was there, beside me on a street in Vestia in broad daylight, hands in his pockets, seemingly happy to run my little errands even though anyone could see us together. The way he looked at me, the way he strolled confidently by my side, his questions about my life, all of it made me feel seen in a kingdom where I felt invisible, important in a place that daily tried to tell me that I wasn't. It was a sensation both unfamiliar and intoxicating.

A feeling so unfamiliar from anything I'd ever experienced with Jae.

"What's next?" he asked, sunglasses once again covering his eyes. Then he reached into his pocket and pulled out a second pair, holding them out to me. "Almost forgot that I brought these since you told me you prefer to avoid attention."

I stopped abruptly. "You brought me sunglasses?"

"Yeah, thought it might help you feel more comfortable."

He walked back to meet me, pushing back the hood of my sweatshirt, his touch lingering in my hair for just a second longer than necessary. Then, with a grin, Max slid the sunglasses onto my face, his fingers brushing against my skin as he adjusted them.

"There." He stepped back to take a better look. "Perfect."

"You're ridiculous," I told him, but the affection in my voice was unmistakable.

He shrugged, still grinning. "Maybe. But I'm having a great time. What about you?"

I looked at him then, really looked, taking in his genuine smile, his sparkling silver eyes, and the way he was going out of his way to make sure I was comfortable. I could ignore the red flags that came along with his association with Jae—maybe I just wanted to ignore them—because right then I realized I was having a great time too, something so rare in Vestia, something I hadn't felt in a long time.

"Yeah," I admitted, smiling back at him. "I am too."

10

MAX

Doing laundry.

Pretending not to peek at Lilly's clothes as she put them in the washer.

Strolling down the sidewalks of Vestia like we were a regular couple having a regular day together.

It was simple, it was normal, it was *perfection*.

But, as always, nothing perfect lasts forever. We hadn't made it more than ten feet down the sidewalk before my watch buzzed. It was Blaise.

Any new details on the target? the text read.

Damn it. I never should have told Blaise what I was doing today. I closed out the text without responding.

"My driver is parked not far from here," I told Lilly. "He'd be happy to drive us wherever you want to go."

She shook her head. "No need. This is a quick errand, and then I'll go back to get my clothes."

"I'll walk you back. Or we can drive. I can tell him where to meet us."

"We're not going far."

When we turned the corner, we were surprised with a burst of color and noise. The sidewalks and street were suddenly crowded, filled with people drinking and dancing, more than a few of them already drunk, all of them streaming around us. Small tents were set up along the sidewalk where vendors were selling tiny replicas of the king's crown alongside plastic toylike versions of the Hellfire throne. And then I saw...

Oh. This was great.

Did Rand know that his photo had been copied and poorly pasted onto cheap T-shirts? Racks of the thin white shirts hung outside the tiny tents, each one adorned with the new king's face scowling in what looked like an official portrait that had to have been fake. Was that even Rand at all? It was hard to tell, but it was certainly intended to be him, and no one seemed to know any different or care. No one was buying them either way.

I couldn't decide if Rand would love these shirts or die of embarrassment at their existence, and I was considering whether I should buy him one when I felt a tug on the hem of my own shirt.

When I looked down at her, Lilly had lifted her sunglasses, and I watched her green eyes widen as she took in the scene, the dancers and musicians, the street performers and food vendors.

She let go of my shirt and leaned closer, speaking loudly over the music. "What is this?"

"Pop-up festival. I've seen these happening all over Vestia ever since the new king was crowned. It's mostly an excuse to throw a party since the king's popularity is so low right now."

"Really? Why?"

"You don't keep up with politics, do you?"

"Not at all."

"They hate that it's illegal to own fae now," I explained. "That Dust is illegal."

The crowd surged around us, and I felt my instincts kick in, sharpened by years of training. The press of bodies, the noise, the potential for danger even in the middle of what seemed like joyful chaos.

The colors, sounds, and smells of the festival were vibrant, but they brought with them a crowd of demons and other creatures, many of whom seemed to take an interest in Lilly as we strolled by. Even concealed in an oversized hooded sweatshirt and jeans, there was something about her that drew attention, a grace and beauty that couldn't be hidden no matter how much she tried.

But I didn't like the way several of the demons were looking at her, the way their eyes lingered just a moment too long, their expressions betraying thoughts I didn't want to dwell on. Lilly seemed oblivious to it all, and I was glad for that.

I found myself drawing closer to her, my body reacting protectively, a silent warning to anyone who might think of approaching. It was an instinctive response, something primal, a feeling I hadn't expected to experience so strongly.

Without thinking, I pulled Lilly to me, my arm encircling her waist to shield her from a group that moved past us.

"Are you all right?" I asked her after they were gone. We had more than enough room on the sidewalk for just the two of us, but I realized I was still holding her.

I didn't let go. I didn't want to.

"I'm fine."

My watch buzzed again, this time against her, and Lilly looked down as well at the sound.

"Work," I explained, reluctantly taking my hand away from her so I could see what Blaise wanted.

"What kind of work do you do again?"

You better not be fucking around, the text from Blaise said, and I could hear him scolding me in my head, complete with his arms crossed over his chest. *We need details for tomorrow night. Call me when you get this.*

I'd call him later.

"Oh, you know, a little of this and a little of that," I said, deleting the text. "It's a family business."

"And your family wants to be involved with Jae? And you? Why do you want to associate with someone like him?" Lilly asked.

I sighed, grateful that my sunglasses covered my eyes. "It's...

complicated. But what about you? Why do you associate with someone like him?"

She bristled. "It's complicated."

"Too late, I already used that line."

"Okay, fair." Lilly lowered her own sunglasses yet still didn't speak. "He gave me a job," she finally said.

"At the club."

She nodded, and while we continued walking, I wanted to press her further on Jae, but it seemed like she was trying to keep something from me. I knew I should keep asking questions since information about Jae would help me do my job and make Blaise shut up for once, but I couldn't bring myself to ask more when she so obviously didn't want to talk about it.

She definitely had secrets, but didn't all of us?

My watch buzzed again, but this time I didn't even look.

"It's okay," I said instead, trying to reassure her. "You don't have to talk about it if you don't want to."

She stopped walking and turned to face me. Her expression was serious, but there was a hint of something else in her green eyes— something vulnerable that I hadn't seen before. She took a deep breath before finally speaking.

"There aren't a lot of options for someone like me here." She stopped midsentence, something seeming to catch her attention.

I followed her gaze. The sidewalk was crowded with demons, but here and there we saw a few wolf shifters in their human forms but still recognizable by their long nails and signature scruffy hair. Wolves were tolerated in Vestia since they mostly kept to their own packs; most of them preferred to hang out with other wolf shifters downtown rather than mingle with demons. They weren't what had caught Lilly's eye, however. No, the wolves were on her left, and Lilly was focused on the right, on a woman looking through jewelry at one of the vendor tents.

A fae woman.

From the moment that fae slavery had been declared illegal in Vestia, the fae had left the kingdom in droves, the majority returning to their faraway homeland of Rowan. Only nobles in Vestia had ever been allowed to own fae in the first place, a status symbol reserved for the wealthy yet envied by many. Now that fae were free, some of those demons who'd never owned one were irritated that they were never going to get the chance. Others still saw fae as property, and they hung on to their lingering prejudices even though the laws had changed.

Yet here was one, a woman who looked to be in her midtwenties, with bright white hair tied down her back in an elaborate braid and large blue wings that glittered in the sunlight. Her wings fluttered behind her as she moved from tent to tent, seeming not at all bothered by the stares she received from those around her. As we watched, another fae stepped out from the shadows beside her. This one was around her same age, a tall man with purple wings and a stern face, his muscular body looking like it was built for combat. Yet despite his appearance, he held out a hand to her, and soon the two of them were in the street, dancing to the music along with everyone else, demon and wolf alike.

"Are you wanting to dance?" I asked Lilly.

"Oh. No." She shook her head. "That's not it. It's just... seeing them. Both of them."

"They seem..." I struggled to think of the right word as I watched the fae man hold the woman in his arms and spin her around. Of the two, he seemed to be the one with any dancing ability, and his blue-winged girlfriend was having trouble keeping up, stumbling over his feet at every turn. Not that either of them seemed to care, judging by the soft way they were looking at each other.

"Brave," Lilly whispered.

"I was going to say happy, but yes, brave. That too."

She nodded, her eyes still on the dancing fae couple. Their happiness was a stark contrast to the guarded expressions of some of the demons around us. Though the law had changed, the disdain and residual anger toward the fae were still very real for many.

The dance continued, the couple's laughter filling the air as they twirled and dipped, lost in each other. And then, with a sudden misstep, the fae woman lost her balance, falling toward the cobblestones.

Before I could blink, Lilly rushed forward. The crowd around the couple parted, a mixture of concern and curiosity in their eyes, and I followed closely, watching as Lilly reached the fae woman and knelt beside her. The fae man knelt in the street too, concern written all over his face.

"Are you hurt?" Lilly asked her.

The fae smiled weakly. "My ankle is maybe? I wasn't even supposed to be here today, but when a handsome man like him asks you to dance..."

The man tried to help her up, but she winced with pain, and he carefully set her back on the ground.

"Damn it, that hurts." She groaned. "I will never hear the end of it if I broke my ankle while dancing in the street of all things. Victor, you cannot tell anyone that this happened. Or that we were dancing in the street."

The fae beside her bowed his head solemnly. "Of course. Can you help?" he asked Lilly, who was already touching the woman's ankle. Her sunglasses were pushed back on her head, holding back her hair. "Are you a doctor, miss? Is she going to be okay?"

Lilly didn't answer, and for a second I wondered if the injury wasn't as bad as it looked. I'd seen my fair share of broken ankles, and judging by the way it was starting to swell, the fae woman at least had a bad sprain.

But then I realized why Lilly was hesitating. A crowd was beginning to form around us, onlookers drawn in by the spectacle of seeing two fae in one place, and now there was the added intrigue of one of them being injured. The situation was attracting attention, and I could feel Lilly's discomfort growing with the weight of so many eyes on her.

"Max, can you use your wings to give us some privacy?" Lilly asked me.

"Certainly." I was happy to oblige, turning around and spreading my wings to cover the trio, glaring at anyone who dared to even think about coming close to them.

"No, I'm not a doctor," I heard Lilly say, "but I can tell she'll be okay. It will probably be fine with some rest."

Then the group was silent, too silent. After a moment I looked over my shoulder, but Lilly was already standing up, brushing off her jeans from where she'd knelt in the street. The purple-winged fae was also standing, his face still as serious as it had been moments prior. He seemed to be about to say something to Lilly but then noticed that I was watching and didn't.

It was an odd tableau. The music, the crowd, the festival itself—it all seemed to fade away in that moment, leaving only the three of them: Lilly, the fae woman, and the man, locked in a silent understanding.

"It will be fine with some rest," Lilly repeated, her tone much colder than it had been a few minutes ago. What had I missed? What had happened between these three? It was the look in the fae woman's eyes that caught my attention—it looked like... shock. Was she that surprised that a human had helped her? Humans did still own fae slaves in Eden, so it would make sense for them to not to trust Lilly, but the two fae had seemed friendly enough only a few minutes ago.

Then Lilly backed away.

I turned to the fae couple, offering a quick apology, and then ran after Lilly. She'd only made it a few feet away, walking as if in a daze.

"Lilly, what happened back there?"

"Nothing," she said, shaking her head. She handed me back the sunglasses I'd given her and I stepped away, not wanting to take them.

"Those are a gift," I told her. "I don't want them back. Can we... Can I...? Did that couple say something rude to you? Tell me and I'll go back and break an ankle for real if they did."

"No. You heard everything. I just need to get home. We've been gone too long." Her voice was flat, emotionless, but her eyes betrayed a hint of fear. It was clear something had happened, something I hadn't seen or understood. The connection between Lilly and the fae woman, her sudden shift in demeanor, it all swirled in my head like an unsolved puzzle.

"Okay, then I'll go with you. I'll fly you—it will be faster."

"I think I'd rather walk. By myself. Sorry, I just need to clear my head."

"Did I do something wrong? Say something wrong? If I offended you..."

"You didn't." Finally Lilly stopped, turning to me, her voice softer. "I'm sorry for walking away like that. I was... overwhelmed."

"That's understandable. There was a lot going on."

The walk back to Lilly's apartment was filled with an unusual silence, and I could feel a tension growing between us. No matter what I thought to say, the words seemed stuck in my throat, and every attempt at conversation felt forced and awkward. It was as if we were both wrestling with thoughts we didn't quite know how to share.

Finally Lilly broke the silence, her voice soft and almost hesitant. "Max, have you ever wished for a different life?"

The question caught me off guard, hitting me like a punch to the gut. How could she know? How could she possibly understand the thoughts that had haunted me, the longing for something else that I had barely allowed myself to acknowledge? My heart raced, and I fought to keep my face neutral as I turned to look at her.

"What do you mean?" I asked, my voice carefully controlled.

She shrugged, looking away as if embarrassed by her own question. "I don't know. Just... something different. A life where you don't have to always be on guard. Where you can be free to be yourself without having to answer to anyone."

I watched her as she spoke, her face open and vulnerable, and I realized she was sharing something deeply personal. The longing in her eyes was a mirror of my own, and I felt a connection to her in that moment that was both terrifying and exhilarating.

"I think everyone wishes for something different at some point," I said, choosing my words carefully.

She looked up at me, her eyes searching my face for something. "Is that how you feel?"

I hesitated, feeling a pressure in my chest as I wrestled with how much to reveal.

"Yeah," I said finally, my voice barely above a whisper. "Sometimes I do."

And as we made our way back to her apartment, I couldn't shake the feeling that something had changed between us. Something had been exposed, as if her question had opened a door, and I wasn't sure if either of us was ready to walk through it.

Before I left, I tried again. "Let me take you on a real date, just the two of us. Dinner, lunch, whatever you want."

She sighed and looked at me, a mixture of sadness and something deeper in her green eyes. "Max, I appreciate it. I really do. But I can't. Not now."

And with that, she turned and walked away, leaving me standing there, my heart heavy and my mind spinning with unanswered questions.

"I'm not giving up!" I shouted after her.

Lilly looked over her shoulder, a small smile on her lips. "I can tell!" she called back.

As I watched her leave, the world around me seemed to fade away, and all I could think about was Lilly and the pain in her eyes. What was she hiding? What was she afraid of? And why wouldn't she let me in?

This feeling of helplessness was new to me.

And I didn't like it.

11

———

MAX

"So then I asked her out again, and she still said no. Well, not *no* so much as *not right now*, which I think is better. She actually said, 'not now,' which might mean something different. But it's been a whole week. What do you think? Should I—"

"You should shut up and focus on the mission."

"Focus on her what now?" I asked Blaise. "Hold on a second. The guy woke up, and I can't hear anything you're saying."

With a deep sigh, I pressed a button on my earpiece to silence Blaise and then turned to the demon on the ground beside me. Why couldn't this guy just stay quiet? I'd thought the gag I'd secured around his head would have drowned out his incessant yelps, but all the noise he was making indicated that I'd been wrong. I was trying to get the rest of the details on the location from Blaise, but how could I when this demon kept scrambling around?

In a fluid motion, I retrieved a knife out of my pocket with one hand and shot it at him, the knife's sharp tip lodging into the ground a few inches from the demon's face.

"Can you behave now?" I asked him.

How did this guy not understand who was in charge here?

The demon flinched back but didn't get far since I'd secured his hands and wings behind him and tied his tail to his ankles with rope. Looking up at me, his silver eyes were wide and wild with anger that quickly shifted to fear when, like the knife I'd used in Blaise's workshop, the one in the ground in front of him started to crackle with the beginnings of fire. But it didn't immediately burst into flames.

I turned the earpiece back on.

"I need you to know that this knife burns slower than the one I used the other day," I told Blaise.

As the crackling turned into a small flame, the demon kicked his feet, trying to scramble away, but his back hit the wall, stopping him.

"What?" Blaise asked in my ear.

"The other one was quicker. Is this knife defective? It's hardly doing anything."

"So you're why those knives disappeared! Damn it, Max, I knew it was you. Those were just prototypes; you can't count on them to work—"

"I'll check in later," I told Blaise, touching my ear to turn off our comms.

Squatting down in front of the demon, I spoke softly. "Let's chat, okay? We have more time than I anticipated actually. You should be grateful."

He mumbled something behind the gag.

Oh yeah. He couldn't talk.

"Before I caught you, you were on your way somewhere," I said as I untied the gag, "so let's start with you telling me why a guy like you had any business in a church."

The demon's eyes narrowed. "Fuck you. Untie me."

I pulled the knife out of the ground. Only the tip was burning, though the rest of it was hot even through the thick fabric of my gloves. I held it close to his face, making him flinch back from the heat. "Let's get something straight. You can walk out of here or you can burn. It all depends on you."

"Do you want money? Take my wallet. My ring. Take whatever."

"I already have those," I said, patting my jacket. "I took them when I knocked you out and tied you up. What I want is information about what you were doing tonight."

"I was going there to gamble, you fucking psycho. Untie me right now. You have no idea who you are messing with."

"Gamble? Really?"

"Are you a cop or something? Gambling isn't illegal."

"I know, so why is it being hidden in a church?"

"I don't have to tell you shit. They'll never let you in there."

"That would have been true, except I took your invitation."

I reached into my jacket and took out a card I'd found when I searched his pockets. As my research had already told me, the invitation was for a night of gambling, all of it hosted by Thornfield Enterprises, a human organization out of Eden. They had a long history of trade with Vestia, all of it through the previous king, who'd paid a high price for fae slaves from Eden. When slavery became illegal in Vestia, the Thornfields were among the first with complaints, their main source of income cut off in an instant. If they were behind these organized card games, it was possible they were using them as a way to make connections and gain influence with some of the most violent and corrupt demons in Vestia.

Demons like Jae.

I patted my jacket and then pulled out another copy of the invitation. The one I'd received from Jae earlier that day. The stupid bastard had been more than willing to invite me along to meet his friends.

"Oh wait, what's this?" I asked him, waving the second card in front of his face. "My very own invitation? How'd that get in there? That's right, I already had one. Guess I didn't need to tie you up after all. My bad."

"You're insane."

"Probably." As I put the invites back in my jacket, my fingers touched something else in my pocket. This time I brought out a flashy silver ring with clusters of green emeralds surrounding a big central diamond. I held it up, the tiny light from the knife's flame shining on the stones.

I'd seen this ring once, only briefly, that night Lilly had broken up a fight in her club. The same ring that had slashed open her friend's face.

"I've seen you before," I said. "Did you know that?"

"Doubtful, you piece of shit."

The reflection of the flames on the diamond caught my eye. "And you're married. What's that like?"

"Untie me!"

"How did you get her to say yes? See, there's this girl, and all I want is one date. For now at least. I'll probably marry her one day though."

"You're crazy!"

"She does make me crazy, you're right. Crazy enough to do things I might regret if you don't give me more information about what's really happening at these gambling nights."

"It's a meeting, okay? A business meeting."

"What kind of business?"

"Nothing that wasn't legal only a few months ago, you psycho!"

"Dust then. As I thought. On that note, I think the gag is going back on." I rammed the knife into the ground beside him, put away the ring, and retied the gag even as he squirmed. Satisfied with my work, I yanked the knife out of the ground and stood back up. "Marriage is supposed to be a commitment between two people, but I know for a fact that your ring has hurt at least one woman who wasn't your wife. I wonder how many others?"

Of course, he couldn't answer. I didn't need him to.

"Have you seen in the news about the women who have been disappearing from downtown?"

He struggled against his bonds, his wings desperately trying to break out while he shouted something behind the gag.

"So you have? Good. It was really nasty stuff. At least five women, all dancers in local clubs, disappeared over the past two years, but only two were found. They weren't easy to identify given the condition of their bodies."

I twirled the burning knife in my gloved fingers, not bothered by the growing heat.

"Since I had your ID, I had my associate run a check on you while you were knocked out. It seems like you were one of the last demons to be seen with each of the missing five women. All unofficially of course, nothing on the record. You made sure of that. Especially since you're married. That would be quite the scandal since you probably thought you had all of your wife's hospital records erased too. The thing is," I said, crouching down to his level, "nothing is ever truly erased. We all carry the weight of our actions."

His eyes widened, and he vehemently shook his head.

"Are you scared?" I asked. "Do you think the women you killed were also scared? Or your wife, forced to live with such a pathetic excuse for a demon?"

Leaning toward him, I brought the knife closer to his neck, close enough that he had to feel the heat from the burning blade. I could feel it against my own gloves, threatening to burn right through them. If I held on for a few more seconds, the entire knife would be on fire. Not wanting to miss my chance, I pointed the tip of the blade right at his jugular.

"And now no one is going to be scared of you ever again."

When I was finished, I stood up and peeled off my gloves, tossing them into the flames. This knife had taken longer to combust, but once it was fully aflame, the blaze was taller than me. I let my wings spread out at my sides, allowing them to slowly fan the fire until it grew even larger.

Touching my ear, I turned the comms back on. "Blaise. I take back what I said earlier about our knife. It wasn't defective at all."

"Hey! No names, you know that."

"It doesn't matter. There's no one around to hear me."

After a few seconds, the orange flames dwindled to nothing, the muffled screams had stopped, and the alley was silent except for the sound of my boots on the pavement as I walked away.

I had a mission, after all.

12

LILLY

Jae's driver deposited me at the penthouse like a lamb to slaughter. The elevator doors slid open to reveal Jae lounging on a black leather sofa, glass of wine in hand. He sat up when he saw me, his black wings spreading out at his sides. His silver gaze raked over me, cold and predatory.

"Come here, pet. We have plans tonight." He crooked a finger at me.

I approached on leaden feet, dread pooling in my gut. What fresh hell had he devised now?

Jae waved a hand at several gowns draped over chairs, different sets of shoes lined up on a rack. "Pick one or I will. I'd prefer you without any of them on, but we don't have time for that tonight."

I picked up the first one I saw, not really caring what it looked like, and started to take it to one of the bedrooms to change, but Jae called my name.

"Lilly. What do you think you're doing?"

"I'm going to put on this dress."

"Do it here." He smirked. "I don't want to miss any details of this experience."

Jae's intentions were clear. I knew he was watching me not just for his own enjoyment but to remind me of my place, of the control he had over me.

With a shaky breath, I unzipped the long-sleeved, short red dress that had caught my eye. It was covered in red sequins, sparkling even in the soft lighting of the room. The dress was formfitting and low-cut, designed to show off the chest. I knew it was provocative and daring, but somehow that made it feel right for the evening ahead.

I glanced at Jae, his eyes fixed on me, a smug smile playing on his lips. I turned my back to him, refusing to give him the satisfaction of seeing my face as I changed. I quickly slipped out of my current clothing, feeling his gaze on my bare skin. I tried to ignore the sensation, focusing on stepping into the red dress.

I heard him stand, and the next moment his hands were on me, his fingers brushing lightly against my back as he pulled the zipper up. The dress hugged my body, and I felt his hot breath, his lips dangerously close to my neck, his wings circling around us.

"Perfect," he whispered, his voice full of admiration and something darker. "You'll be the center of attention tonight, Lilly. Just as I want you to be."

I was about to turn away, to put some distance between Jae and me, when he held up a syringe filled with a pink liquid. I felt a shock of recognition, my eyes widening as I realized what it was. It looked like the poisonous Dust he'd taken that night at the club. The night he'd made me heal him after he got high out of his mind.

"What is that for?"

Jae's smile was a chilling thing. "This is your task for the evening, my precious Lilly. You're going to use this to get information from a demon who will be at the card game we're attending."

My heart pounded in my chest, and I felt a fresh wave of revulsion for Jae. But I knew better than to show it. "You want me to poison someone?"

Jae huffed a laugh. "This won't kill him. Not this much. He wouldn't be able to handle what I can. Think of it more as persuasion," he said. "I'll get you time with him, and then this will make him more pliable, more willing to talk. And you, my lovely Lilly, will extract the information we need."

"What will happen to him?"

"He'll feel good, and then he'll most likely just fall asleep."

"Most likely?" I asked, and Jae shrugged.

I looked at the syringe, terror and disgust warring within me. This was a dark path, one I had never wanted to walk, but I knew that refusal was not an option. In fact, in this moment, Jae had power over me, but he also needed me. And in that need, I realized, could lay my opportunity. If I played along, if I made him believe I was his to command, if I never ended up using the syringe at all and one day used it on him instead, I might find a way to turn this situation to my advantage.

"How do you propose I carry it?" I asked, my voice cold.

Jae's eyes flicked to the low cut of my dress, and he handed me the syringe. "I think you'll find a way."

I took it, my hand trembling, and tucked it into the top of my dress, feeling the cold glass against my skin. I met Jae's eyes, forcing myself to show no fear, no hesitation.

"Who is it?"

"You know him. Dominic Ellerby. I think the little fucker has been causing problems with my supplier. I'll go over the details with you in the car."

Dominic? That guy?

"I'll do it," I said, my voice firm. "But remember, Jae, I'm doing this for you. Don't ever forget what you owe me."

His smile widened, but his eyes were like ice. "I never forget anything, Lilly. Now let's go. We have a game to win and a kingdom to conquer."

As we left Jae's penthouse, my mind was a whirl of thoughts and emotions. Jae escorted me downstairs to his waiting limousine, gripping my arm in a bruising hold. "Remember, you're to stay by my side and do exactly as I say. No wandering off." His nails bit into my skin, a silent warning. "Understand?"

I gritted my teeth. "Perfectly."

"Good girl." He released me, patting my cheek before sliding into the limo.

Bastard.

The drive passed in tense silence. My gaze flitted to Jae, watching for any hint of his plans, but his expression remained smug and unreadable. He enjoyed keeping me in suspense, dangling information just out of reach to keep me anxious and malleable.

When we pulled up outside an old church, Jae's hand clamped over my knee, squeezing hard enough to bruise.

"Remember," he said softly. "One wrong move and you'll regret it."

Message received. Tonight I would play my part.

13

MAX

"I confirmed that this is a meeting of Dust dealers. You have my location?" I asked Blaise.

"At an old church," Blaise confirmed. "Didn't know many of those existed anymore."

Blaise was right. It was surprising to see a church in the city these days; most in Vestia had closed long ago. As the capital became the world's hub for tech and innovation, the priests of the old religion had become millionaires overnight when they sold their properties to developers looking to build the next big skyscraper.

It was a pity; the stained glass windows and ornate statues that decorated the outside of the churches had been torn down and replaced by steel and concrete one by one, all over the kingdom. The demons of Vestia gradually chose to worship at the altar of science instead of religion.

Such was life in Vestia. I'd learned a long time ago that if I wanted the citizens of Vestia to have a better life, I'd have to answer their prayers myself.

All I needed to do was gather information and find out who was meeting and if it was anything illegal. Easy enough.

When I opened the heavy wooden door into the church, I was

first hit by the rich aroma of incense, spicy and sweet and totally overpowering. The air was so thick with the scent that it felt like I was wading through the smell as I walked toward the altar. The church itself was dark and empty, the only light coming from the soft glow of candles and the incense burning on the top of the altar.

"You in yet?" Blaise's voice came through clearly in my earpiece.

"Sort of," I muttered back, keeping my voice low. I didn't see anyone in the church itself, but I couldn't be completely certain. "Seems empty."

"Remind me again why you get to go play card games and I'm stuck down the street monitoring you."

"Because you're so damn good at it. I'll check back in. Watch my location, but give me some time," I whispered before pressing a small button to turn off the earpiece.

It was true that I seemed to be the only demon in the church, but then why was the incense still burning? And so much of it? I checked the invitation again, but it seemed more like a business card than an invitation to anything nefarious. Still, I had the right address; they had to be around here somewhere.

My footsteps echoing on the stone floor, I made my way behind the altar and found a hallway leading to what appeared to be the priest's chambers. There was a small bed, a dresser, and a closet, but still nothing out of the ordinary. Back in the hallway, I moved farther into the back area of the church, and as the scent of incense seemed to fade behind me, I smelled something else.

Smoke.

Now that was a scent I knew.

It wasn't the sharp scent of smoke from a fire though; this was heavy and earthy and definitely coming from somewhere close. I followed the scent to a set of stairs lit by only a few candles, the lights casting long shadows on the walls as the steps led down. Cigars, I knew as soon as I got to the door at the bottom of the stairs. The incense had been a cover in case anyone wandered into the church.

I knocked once and the door creaked open slightly. A pair of silver eyes stared back at me as I dug out my original invitation and handed it to him.

The demon didn't answer but gave me a long look over. I held my breath, but I quickly relaxed when he started taking out his keys to open the door.

"Most of the games have already started," he said.

"I'm sure I'll find something."

A heavy haze of cigar smoke and thick cologne enveloped me as soon as the bouncer opened the door. I scanned the room, taking stock of my surroundings. In the dark space with its low ceilings, the sounds of laughter and the clinking of glasses echoed off the stone walls. Fifteen or twenty round tables were set up in the room, each one surrounded by four or five demons playing various card games.

On one wall there was a long wooden bar and bartender; other than a few lamps on the bar top and one each table, the room was mostly dark, cigar smoke swirling in the air. There was no sign of the infamous CEO of Thornfield Enterprises, Marion Thornfield herself. I doubted the head of the company would make an appearance at a meeting like this anyway. She'd send someone else. My eyes scanned the room, finally settling on the bar where a human was drinking by himself.

The bar was as good a place to start as any.

The guy couldn't have been older than twenty-five, blond hair hanging in a disheveled mess over his forehead while he nursed a dark liquor. Unlike the rest of the crowd, which was dressed in suits and jackets, he was dressed in a worn-out leather jacket, one that had definitely seen better days, with a simple T-shirt underneath. Dark jeans, rough boots; the casual, almost rebellious look was a contrast to the rest of the room. As he leaned over his drink, his blond hair hung down to hide most of his face.

"What's good here?" I asked him.

He turned his head slightly, his eyes meeting mine for just a second, sizing me up before turning back to his drink. His eyes were red and glazed, telling me what I already suspected—he had recently taken Dust.

"You're new," he said. Not a question, a statement of fact.

"Is it that obvious? My buddy invited me, told me I could—"

"Don't care." He gestured to the bartender, who started to make another drink.

Well, all right then. Time for a new tactic. I was about to ask the bartender for something myself when a hand clapped my shoulder.

"Get him something sweet."

I spun the stool around to see a familiar demon. Big, muscled arms strained against a bright blue suit, and more than a couple of gold necklaces hung around his neck. It was Lilly's boss, smiling at me around his cigar like I was an old friend.

Disgusting.

"Glad you could make it." He held the cigar out between his ringed fingers, letting the ash drop onto the floor. "You like that sweet shit, don't you?"

"You've done your research. I'm flattered."

Jae's silver eyes gleamed with self-satisfaction. "Of course. I know everything that goes on in my clubs. They are mine, after all. I wasn't sure if you were coming tonight."

"I'm always up for trying something new."

"Glad to hear it. I won't be the only familiar face you'll see tonight."

"Oh?"

If there were other demons who came to the Red Rose that I could connect to the illegal Dust, all the better.

"You'll see later. You met Patrick?" he asked, nodding to the human at the bar.

There it was. The introduction I needed. "Something like that. Patrick," I said, the man not even bothering to look my way, "a pleasure to meet you. I'm Max. Is this your first time in Vestia?"

Patrick grunted, still scowling into his drink.

"Ignore him. He's a touchy little shit. Thinks being the Thornfields' lapdog gets him the ability to act like fucking royalty around here. He's pissed that I didn't bring more girls for him. Care for a game? Come on," Jae said, draping an arm over my shoulder.

He started walking us toward a table where several demons were already seated. After exchanging some money, the dealer got us set up for a new game.

As the cards were shuffled and dealt to each of us, Jae leaned back in his chair. "Next time you're at the club, come see me. I think we can work out something to benefit us both."

The sight of the arrogant demon made me physically ill, but I wasn't going to let him know that, not if he was insisting on us being friends.

I leaned forward, resting my elbows on the table and feigning consideration. "I'm definitely interested. Especially after the other night."

"Lilly caught your eye, eh?"

"You could say that."

"I'm not surprised." Jae chomped on his cigar and threw some chips onto the pile.

The demon to my left, a young guy with small wings I'd seen a few times at the Red Rose, leaned back in his chair and licked his lips. "Are we talking about that hot human at your club?"

I gripped my cards tighter, nearly tearing them.

Dominic Ellerby. The youngest son of the owner of Vestia's largest shipping companies. A spoiled, irritating demon with a drug and alcohol problem, both of which had led to his multiple arrests for fighting, public intoxication, and domestic violence against a few supposed girlfriends. His father had bailed him out each time, and he'd ultimately never served any real jail time.

Like Jae, Dominic was decked out in expensive jewelry, all of which I assumed he'd purchased with either his father's money or from his own drug dealings. I'd seen him at the Red Rose, waving around money like a fool, grabbing at girls who obviously wanted nothing to do with him no matter how much money he was offering.

Jae nodded. "Yep. That's the one. I've known her since she was seventeen. She's a wild one, that one, if you know what I mean."

Seventeen? I wanted to throw up. That wasn't in any of the information I'd been able to find on Lilly. In fact, I'd found basically nothing on her other than the lease for her apartment, which wasn't even in her name. It was in Jae's name. All of her employment records were either missing, or more likely, they'd never existed in the first place and she was being paid off the books.

I didn't even know if Lilly was her real name.

Underneath the table, my tail started tapping against the floor, a telltale sign that I was irritated, but I tried to keep my face composed. "Damn. Seventeen, huh? How'd you manage that?"

Jae looked smug, and I couldn't decide if I wanted to slit his throat or punch him in the face and *then* slit his throat. "Let's just say she was a family friend who needed some help. Help I was more than happy to provide."

"I could help that girl, all right," Dominic continued, completely oblivious to the rage kindling inside me with his every word. He let out a low whistle. "I'd kill to have a taste of her."

Jae chuckled as he puffed his cigar. "Maybe you'll get a chance, Dominic."

"Doubtful. She never has time for me."

Probably because you're disgusting.

My skin crawled as I watched Jae smirk at the guy, and I curled my tail around my chair leg to keep it from showing my growing anger.

"I bet we can change that." Jae snapped his fingers, and a server came by. He whispered something to him before the server rushed off, then signaled the dealer. "You, let's start this game."

The dealer obeyed instantly, starting a simple game of cards. We were about to finish the second hand when Jae put down his cards.

"There you are," he said. "My good luck charm."

I wasn't sure what I was expecting to see, but I know it wasn't Lilly herself.

Lilly wore a deep red dress, long-sleeved and made of skin-hugging satin covered in sequins. The front had a low V-shaped neck-line that left much of her skin exposed and a hem that stopped short of her knee. She'd tied up her brown hair, but a few pieces had been pulled out to frame her face, making her green eyes that much more striking.

In short, she looked stunning.

Lilly froze when she saw me, her eyes locked on mine. Slowly the other people in the room began to notice her presence, and soon everyone was looking at her. She seemed confused at first, but then she smiled, that fake smile I'd seen her give other men at the club. She took an awkward step forward, her body tense as she stood behind Jae's chair, clearly uncomfortable no matter how much she smiled.

But Jae didn't seem to notice or care; he motioned for Lilly to join us.

I swallowed hard, wanting Lilly as far away from these fools as possible. She glanced my way, and it took everything in me to not stand up right then and whisk her away.

"Good to see you again," I said to her, trying to match her smile. "Can I get you a chair to join us?"

"What? No. Didn't you say that you had her the other night?" Dominic whined at me. "Come sit with me tonight, sweetie. For good luck."

She smiled sweetly. "I doubt a guy like you needs much luck."

"I don't know about that. I'm always down to get lucky."

For fuck's sake.

My elbow hit his drink, knocking it over on the table, some of the dark brown liquor splashing on what I hoped was an expensive shirt that would be costly to clean.

"Will you look at that?" I asked loudly, signaling over a server to help clean it up. "My apologies. That was an accident."

"Make it up to him by giving him some attention, Lilly," Jae said, nodding to Dominic.

Wait. No. That wasn't what I had intended.

She glanced my way, and I wanted her to know...

No, I needed her to know...

I don't know what I was hoping to tell her, and it didn't ultimately matter since I couldn't say anything at all. It felt like a stone had sunk in my stomach when I saw Dominic push back his chair and pat his lap before she sat down.

The game began anew, and I picked up my cards, trying to focus on the cards to take my mind off the way he held Lilly in his lap. The way his fat ringed fingers squeezed into her flesh.

The sight was like a punch to the gut. Lilly, radiant and alluring, perched on Dominic's lap, her subtle laughter to whatever idiotic thing the demon was saying. It was a twisted show, a dance I couldn't bear to watch but found impossible to look away from. Dominic, that lowlife—his hands explored territory I longed to call my own. His oily smile, his brazen confidence, it all grated on me, fueling a fire of anger I had to keep carefully concealed.

She looked beautiful, as she always did, but the way she was positioned, the way she moved—it was maddeningly sexy. A part of me wanted to storm over and pull her away from him, but I knew I couldn't. The situation, Dominic's wealth, his family's influence, it all made him untouchable, at least for now.

Occasionally Lilly adjusted her dress, and I thought I caught sight of... something. What was that?

When I made the mistake of glancing away from my cards, I saw the look of the other men at the table, their own eyes not even trying to hide their hidden desires. I clenched my fist, anger simmering within me, mixing with jealousy and a helpless desire. Lilly didn't know how I felt, how I ached for her, and watching her in that man's arms was a torment I hadn't been prepared for. The job required me to keep a clear head, to focus on the mission at hand, but in that moment, all I could think about was the distance between us and the cruel reality that kept me from crossing it.

"Dom, I invited Max here tonight so we could talk about our upcoming partnership."

"It's a little early to call it that," I said, my eyes back on my cards. "Verdict is still out. Raise," I muttered, tossing chips into the pot as if they were worthless trinkets. It was all worthless if I couldn't protect her.

Jae smirked in appreciation. "Bold. I like it. I'll do the same, but I propose an even bigger wager. An hour with the lovely Lilly here, if either of you can beat me, for whoever wins this hand. If I win, I take all your winnings since I already have her. Who's in?"

Like hell I was going to let anyone at this table other than me win anything.

But then Lilly did something unexpected; I hardly even saw it, but I knew that I had. She shook her head at me, a silent signal telling me to fold. But I couldn't let them win this easily—not at this point. So instead of folding, I pushed all my chips into the center of the table with a fierce determination that surprised even me.

Jae clapped his hands and smiled. "That's the spirit."

Dominic followed suit, throwing in the rest of his chips eagerly.

I was going to win. I knew I was going to win. I'd already been counting cards before Lilly even sat down at the table, and now that she was there next to me, in that fucker's lap, I was following the game more closely than ever. Thankfully, I knew my hand was going to win, and with each second that passed, I could feel my heart racing, my mind calculating each possible outcome to confirm it.

Until the dealer called the end of the match and I lost.

I fucking lost.

I stared in disbelief at all the cards spread out on the velvet tabletop.

There was no way.

I'd counted all the aces. I'd seen which ones were played. There was no way that Dominic had won. Unless he'd cheated. That had to be it. He had to have cheated, but how? I'd been watching the cards the entire time. Unless the dealer had been in on it too. Unless this had been a setup from the very moment I sat down at the table.

My eyes snapped from the cards to Lilly, but she looked away. I could feel my chest tightening and my throat going dry as I watched him take her hand and lead her toward the stairs. All I could focus on was their intertwined fingers—his filthy hand tightly gripping hers.

Jae was talking to me, but I wasn't listening.

I'd *lost*.

With a murmur of an excuse about getting a drink, I got up from the table and bypassed the bar, heading up the stairs, taking them two at a time. I touched my earpiece.

"You there?"

"I heard," Blaise answered.

"I'm going to start with smoke bombs. Then, on my signal, I want you to light this place up."

14

LILLY

I pretended to adjust my dress in the mirror, but really I was checking to make sure the tiny syringe I'd stashed in my dress was still there. This was part of Jae's plan, a twisted scheme that had left me shocked and unnerved when he first proposed it. But as I looked at Dominic's smug face behind me, I knew I was willing. I wanted to forget every lecherous glance, every unwanted touch, every moment I'd been forced to endure with him.

If only the syringe could erase those memories from my mind as well.

I glanced at Dominic's face once more, steeling myself for what I had to do. This was a path I'd never thought I'd tread, but in this dark world, it seemed there was no choice but to walk it.

Once I stabbed Dominic with the needle, he would fall asleep and I'd be able to get the fuck out of there.

Easy-peasy.

Right?

The door clicked shut, and Dominic locked it behind him. Grinning at me with his gross yellow teeth, he leaned against the door, his thin tail slowly dragging back and forth at his feet.

"Luck sure was on my side tonight, wasn't it?" he asked.

"If I'm your luck. If I hadn't given you that ace, you would have lost that game back there."

"Aw, does my sweetheart want a kiss for her good behavior?"

So gross.

"See," he said, coming closer, "I knew you liked me." He kept grinning, his tiny wings fluttering behind him. "I knew you liked me better than that pretty boy anyway. That's why you helped me win and not him."

No, you fool, I helped you win because I want something from you.

I'd known Jae was going to use me as bait tonight. What I hadn't known was that Max was going to be there too. Why had I expected anything else? If they were going to be business partners, it made sense that they would associate outside the club.

Dominic wrapped a hand around my waist, bringing me closer, and I had to channel everything I'd learned from working at the club to not throw up from his breath. He reeked of smoke and cigars in the worst way.

I pretended to touch his arm but actually wiggled back a step, trying to put some distance between us. "Why don't you lie down and we can start with a massage? I hear my hands are magical."

His eyes lit up at that. "I can't wait to find out."

It took a remarkably small amount of convincing to get Dominic lying face down on the bed. I said a silent prayer of thanks to whatever god would listen that I no longer had to look at his face and that he couldn't see the look of disgust on my own. I sat beside Dominic on the bed, not far enough away to no longer smell the smoke on him, but at least it was something.

Before I started, I took the syringe out of the top of my dress and placed it in my lap, making sure it was ready. I started with running my fingertips along the edge of his wings, knowing that would get him to relax. Then I moved to the area right between his wings, kneading my knuckles into his back.

"Damn, your hands feel good. Whenever you're ready to leave Jae's club, I can find you a new gig."

"Oh? Why would I leave Jae?"

"Whatever Jae is getting you, I can get better, I promise."

Dominic's words slurred, and I leaned over to see that his eyes were closed. This fool was already letting down his guard around me? He wasn't going to be much of a challenge.

I hummed as I continued to rub into his back, trying to ignore the revulsion that crawled through my skin each time my fingers came in contact with him. Yet I had to play along, had to coax information out of this vile demon.

"That sounds intriguing," I purred, my fingers working at the knots in his shoulders as I continued to massage him. "But why should I believe you, Dominic? What makes you think you can offer more than Jae?"

He chuckled, a sound that made my stomach turn. "Oh, Lilly, my dear, you have no idea what I've got in the works. The deals I'm facilitating, they'll make me richer than you can imagine. I'm talking about big money, sweetheart, money that will make whatever Jae can provide look like pocket change."

I bit back the disgust that threatened to creep into my voice. "Really? That does sound promising," I said, injecting as much interest into my tone as I could muster. "But what kind of deals are you talking about?"

He shifted slightly on the bed, and I held my breath, fearing I'd pushed too far, but then I saw him grin again. "Can't tell you everything, beautiful, but let's just say some new players are in town. Humans like you. And they want to do business with me, not Jae. They're tired of him."

His words were the confirmation I needed, but I still had to keep up the act, had to keep pretending to be drawn to this loathsome creature. I continued to massage him, my mind racing, piecing together the puzzle.

"Humans like me," I repeated.

"Yep. Jae distributes Dust for those rich human friends of his, right? But I have better connections. My dad knows all kinds of newer, up-and-coming families in Eden."

"Your dad, huh?"

"Yeah. They'll ship direct to him, I mean to me, at a cheaper price. You should leave that demon and stick with me instead. I won't make you work in any nightclub. I'll keep you safe at my home, I mean my parents' home, but I live there too, you know. One day it will all be mine."

"As great as that sounds, why would I want to do that when you just said Jae has rich friends?"

Dominic huffed. "Things are going to change in Vestia soon, starting at the top. You need to be smart about who you ally yourself with, and Jae isn't being smart. If those Thornfields make a move and are caught—"

Without even thinking about it, I dug in with my knuckles, hard. He flinched, and I quickly muttered an apology.

Thornfields?

Had I heard him correctly?

"Why'd you stop? Oh well, doesn't matter. I'm bored with this."

He flipped over and suddenly grabbed me, my syringe falling onto the floor.

"Wait!" I said, trying to push him away. "Shouldn't we get to know each other first?"

"Look, we don't have much time, so how about you do a little less talking?"

In an instant, his nasty hands were all over me, and he kept mumbling about how I should leave Jae for him. Swatting him away, I tried to reach for the syringe on the floor, but it was just out of reach.

Damn it.

"Stop," I said, but he didn't. As hard as I pushed against Dominic's chest, he just seemed to get more and more aggressive. But then I sniffed the air. "Do you smell something?"

"Only you, baby."

"No. Oh shit, the door!"

His eyes followed to where I was pointing, to where smoke was seeping around the doorframe. The burning smell was growing stronger by the second. Dominic jumped up and hadn't taken two steps toward the door when it suddenly swung open.

"Max!"

There he stood, chest heaving, his wings expanded to fill the entire doorframe. He wasn't looking at me though. Max walked forward over the broken door without a word, and in one swift movement, he grabbed Dominic by his neck and lifted him off me and into the air. Dominic's wings and tail flailed behind him as he tried to hit Max, but Max held him firmly, not letting go.

"What the fuck, dude? Put me down."

"Hmm... Nope."

"Max!" I shouted his name, but he didn't even look at me.

"Is this about me winning that game?" Dominic tried grabbing at Max, using his nails to scrape at Max's arms and chest, but Max didn't budge. Even when Dominic's long, thin tail whipped against Max's legs, he stayed still, unmoving, terrifying.

"Look, call my dad, he'll give you whatever you want."

Still holding Dominic in the air by his throat, Max cocked his head. "What I want to do is take off each one of your fingers, one by one. That's for starters."

What the hell?

Was Max about to kill him?

The plan had been to knock him out and erase some of his memories, not murder the guy. But if Max continued liked this, I wasn't sure what he would do.

The syringe on the floor caught my eye, and I grabbed it. Lurching forward, I stabbed Dominic right in the back of his throat. Max stared at me in confusion, but then Dominic's body went limp.

Max dropped him unceremoniously on the floor and stared, open-mouthed, at me. "The fuck?"

"I'll explain later!"

We both took a step back when Dominic coughed a few times, several droplets of blood flying out of his mouth and spattering the floor. I stared at the syringe in my hand in horror. I'd thought Max was about to kill him, but was I going to end up being the one responsible? What the hell had been in that syringe? He was just supposed to fall asleep.

Thankfully the coughing stopped and his body went still. The demon was still breathing, thank the gods, so I stepped over the sleeping Dominic and grabbed Max's hand, pulling him behind me through the door and out into the hallway. From somewhere I could hear the crackling of fire and smell its acrid smoke. It seemed to be coming from the main sanctuary of the church, right where we needed to go if we were to get out.

"What's going on?" I coughed, swatting away the growing smoke. "Did some of the candles fall over and start a fire?"

"I'll explain later."

"That was my line!"

His eyes darting everywhere, Max stepped forward, his wings expanded, and he flew up above the smoke. Shielding my eyes, I could see him looking around. Suddenly he swooped down, landing in front of me.

"Come on. Let's get out of here."

"Wait! We can't go through the fire!"

But Max wasn't listening. "We're taking a shortcut. Come here." He held out his hand. "Let me rescue you this time. Please?"

It wasn't like I had much choice.

I gave him a small nod, and we were immediately airborne. He wrapped an arm over my head to shield me from the smoke as he flew over the growing fire inside the sanctuary and to the front entrance.

Once he'd shoved open the doors and we were outside, Max kept his arms tight around me, and I held on to his chest as his massive wings extended at his sides, slowly pushing us higher and higher into the night sky. I could feel the flex of his chest muscles with each stroke of his wings; I hadn't ever thought about the strength that would be needed to move wings of this size, but it had to be immense.

I had never felt anything like it before. The rush of wind against my face, the ground falling away beneath us, the wild beating of Max's leathery wings—it was terrifying and exhilarating all at once.

I glanced back at the old church, now consumed by fire, a hellish glow against the dark Vestian sky. But my fear was soon overshadowed by the sensation of flying, a feeling so foreign and yet so liberating.

My entire life had been confined by rules and expectations. The rigid demands of my family, then of Jae, not to mention the unspoken code of conduct at the nightclub—they had all tethered me to the ground. But up here, in Max's arms, those constraints felt distant and insignificant. If I could forget what had happened earlier in the night, forget about Jae and Dominic and all that disgusting business, I could truly feel what was an unspoken promise of freedom in the way we soared over the city, something I had never dared to imagine.

We glided over downtown Vestia, the twinkling lights forming a mesmerizing pattern below. The city looked different from this vantage point, both more beautiful and more remote. My heartbeat raced, not just from the adrenaline but from the close proximity to Max.

I barely knew him, and yet he had just saved my life. I could feel the warmth of his body against mine, the strength in his arms, the peculiar sensation of his long tail, tipped like an arrow, balancing us in the air. His presence was both comforting and disconcerting, his very existence defying everything I thought I knew.

We flew around grand skyscrapers and over bustling city streets until the buildings became older and smaller. The humid night air grew thicker as we approached my apartment. It was a far cry from the elegance of the downtown we had just flown over. The contradictions of my feelings mirrored the dichotomy of Vestia itself, a city of both splendor and decay.

Max's voice broke through my thoughts. "Hold on tight," he said, his voice soft yet firm as we began to descend. I tightened my grip, my mind a whirlwind of emotions. Part of me wanted to cling to him forever, to continue this aerial dance and never return to the ground.

We landed softly outside my apartment door, Max's wings folding neatly against his back. He released me, but I still felt the ghost of his touch, the echo of our flight lingering in my senses.

"Are you all right?" he asked, concern in his eyes.

I nodded, unable to find the words to describe what I had just experienced. The fear, the exhilaration, the freedom, the strange allure of Max himself had all merged into a heady mix that left me breathless.

I looked up at him, my emotions still in turmoil, and for the first time, I allowed myself to acknowledge the attraction I felt for this mysterious man with the black wings.

Then the realization hit me.

"I don't have my keys."

"Not a problem."

Without another word, Max swung his leg back and delivered a powerful kick of his boot square against the middle of my apartment door. The wood quivered for just a second before giving in and slamming open.

Well, damn.

I stared in disbelief at the splintered remnants of my door, anger and frustration welling up within me. Max stood in the entryway, not even having the decency to look flushed or even bothered from the effort of breaking it down. Just how strong was he if he could bust through a door without breaking a sweat?

I wasn't sure what to say. Part of me was horrified at how fragile and unsafe my door had really been while another part couldn't help but be mildly impressed by how easy that had been for Max. The problem was now that I didn't have a door.

"What am I supposed to do now?" I asked him as I shuffled past him into my apartment. Max stayed in the open doorway, now letting his wings spread wide to block anyone from seeing inside.

"Grab what you need," he said over his shoulder. "You're not staying here."

"That much is obvious. My door is broken, and my landlord is going to have my head for the repair cost."

"Like hell he is." He left my doorway then, storming into my apartment. His silver eyes scanned the room as he paced around.

"You could have at least tried to pick the lock or something. Now I can't even lock my door, and I won't be safe staying here."

Max's eyes narrowed, his irritation evident. "Safe?" he growled.

"You think you'd be safe here after leaving with me? Jae's not going to just let you go like that, Lilly. He'll come looking for you, and if he finds you here..."

His voice trailed off, but the implication was clear.

"I can handle him," I told him.

Max's jaw tightened. "You're not thinking clearly," he said through gritted teeth. "You can't go back to the way things were. You can't just return to Jae's world and pretend nothing happened."

"I said I'll handle him. I always do. You can't just destroy my home and expect me to be grateful, Max."

Max's face contorted with rage, his wings twitching involuntarily. "Your home? This place?" he shouted, his voice rising. "This isn't your home, Lilly. This is a cage, a trap set by Jae. Do you have a suitcase? I'll throw some things in. No, wait. No need. Let's just go," he said, taking my hand and tugging me back toward the open door. "I'll buy you new things."

"Max, stop," I said, pulling back, but he didn't let go. "What are you saying?"

"I'm saying that your boss deliberately set you up tonight." I could hear the unbridled anger and frustration in his voice, both of which were so new to hear from him. "If Jae dragging you there in the first place wasn't bad enough, it was all a setup. That guy cheated. He should never have had that ace."

"How did you know that?"

"Because I cheated too."

"What?"

"What?" Max echoed, mirroring my confusion. "I was counting the cards."

"And I gave him the extra ace."

Max looked at me for a moment and then clenched his fist. "I knew he didn't beat me on his own! If you knew he was going to win, you knew you were going to end up alone with him. That's why you had that syringe. I see... That's kind of cool. Way to go. I'm impressed with your execution."

"What?"

"Wait," he said, "if this was planned from the start, why did I set the building on fire?"

"That was you? Oh my gods... Max, what if that guy died? We left him there... by himself... with all that smoke."

Max shook his head. "Dying from smoke inhalation would be better than if I'd torn his throat out."

I looked at him incredulously. "Is that what your plan was?"

"Do you really want me to answer that?"

With a deep sigh, I took my hand away and sat down on my couch. I started rubbing at my temples, trying to make sense of what he was saying and everything that had happened.

"I'll figure something out," I said. "If Jae comes here, it will be so much worse if you're here. As it stands right now, I can still come back from this. I'll tell Jae I was scared and ran. I'll come up with an excuse about the door."

"You think he'll believe that?" Max's anger seemed to deflate, his shoulders slumping. He took a step toward me, his eyes softening as he crouched down in front of me, his eyes searching mine. "Why bother telling him anything? I know you understand what kind of demon that monster is. He sold you out to that man without a second thought."

"I know. Just like how I know I can handle this myself. Just like I would have handled Dominic myself until you showed up and made it ten times worse."

"I don't understand, Lilly."

"What don't you understand?"

"Any of it! All of it!"

"I never asked you to understand me or my life, Max. You probably think I'm dumb for going along with Jae's shit—"

"I never said that," he interrupted, his voice gentle but firm.

I closed my eyes and put my head in my hands, not wanting to see the look of pity from him that I knew was coming. "You didn't have to. You and Jae are going to be partners, right? You were ready to murder that demon. You set fire to a church, Max! All because you thought I needed rescuing? You all think I'm this weak—"

"I'll tell you exactly what I'm thinking."

"I don't want to hear it."

"I'm thinking about how I don't understand why someone so smart and beautiful thinks so little of herself."

My eyes popped open, only to see Max kneeling in front of me, his silver eyes staring at me expectantly. "What?"

"I'm thinking about how much I care about you. And I'm thinking about how I'm going to kiss you right now."

His words hung in the air, the tension between us thick and tangible. In that moment, when Max moved toward me on the couch and took my head in his big hands, all that mattered was the connection between the two of us. There wasn't time to unpack what this meant, what any of it meant, when his wings curled around the both of us, creating a dark, warm cocoon that surrounded us when his lips first touched mine. His kiss was gentle, careful, our lips barely pressing against each other's, but it wasn't enough.

My own hands clung to his face, my fingers tucking behind his ears and tugging him to me. After all the confusion of this night, right then I needed him closer. I *wanted* him closer—on me, against me, all over me. Max followed my movements, rising up and matching my intensity until there was no space left between us. His mouth slotted against my own, I tasted the faintest hint of a sweet alcohol on his tongue. I wasn't sure if I'd ever tasted anything as delicious.

After a moment, Max pulled back but stayed close, his warm hands still gently holding my cheeks, as if I were something so fragile that I might break at any second, despite how passionately he'd kissed me moments before. His gaze left me speechless. As I met Max's eyes, I saw something new and unexpected—a warmth I'd never seen in anyone else's eyes. Many men had looked at me before, but never, ever like this, never with this intoxicating mix of intensity and tenderness.

"What are you thinking now?" I dared to ask.

Coming closer, he brushed his lips over my own, and I felt him smile against me. "I'm thinking about kissing you again," he said, his voice a low whisper. "Is that okay with you?"

It was more than okay.

I'd barely nodded before his lips were on mine again, his body moving closer until he was fully on the couch with me. Now that he knew what I wanted, what we obviously both wanted, the kiss was stronger, hotter, messier, his hands exploring everywhere they could reach, my body arching into the warmth of his touch.

Only at the surprise of his tail starting to curl against my leg did I open my eyes, suddenly remembering where we were and what we had been doing.

"The door," I mumbled between breaths.

"Fuck the door."

Max dove his head back down, dotting kisses along my jaw. I didn't want him to stop, but my apartment door was open to the night air, and there was no way to know who might walk through at any moment. We were on borrowed time, and I didn't want to think about the consequences of Jae showing up while we were together like this.

Max must have realized it too, because with a frustrated murmur, he leaned back, keeping his forehead against my own. "You do realize that you're coming with me, right? It's not safe to stay here without a door."

Gently I pressed one hand against his chest and tried to ignore the muscles I felt underneath my palm as I shifted him back away from me. The distance helped clear my head slightly, my mind catching up with everything that was happening. There was no way to deny that the chemistry between us right then was off the charts, but what did I even know about Max? I knew he came to the club, he was rich, and he hung out with the same demons as Jae. Not a great combination. I didn't even know his last name. No matter what my body was telling me to do—no, *screaming* at me to do—I had to be smart.

"Since you broke my door, I want you to fix it. Tomorrow. Tonight you're going to pay for a hotel where I will stay... by myself."

Max's wings drooped behind him, and I had to bite back a chuckle at the sight of this demon pouting like a puppy.

"And then what?" Max frowned.

"And then I'll talk to Jae and sort everything out."

"Why bother? Lilly," he said, his hand touching the side of my face, "don't I get some kind of reward for rescuing you?"

"I didn't need rescuing."

"The building was on fire."

"Apparently because of you."

"Semantics. I want a date with you."

The idea of stepping into the unknown with him made me hesitate. But the longer I didn't say anything, the more Max continued to stare at me with those gorgeous silver eyes, his fingers gently holding my cheek.

"Okay," I finally said.

His eyes lit up, his tail suddenly tapping against the floor. "You're not arguing with me?"

"Nope."

"There's a work thing in a few days. A big event for other businesses I'm thinking about investing in. Be my date."

I considered that. "Okay."

His wings no longer drooping, Max stood up and held out his hand for me to take. "Then let's get the hell out of here."

I woke up shivering.

The room was dark, the windows covered with heavy curtains. The fireplace still wasn't lit. They were all probably too busy with my stepmother to worry about the fire in my room, but without it, I was freezing. The ice had been so sharp and the water so cold. At least my hair had been dried and my clothes changed since they'd been soaked by the lake. Groping for blankets in the dark, I realized that I'd kicked all of them off, but I soon found my heavy comforter and pulled it around me, the familiar weight at least taking away some of the cold.

Wait.

I blinked, and I was back in reality. I wasn't home at all. I was lying in a bed in a hotel room in Vestia, not my old home back in Eden. Air-conditioning was cooling the room, not the ever-present snow that always surrounded our estate. These weren't my blankets, and this wasn't my room. That life that I'd known in Eden was gone. Long gone.

And you know what? Good riddance.

After gathering up my things, I did the best I could with my hair, splashed some water on my face, and pulled on the jeans and sweatshirt I'd changed into last night. For once I was grateful that expectations for humans were so low, since most of the demons who would see me leave the hotel that morning probably wouldn't even glance my way.

The chaos I was living with in Vestia was temporary; once I was done with Jae, I could determine my own destiny, something I'd never been allowed to do back home. Before zipping my backpack, I caught sight of the postcard I'd tossed in at the last minute. One side of the card, the edge ragged with age, was blank, but the other had a picture I'd stared at so often I had it memorized: a seaside port, the sun reflecting off blue water that crashed against a rocky coastline dotted with quaint cottages. When I was finally free of Jae, I'd make my way to that port. I'd start over there.

Speaking of Jae, I needed to come up with an excuse for vanishing the night before. I didn't want him to know about what had happened with Dominic either, so I needed to pretend I knew nothing about it. *I saw a fire, so I ran away.* That might work. But he'd want to know why I didn't bother to look for him or call him. *My phone burned in the fire.* That was plausible, but he'd just buy me a new phone.

Slowly opening the door just an inch, I peeked outside to see if I was alone. What I didn't expect to see was Max sitting on the floor across from my door, his back against the wall, completely and totally asleep. He'd drawn his knees up against his chest, his wings curling around his body like a blanket. With his head tucked into his arms, all I could see was his black hair moving as he took slow, steady breaths in his sleep. There was a peaceful silence in the hall, broken only by the gentle sound of his breathing.

Had he waited out here all night? To watch over me even though I wasn't in any danger and no one knew where I was? It was ridiculous, it was absurd, it was… sweet.

What the hell was I thinking? Why couldn't I be attracted to normal guys who work in offices or do something on computers? Really, anything that wasn't dangerous or illegal. The more time I spent with Max, the more I felt like I might be falling back into the same trap I'd fallen into with Jae, and I knew where *that* had led.

No. This was different.

Max was different. He'd proven that last night.

Hadn't he?

I scooted closer, close enough to feel the heat of his body, to smell the scent that I now knew was distinctly *Max*. Whatever that meant.

"Who are you?" I whispered.

"Lilly."

I shrank back, thinking he'd woken up. I breathed a sigh of relief when I realized he hadn't. Max was still asleep, just mumbling to himself. But he'd said *my* name, I realized, my heart starting to race. Was he dreaming about me? Did he know I was right beside him?

"I'm here," I whispered.

I couldn't leave him like this, but I didn't want to wake him up either. Quietly digging around in my backpack, I found a pen and the only paper I could find—the postcard I'd thrown in there. The postcard with the picture of Cambria on it, with its sparkling water and sunny skies. I'd carried this card with me for years because it represented hope, or at least what I hoped my future could be.

I scrawled a quick note on the back of the card and then placed it at Max's feet, careful not to wake him.

Maybe, after last night, I could have a different kind of hope instead.

15

MAX

*D*ear sleeping beauty, when's our date? PS: You owe me a door.

Pressing the card against my chest, I smiled. She called me a sleeping beauty, which meant...

Lilly thinks I'm beautiful.

I flipped over the card to see a photo of Cambria, the port town on the edge of Vestia, the place Lilly had told me that she wanted to go see one day. When she'd packed her bag at her apartment, this card had been one of the few things she'd brought with her, so it had to be important to her.

And she'd left it with me.

I wanted to feel grateful that she'd written a message at all and even more grateful that she'd left this important possession with me, but I couldn't ignore the twinge of sadness I felt too. I'd make it up to her.

Tucking the card carefully into my jacket, I headed home to change. I still smelled like smoke from last night and was in desperate need of a shower, but when the doors opened to my apartment, two of the last demons I felt like talking to greeted me instead. I already knew what they wanted, so I walked right by them, tossing my jacket behind me.

"For the last time, I don't give a shit about the entertainment, Sam," I told them. "And Kal, if you bug me about the color of table-cloths one more time, I'm firing both of you."

They trailed behind me, and Kal scooped my jacket up off the floor.

"But what about the entertainment?" Sam asked. "What if we got a fire dancer since, you know, you like fire and stuff."

I spun around to stare at them in disbelief. "Have you lost your mind?"

"It was Kal's idea."

"It was not!"

I held up a hand to silence them both. "Male or female?"

They exchanged a look. "I'm not following...?" Sam said.

"It's just that I don't think Lilly would like to see a female fire dancer in my apartment, so it would have to be a guy."

"Lilly, sir?"

"We are not having a fire dancer in this apartment," Kal insisted.

"Although I don't mind the idea of making Lilly a little jealous. No. I don't want to scare her away anymore. No fire dancers."

"Aw, man..."

"Yes, sir," Kal nodded, already taking notes on his tablet, no doubt adding my request to his ridiculously long to-do list. The thirty-year-old demon was nothing if not particular, in both his tall, muscular appearance that he hid behind dark, stuffy suits and his work ethic, which was one reason he was the ideal demon to help me clean up after my missions. Whether for a covert job or an upcoming party, Kal was excellent at making problems of all shapes and sizes disappear, no matter how bloody. He followed orders, worked hard, and kept his mouth shut—the perfect combination in this line of work.

Sam, however, the other demon I'd hired to help, was... not.

Sam was young, barely eighteen, with shaggy blond hair that

always looked like it needed a brush. He was small, probably from how poor he'd been growing up, and had only minimal education. Not that it mattered. Sam had street smarts gained from his years trying to survive the slums on the outskirts of Vestia as a child, and we met a few years ago when I was still working with my father. If not for my father, Sam's story might have ended a long time ago, courtesy of the gang that had kidnapped him. But since it didn't, Sam made up for any of his shortcomings with an outpouring of enthusiasm and loyalty.

I had clothes covered in blood? Sam would wash them and return them cleaner than ever. A body needed to disappear? Sam made it happen with some assistance from Kal in moving the remains. I needed a latte ASAP? He was happy to make a coffee run.

I preferred to work alone, but these guys were part of the intimate circle of demons who knew the truth of what I really did.

But when they bugged me about stupid shit, I considered making that circle smaller.

"Oh! If not fire, what about ice sculptures?" Sam clapped his hands. "I read about those once! I heard they were really popular with the humans in the north, so it would be something unique here."

I pinched the bridge of my nose. "Sam. How long do you think an ice sculpture is going to last in this city?"

"Sir, it's just... this guest list includes some pretty influential demons," Kal said. "We know you want to appear as someone with both class as well as a far reach. We want the event to be impeccable, to portray you as capable and responsible."

"Are you saying I'm not responsible?"

Kal's eyes flicked to my jacket, which he'd just picked up off the floor. "Sir, we simply want everything to be perfect."

"Please can we get an ice sculpture?" When Sam pleaded at me with those big eyes, I had a hard time saying no to the kid.

"Fine. Whatever. Try an ice sculpture. But you're cleaning it up when it melts everywhere."

Kal grumbled something about how he would end up being the one to actually clean it up, but I had another idea.

"And I have another task for you both in the meantime."

"A side quest? Awesome!" Sam pumped his fist into the air. "You can count on us!"

"Tonight you're going to report to the Red Rose downtown—"

Sam's mouth dropped open. "Uh, are we allowed in there?"

"I'll get your name on the list. There's a human who works there. Her name is Lilly. Keep an eye on her and report back. Consider it your most important assignment for the evening."

"More important than the ice sculptures?" Sam asked, no longer looking as excited.

"By far."

"Sir, may we ask why we are watching the young lady?" Kal asked.

"Because I want to make sure that nothing happens to my future wife."

Sam's hands flew to his mouth, and he squealed. Kal looked like he was about to have a heart attack.

"I was not aware that you'd become engaged," Kal said slowly.

"Yeah! When were you going to tell us, boss?"

"I'm not. Not yet. But I already know."

Sam and Kal left me alone then, finally, the two of them already bickering about wedding plans. All I could do was shake my head. My watch pulsed, and when I looked down, I saw a text from Blaise.

Why the fuck were you at a hotel last night?

I texted him back, letting him know I was on my way.

16

LILLY

The bar was even busier that night, and I couldn't stop thinking about him and last night.

The press of his hot mouth against my own. The weight and feel of his body. The softness of his wings.

Fuck.

At least the bar was busy with more new customers than normal to take my mind off the sinful images that kept running through my head. Jae had accepted that I ran away when the church caught fire, and he seemed pleased when I told him what Dominic had revealed about his father's own supply chain attempting to rival Jae's. Jae assured me that Dominic was, in fact, alive, but I wondered for how much longer.

I was cleaning up a table near the bar when I heard two new guests—a demon with messy blond hair who seemed too young to even be in the club and another one, older than me, looking stiff and awkward—talking to each other in low tones.

"Do you think the boss wants us here every night?" the younger one asked.

"I hope not. We have too much to do," the older replied.

"I'm not complaining though. At least we get to drink on the job and look at pretty girls."

"I will admit that this job is better than cleaning up his messes."

Job? With the amount they'd been drinking, there was no way they were security, yet he'd just said that they were assigned to work at the club. I hadn't seen them interact with our actual security, so who the hell were these guys?

I kept a casual eye on them both. The way they were talking, the words they were using, it all seemed to suggest something underhanded.

"I heard the last job went sideways," the younger demon said, his voice dropping even lower. "It was a mess, wasn't it?"

"Shh! Don't talk about it here." The older one glanced around nervously. "You never know who might be listening."

"But we're fine now, right? We've got a solid plan?"

The older demon sighed, rolling his eyes. "Of course we do. But the less said about it in public, the better. Focus on tonight. That's all that matters."

I waited until the younger demon got up from his seat to head to the bathroom before I followed him. Just as he turned the corner to go down the hall leading to the bathroom, I walked faster, going past him and bumping into him along the way. Realizing what had happened, he looked down at me, mumbled some excuse, and tried to walk around, but instead, I stepped in front of him, blocking his path.

"Hey. You."

"Uh... me?"

"Yeah, you," I repeated. "I don't know what kind of game you're planning here, but you and your friend need to take it somewhere else."

"I'm not planning anything."

"Liar. I heard the two of you talking just now."

"You heard us?"

"Of course I did."

He paled. "Shit."

"Shit is right. If you and your buddy are planning on causing trouble in this club tonight, you need to—"

"Damn it, I knew Kal should have been quieter. It was probably that last beer. He's a big guy, you know, but he's really a lightweight. This job is going to be hard on him. Please don't tell the boss you heard us."

It was my turn to be confused. I stared at him blankly. "Huh?"

Were these two demons actually employees here? When had Jae hired them?

"If the boss finds out you know why we're here, Kal and I will both be on his shit list."

I had no idea what he was talking about, but he seemed to think I did. I could work with that. "Riiiight," I said slowly, nodding my head as if I understood. "You better hope I don't say anything then."

"Please don't. I haven't had a job this easy in forever. If I'm not here watching you, he'll find more bodies for me to clean up and then—"

"Hold on. Watching *me*?"

"I don't mean it like *that*!" The demon held up his hands as if he was surrendering. "Max would kill me if he thought I was looking at you like that."

I wrinkled my nose. "Max?"

"Yeah, Max."

"What does he have to do with this?"

His silver eyes went wide. "Oh shit."

"Is Max your... boss?"

"Shit." He threw back his head and groaned. "You didn't know. Shit. Shit. Shit."

"Of course I knew." Nothing like a good bluff. "Obviously. But I need you to repeat it all to me as if I didn't. Tell me everything. Right now."

"No way!"

He started to dart away from me, but I grabbed the edge of his wing and pulled. I'd lived in Vestia long enough to know how sensitive their wings were, so I yanked back hard enough that it would hurt.

"Ow! Let go! You're a lot stronger than you look, you know," he said when I released him, rubbing the edge of his wing where I'd grabbed him.

"I'm not apologizing for that. Start with the basics. Who are you?"

"I'm Sam."

"Okay, Sam. You work for Max."

"Yeah..."

"Are you telling me that Max has assigned you to come to this club?"

"Yeah..."

"And he's paying you for that?"

"Well, yeah. Of course. I don't work for free."

"Why?"

"Um... What?"

"Why is he paying you to come here?"

Sam rolled his eyes, seemingly exasperated by the question. "Because I'm good at stealth operations obviously."

"Which is why I was able to overhear you earlier."

"That was Kal's fault, not mine."

"Tell me why he's having anyone spy on me at all."

"No way. I've already said enough. If the boss finds out that I even talked to you, I'm going to be in deep shit."

"If you don't tell me more, I will grab that wing again and twist until it won't fly anymore. I swear I will."

Despite my threat, Sam grinned. "Damn. At least now I see why Max is so in love with you."

Just like that, the world stopped moving.

"He... What?"

Sam's grin vanished, his jaw dropping open. "Oh shit. I did it again. Forget everything I said!" He started to dart away, and I chased after him.

"Get back here!" I yelled, and he stopped finally. "You're going to do something for me."

"Whatever it is, please let this job keep going. Let me just come here and drink on the job, please."

"You're not in a position to make demands. Call your boss and tell him to come here. Now."

"I can't. Please don't make me." His eyes bugged out. "He'll kill me."

"Not if I kill you first."

"Then you won't get this invitation!" Sam scrambled to find something in his jacket pocket, pulling out an envelope. "He said to leave this at the bar for you, but you might as well have it now." He shoved it at me. "Just take it and please don't say anything about this. Please? If he's mad at me, I'll never get him to agree to the ice sculpture."

"What?" Ignoring whatever he was rambling about, I took the envelope and opened it up. It was my postcard, the one I'd left with him. Underneath the note I'd left for him was scrawled two handwritten lines of his own. This was the first time I'd seen Max's handwriting, and it seemed to suit him. Printed letters, a random mix of capitals and cursive, and overall messy.

Hope you like the door, my first gift to you.

I rolled my eyes. The door he had kicked in with his big-ass boot. No way was that going to count as a gift.

Meet me at the address below tomorrow night.

17

────────

MAX

Blaise's gym was our sanctuary.

The whole building was nothing more than a run-down, abandoned storefront above Blaise's workshop, the rare building in Vestia that hadn't been demolished and rebuilt in the glossy steel-and-concrete aesthetic of the rest of the city. Even though it was in the middle of the capital, Blaise's building had been long forgotten by developers simply because they knew that stubborn asshole was never going to sell.

I didn't know how much he'd paid for the building, but it wasn't like he used any of his money to fix the place up. The peeling paint on the walls and high ceilings, the low hum of the old cooling system struggling to survive in the constant, suffocating heat of Vestia, the vague scent of oil and steel from Blaise's workshop below—it was all part of the ambiance, something a more polished gym could never replicate. It was gritty, it was real, and it was ours.

In contrast to the rest of the building, Blaise had built a brand-new boxing ring on the ground floor that was made of the most expensive and highest technical specs you could find. It had an elevated center platform covered in a foam mat that I was pretty sure used to be blue but was now dark with use. Since you never knew what might happen when two demons were flying around in the air, Blaise had installed tall posts in each corner of the ring, each one soaring almost all the way to the ceiling, connected to the other posts by thick white ropes to catch us in case we fell against them.

On opposite corners of the ring, we both hovered a few feet off the air, watching the other. I stared down Blaise, the familiar clench of anticipation deep in my gut as I readied my first strike. Blaise's insane physique had been honed from hours working with heavy metal and tools in his workshop, but he was still able to move with a speed that matched my own. If I really admitted it to myself, with his strength and speed, Blaise was a better all-around fighter than me and always had been, but I never backed down from a challenge.

A shared glance and quick nod meant that we were ready to begin, and Blaise flew at me fast and focused with a strong right hook. The attack was powerful and direct, just like him. It was also predictable as hell. Just like Blaise.

Easily dodging the hit, I used my wings to push me higher and spun at the same time, my tail lashing out against his face. He swerved to the side to avoid, as I'd known he would, giving me an opening to rush at him with my full strength. Locking my arms around his waist, I pulled us down, our bodies crashing against the foam padding as we hit the mat.

"That's one point for me," I said, jumping up and stepping back to my original corner.

"Fine. It will also be your last."

He wasn't wrong.

Blaise was a powerhouse, a mammoth of muscle and determination. His attacks were ferocious, each one a hurricane of unrelenting blows, all of them aiming to overwhelm and overpower.

That just meant I had to work smarter, not harder.

As we continued to spar, the grunts and thuds of our match continued to echo throughout the empty room.

"Do you have something to prove today?" Blaise asked between blows.

"Maybe."

I continued to weave and dodge in the air, each of my movements a strategic counter to his raw power. I could tell he was aiming for a quick, decisive victory, but I wasn't about to give in so easily. My wings flapped harder as I pushed upward to avoid his sharp dive, and I threw a counterpunch that barely grazed him.

"You're too slow," he said.

I blocked his next blow, but he came back with another combination that I was only barely able to dodge.

"I can handle it," I shot back, trying to regain my footing as Blaise landed a quick jab to my ribs that knocked me back a step.

"Doesn't look like it. Why are you so quiet? Normally I'm constantly telling you to shut up."

"You want me to talk more?" I asked him. "I would be happy to talk you about ice sculptures. Did you know they're popular with humans?"

"What? No. I don't care about ice sculptures. I'm just saying that this isn't normal."

"I'm not normal."

"I fucking know that better than anyone. Something is off with you. Like last night, that mess? Is this all because of...?"

He left the sentence hanging in the air unfinished, but it wasn't like Blaise to talk in riddles or leave things unsaid.

I landed on the mat, my feet planted steadily beneath me. "Just say it."

Blaise landed on the mat in front of me, his wings folded behind him. He crossed his arms over his chest and stared at me. "Fine. I will. This human is making you lose your focus on your work."

"All I've ever done is pay attention to work."

"Then now isn't the time to change anything."

"Says the demon who suddenly wants to chat instead of fight. Shut up and beat me if you can."

Blaise cracked his knuckles and grinned. "Gladly."

As we sparred, I stayed silent and paid attention to his movements, to the way he was watching me closely.

"I'm going to tell her," I finally said.

Blaise stared at me. "Max. She is connected to the very bastards we are trying to take down. If you tell her, it puts us and our mission at risk. It puts Lilly at risk too."

"So I should keep lying to her? She'll understand if I tell her. I know she will."

"And if she doesn't? What will you do then with someone who knows who you really are, who knows what you really do? Does Rand know you're going to tell her?"

"What, are you going to snitch on me? Come on, Blaise."

"I didn't say that."

"We're going on a date."

"You have time to date?"

"Well, I invited her to that party I'm throwing."

"Does she know that it's a setup for you to connect with other suspected drug lords?"

"Ah... well... not exactly."

Blaise rolled his eyes. "You're an idiot. I don't know how you got it into your head that you can just fly off into the sunset with your girlfriend and live happily ever after. Not in our line of work, Max. No one gets to have it all."

I smiled and took up my stance again. "Just watch me."

The match continued, both of us with a renewed desire to win, to prove the other wrong. He wouldn't back off, continuing to strike with a flurry of punches. But there was something I knew about Blaise. He was a big guy, and big guys like him tired easily. I could see the smallest hints of fatigue in his punches, and when finally Blaise sent a powerful punch toward my head that moved a second slower than normal, I ducked low and swept my leg under his feet, causing him to lose balance and fall back.

Blaise hit the mat with a loud thud. He stayed like that, his wings spread out underneath him, not making any attempt to get up.

"That was a cheap shot," he muttered from the mat.

"Yet you didn't see it coming." My chest heaved as I caught my breath, but a wide smile broke out over my face as I stood over him triumphantly. "You might be right that no one gets to have it all, but sometimes you can get just enough."

18

LILLY

odies shuffled around in the crowded elevator, their wings brushing up against me as I squeezed past them toward the back.

"Can someone press twenty-five?" I asked.

Not a single demon moved. I would have pressed the button myself if I could have, but these jerks were so much bigger than me, with their big wings taking up so much space.

I cleared my throat. "Twenty-five please."

The bulky demon in front of me glanced over his shoulder, scowling as his silver eyes gave me a once-over before he turned back to face the door. "It's already pressed."

Oh.

Well, okay.

Someone could have said that earlier.

The rest of the elevator ride was silent, and I kept expecting the demons to get off at one of the other floors, but they didn't. All of us rode to the top floor together, and when the doors finally opened, we all shuffled out into the hallway, their massive wings bumping me as they passed.

Keeping my head down to avoid their sneers, I followed the group down the hall to where even more demons had lined up, each one giving their name to a security guard with a clipboard.

Once they let me in, I knew I'd been wrong about the elevator taking me to the top floor, because now I saw a grand staircase in the middle of the room, which meant this apartment had not one, but two floors.

And right in front of the staircase, with demons surrounding it and pointing out different aspects of its carvings, was an enormous ice sculpture.

It was an imposing sculpture of a fiery phoenix, wings spread as if caught midflight. Its elaborate tail plumage cascaded down, each feather perfectly carved from the glistening ice. Frozen flames wreathed its neck and head, each flame rendered with almost lifelike movement yet forever stilled in time.

There was a low murmur surrounding the sculpture as demons marveled at the craftsmanship, but I barely heard them. I'd seen sculptures like this before, back when I lived in Eden, but never in Vestia, and never any of this size. To have ice of this size in Vestia meant the person who owned this apartment must be ridiculously wealthy. Vestia was hotter than anywhere else on the planet, and while technology was able to keep most buildings cool, nothing frozen ever lasted long. To have commissioned the piece, paid to have it shipped, and keep it cool through the party—I couldn't imagine the cost.

The phoenix's frozen eyes seemed to follow me as I approached, its beak open as though crying out in a silent scream. Its talons stretched forward, emerging from within the icy blaze that surrounded its body. A flickering light from the overhead chandeliers danced across the frozen creature, as if the phoenix might burst into real flames at any moment.

Gazing up at the towering ice sculpture, I felt that same chill deep in my bones that had seeped in the day I fell into the lake. The heart-stopping shock as the frigid water surrounded me, the way time seemed to slow down as I sank, the knowledge that no one was going to help me only adding to my desperation. With a shiver, I turned away. Some things were better left in the past.

"Excuse me," someone said behind me.

When I turned around, it was two demons, both ladies with perfectly beautiful hair and perfectly dainty black wings. Their long fingernails clicked around wineglasses, and their jewel-tone dresses sparkled under the room's lights, making me more aware than I had been before of my simple black dress.

"Do I know you?" the one with blond hair asked.

"No, I don't think so," I said. "I'm—"

"I didn't think I did." She raised a perfectly sculpted brow. "I didn't realize humans were invited tonight."

"I'm meeting someone," I explained.

The one whose dark brown hair was curled with perfect sophistication narrowed her silver eyes as she stared at me, her expression completely unimpressed. "Who? Give me their name so I can remind them not to bring their pets with them."

"Excuse me?"

"Is there a problem here?" Suddenly Max was standing between the two women, their faces looking like they'd seen a ghost.

"Max." The blonde purred his name, the sound of it coming from her mouth making the hairs on the back of my neck stand up. "So good to see you."

They swooped toward him, each one taking one of his arms and holding on.

"Except some idiot was dumb enough to bring his pet human with him tonight, it seems." The brunette gestured toward me, the blonde joining her in a disgusting cackle while my blood raged.

Shrugging them off, Max held out his hand to me with a smile. "I'm glad you made it, Lilly. I'm honored that you accepted my invitation."

I took his hand, a smug smile on my face, and both demons gasped as Max and I walked away from them. I would have done anything to have turned around to see the looks on their faces.

"Those ladies weren't bothering you, were they?"

"They wish," I muttered.

Max chuckled under his breath as he led me away. "They're jealous right now, you know."

"Jealous?" I asked, wrinkling my nose. "Of what?"

"Of you, kitten."

It was my turn to laugh at the absurdity of the idea.

"What did you think of that ice sculpture?" he asked. "It seems to be the talk of the party."

I didn't want to think about ice any longer. "It is fine."

"Just fine?"

"Just fine. It's very well done. They used to be very popular in Eden, but I've never seen any quite like that one."

"Really? I'd love to hear more about your time in Eden," he said. "Come outside with me." Max gestured toward the large glass double doors. "We can talk out there with a little more privacy."

I followed behind him, letting him hold the door open as we stepped out onto a large terrace. Several tables and couches were set up across the terrace, all of it overlooking the city so many floors below us. I couldn't help but gasp at the amazing view. The city appeared as a sea of twinkling gems and polished towers stretching to the horizon. This high up, I felt like I could reach out and pluck one of the winking stars right out of the sky.

"Pretty, huh?"

"That's an understatement," I told him. "This view is incredible. From this height, you can see so much. You can see all the way to the square."

"I had a great view of that obnoxious statue of the old king before they tore it down."

Ah. My suspicion had been right.

"I never saw the statue," I admitted. "But right now I can see... everything. Is the view why you bought this place?"

"That and I liked how high up it is. Makes flying more fun."

"I see." So the place was his.

Max paled, realizing what he'd revealed. I'd been telling the truth though. I could see so much of Vestia from this terrace. My own apartment only had one window, and it faced another brick wall just as unpleasant as the brick walls inside my apartment. It wasn't even worth opening the curtains.

But this, this was magnificent.

I breathed in the warm night air and tried to imagine waking up each morning in a place like this, reading a book on one of the couches on the terrace, enjoying a cup of coffee as I watched the sunrise.

No, the glittering lights of Vestia only reminded me of the huge gulf between Max's world and my own.

"So you're right. This is my apartment," he said. "I'm sorry I didn't say anything. I just didn't want you to be uncomfortable."

"After you saw where I live?"

"Truthfully, yes."

"I'm not—" A look from him silenced me. "Okay, fine. I am. A little. Your home is... amazing."

"Thank you. It's just an apartment though."

"It's not 'just an apartment.' Why am I here, Max? You're obviously very successful. There are jealous demons lining up for you. Why do you keep pursuing me? This isn't adding up."

"Well, for starters, you're strong."

"Because you saw me swing a pool cue one time?"

"That's not the kind of strength I meant."

I stared out at the city, unable to meet his eyes. "Oh. Well, you're wrong about that too then."

But then he was right next to me, leaning against the railing by my side. "You live alone."

"You know I do."

"In a city hostile to humans. That must mean that you left your family and everything you knew to come to Vestia. Even though you've never told me why, you made a huge change in your life."

I didn't answer since we both knew that was true.

"Again, you did that all on your own. If that isn't strength, what is?"

"You're leaving out some key bits of information, Max. I work in a nightclub where I make barely enough money to pay rent. If the club didn't sell food, I wouldn't even eat most days."

I left out the part about the jealous, violent demon holding a debt over my head who also happened to be my boss.

"And yet here you are."

"Yeah, here I am," I said, looking around at this magnificent apartment and terrace, the city spread out before us both. "Even though I'm not sure how."

"When are you going to start seeing yourself the way that I do?"

I huffed out a laugh.

Weak. Pathetic. Stupid. I'd heard all those lovely terms more times than I could count. I'd heard them when I lived in Eden, and Jae never missed an opportunity to let me know exactly pitiful I was.

"Thanks for the pep talk, but it's probably best if I go. This isn't really my scene. I'm sure I'll see you at the club sometime, right?"

I turned to go but bumped into a server with a tray of drinks. The glasses and tray went flying, crashing on the concrete floor of the terrace. "Oh my gosh, I'm sorry! Are you okay?" I immediately started helping pick up the pieces when I felt a hand on my shoulder.

The server looked from me to Max nervously. "I'm so sorry," he apologized. "This was completely my fault. I should have said something to let you know I was right there. I didn't even think—"

"It's fine, Andrew," Max said. "Go back inside. I'll get someone to clean this up."

"I'll help," I offered.

"Lilly, you don't have to do this."

"It's fine. It's partially my fault."

Another demon stepped to Max's side, whispering something in his ear. Giving me an apologetic look, Max told me he would be back in just a minute. Meanwhile, a group of demons came out onto the terrace, their laughter loud as they shuffled out the large doors. I'd picked up the larger pieces of glass and stood up with the tray when one of them held out a hand with an empty glass in it. Scrunching up my face, I just stared at him.

"Go get us a new bottle, would you? Thanks, dear." With hardly a second glance, he shoved the empty glass toward me again.

"I…" I didn't even know what to say. They thought I was working the party rather than attending it. This was exactly why I shouldn't be there.

Before I could formulate a sentence, Max was back beside me. Brows knit, Max looked from the other demon to me and back again, sensing that something had happened. "What's wrong?"

The other demon sighed. "You might want to hire a new catering company, Max. I understand having eye candy flounce around the place, but that's all this human seems to be capable of doing."

I'd opened my mouth to speak when Max punched the demon straight across the face. Everyone out on the terrace gasped.

"Damn it, Max. What was that for?" the demon asked, holding his face where Max had hit him.

I didn't want to see any more. I'd had enough of men who used their fists instead of their words. The lying, hiding how wealthy he was, and now this? I didn't need any more red flags.

"Good night, Max," I said, leaving him on the terrace. Desperate to put some distance between the two of us, I pushed the door open and hurried through the apartment, past the demons I knew were watching me. Trying to make it to the main room, I turned down one hallway and then another, none of them seeming to lead out.

Cursing under my breath, I backtracked and tried a different direction, but his stupid penthouse was stupidly large, and the sleek minimalist decor of the whole place only made everything look the same. Finally I threw open a set of double doors, hoping it would at least lead to one of the main rooms, but instead, I found myself in a palatial bedroom suite. Max's bedroom.

"Damn it!" I yelled, my voice echoing off the high ceilings. I whirled around to leave but stopped short when I saw him.

Max stood in the doorway, his wings expanded to block my escape. "Lilly."

"I'm going home."

"Why won't you let me protect you?" Max took a step toward me, leaving the doorway and coming closer. "Come on, Lilly. I'd have to be blind to not see the scars all over your arms, and I'm sure that's only the tip of the iceberg."

Instinctively I pulled my sleeves down. "You don't know what you're talking about."

"Oh, I don't? You think I don't see how you try to hide them under the long sleeves you wear?"

"It's not your problem."

"You're right. It's yours. And I can't figure out why you aren't doing anything about it."

I flinched at his words. So that's what he thought. I should have known. Of course someone like him thought this was a problem I could simply fix, just like that.

"Lilly, I didn't mean—"

"I know exactly what you meant."

"Let me explain."

"I don't need your explanations. Good night, Max."

"I want to help you."

"Then leave me alone."

"No."

I tried to walk past him, but his wing shot out at his side, stopping me. When I looked up at him, my heart melted when I saw the determined look in his silver eyes.

"What did you just say?"

"I said no. I won't. Lilly, I just punched that guy for you. Can you at least give me a few minutes of your time?"

He was right. He'd punched someone. For me. The emotions in me swelled, threatening to break through to the surface. I'd spent so long fighting for myself—so, so long—but no one had ever fought *for* me.

"You can't say stuff like that," I said quietly, all the anger gone from my voice.

"Then can I say there's an apartment full of people back there, but I'd like all of them to leave so I can be alone with you? Or can I say how gorgeous you look tonight and what morons those demons are for acting like they are somehow better than you or anyone else?"

And then he was there, right in front of me, his hands cupping my cheeks.

"Is that okay to say?" he whispered.

With a quick nod of my head, no more words were needed.

Max's lips gently brushed against my own, tentative and careful, his breath like a whisper, and I could feel each time he exhaled as he held me close to him. The heat of his body seemed to radiate around us, as if the air had been charged with electricity, and we were the only two souls in the world. That warmth made me relax, my concerns from earlier fading away until all that remained was Max and me—our mouths, our bodies, all tangled and needy, melting into the moment.

It wasn't enough.

I wanted more.

My hands reached up, grasping his arms and pulling him closer to me, deepening our kiss until I felt like I was being consumed by it. Max responded in kind, devouring me as his hands made their way down my body, tracing patterns against my dress as he explored my curves. When his hand cupped my breast, I gasped, and Max stopped kissing me long enough to look down at me and smile. His gaze was so full of lust and desire, surely mirroring my own, that I couldn't deny it anymore. I wanted him. I didn't know if I should, but I did.

He spun me around so that I was facing the wall, and a large hand engulfed both my wrists, holding them above my head and pressing them into the cold wall. He leaned forward, his body pressing against mine as he spoke directly into my ear. "Can you be good for me, kitten?"

"Mm-hmm." I nodded, my cheek brushing against his.

"Good girl. Be quiet now."

With his other hand, he scrunched up the fabric of my dress, pulling it up and over my hips. "Look at you." He whistled, one hand running over my ass cheek. I pushed out my ass for him, and his fingers tugged on the hem of my panties before letting go, the fabric snapping back against my skin.

"These are cute, but they have to go. Stay still."

I didn't dare move as his finger hooked under my panties and slid them to the floor.

"There. Much better."

I shivered as I felt a finger drag across my now bare pussy. He pushed it back and forth, giving me just a hint of friction, enough to make me whine and press my ass back against him. "You're such a tease."

"It isn't teasing if I follow through. Want me to make you come from just my fingers?" He angled his fingers up just right, and I gasped as he pushed one large finger up into me, gently thrusting it in and out. "Because I can do that."

"No." I shook my head. "I want more."

"Then turn around."

He let go of my hand and I spun around, his mouth crashing against mine. His hand wandered back down my body as we kissed.

Then he crouched down in front of me.

"Give me this leg." He easily moved my leg over his shoulder, my ankle dangling against his wing. "Fuck, you're beautiful."

He flattened his tongue against me.

The feeling of his warm tongue on my cunt sent a shiver up my spine and I groaned, my hands flying to grab at his hair. Not satisfied with simply lapping at my lips, he planted a kiss on my clit before latching on and sucking, sucking hard while a finger pressed against my wet pussy.

"Oh fuck. Fuck. Fuck." The words tumbled out of my mouth like a chant as the orgasm washed over me and my whole body clenched. He didn't stop, eagerly slurping and fingering me as I rode it out until finally I couldn't take any more and I let go of his hair. Panting, I leaned back against the wall, my legs wobbling, but he only gave me a minute to breathe before he spun me around and pressed me against the wall again.

Still trying to catch my breath, I leaned against the cold wall and heard the sound of a zipper behind me. Then he shoved forward, his dick sliding between my legs, rubbing back and forth against my soaked and swollen pussy. I hardly had the energy to stand, but it didn't matter. With one hand, Max held on to my waist and with his other, he reached around in front of me, rough thumb rubbing against my clit. With him groaning in my ear and my clit so tender from earlier, every touch sent electricity straight through me.

"Max, you back there?" someone shouted outside the door, and I froze.

But Max didn't.

"Ignore it," Max whispered, continuing to thrust between my thighs.

"Max?" I heard again.

Max growled under his breath but didn't stop, his dick sliding back and forth, creating the most delicious friction and rubbing right against my clit with each thrust.

Suddenly his hand left my hip and was in my hair, wrapping around a fistful and yanking my head backward. "Fuck, kitten," he said, his voice deep and heavy with lust, "you feel so good."

He kept fucking between my thighs. With a strangled groan he shoved forward, both our bodies jolting toward the wall before he pulled back. "Don't move," he growled, and I felt hot, sticky ropes of cum hitting my ass as he came.

"Fuck," he whispered as he took in the sight of my skin covered in a sheen of sweat and semen.

I stayed still, catching my breath as he wiped it off me with his hand.

"Open," he commanded, and dutifully I parted my lips for his fingers, He pushed them into my mouth while my tongue swirled around them, tasting the salty cum from his fingertips, licking them clean.

He pulled my dress back down, smoothing the fabric against my bare ass.

"Next time, kitten." Max leaned close against my back, his breath tickling my ear. "Next time I'm going to fuck you for real."

My body stiffened at his words, trembling at the implication of *next time*.

"You could stay the night," he whispered. "I'll kick them all out right now."

I wanted to. Damn it, I really wanted to.

But I knew that he had an apartment full of demons just outside the doors of his bedroom. "Go back to your party."

Max groaned and rested his head against my shoulder. "I don't want to."

"You need to. You're the host."

"I don't care."

"Next time just you and me, okay?"

He picked his head up at that, a goofy grin on his face. "There will be a next time? You promise?"

"Yeah."

The whole taxi ride home—because there was no way Max was going to let me walk home alone—I kept replaying everything in my mind. Here was a handsome, rich, sweet guy who liked me, who wanted me to spend the night, and I'd just turned him down? What was I thinking?

As I opened my new door on my shitty little apartment, I realized I could have been having sex under what I imagined were his million-thread-count sheets. I smacked myself on the forehead with the palm of my hand. Something must be wrong with me.

"Now you're hitting yourself?"

I jumped back.

"Jae." I spun around and there he was, standing in my doorway.

"You changed your locks."

"I..."

Jae's skin was shining, eyes glowing. He'd been doing Dust again, I could tell. How much had he taken?

"Heard my pet was whoring herself out tonight. Time to explain."

"Jae."

"How long have you been fucking customers on the side?"

"Jae. Listen—"

"Shut up."

I took a step back as he came into my apartment, his black wings spread out behind him. I froze, unsure if it was best to try to run or if that would only make this worse. Now that I could see his face more clearly, I noticed the way his silver eyes were bright with a wild intensity as he loomed over me.

Slowly, as if in some mockery of real care, Jae folded his wings around me, bringing me to him before whispering in my ear. "Do you think any demon wants half-blood scum like you for anything other than a quick fuck?"

Tears of frustration were forming at the corners of my eyes, and I wasn't sure I could hold them back. A part of me wondered if he was right.

"If that's how you see me, why do you keep torturing me, Jae? Why can't *you* leave me alone if I'm so worthless?"

"Because I know the truth about you. I know how useful you can truly be." Jae ran his hand down the back of my head, stopping at my neck.

"Please," I insisted. "Please just leave me alone."

"You will always be mine. I thought you knew that, but then I hear from a friend that you're at some fancy party. The only human there actually, and you thought I wouldn't find out?" Jae leaned into me, his sadistic silver eyes wide and feral. "Well, mostly human."

"I can do what I want," I said, knowing how pathetic my trembling voice sounded as my tears blurred my vision.

"And so can I."

Jae reached into his pocket, and I heard he familiar click of his knife. He held it in front of me, its sharp glint reflecting off his eyes as my entire body trembled in his hold.

Would he kill me right here, right now? I wasn't sure.

"Pitiful, pathetic." He grabbed a fistful of my hair and yanked back, exposing my neck as he brought the blade closer to my face. "I own you. I will always own you. If you're around other men, it is because I allow it, not because it's your choice."

The blade pressed in against the delicate skin under my eye.

"And I will kill you before I let someone else have you."

19

LILLY

"What do you mean, my rent was already paid?"

The demon's sharp fingernails clicked and clacked across the keys of her computer, slightly louder than they had a few seconds ago when I'd first come into the office to pay my rent.

"Do you not believe me?" she asked, not even bothering to stop typing to look at me.

"I just don't understand. If I don't pay today, I don't want you guys to accuse me of not paying rent and kick me out."

She finally stopped typing and spun in her chair to face me, her silver eyes narrowed. "Are you accusing me of lying? I swear, all of you humans are the same," she muttered.

I adjusted the sunglasses I was wearing, big round glasses that hid the cut Jae had left under my eye. "I never said you were lying."

"Do you want me to delete those transactions?" she asked, turning back to her computer, hands poised over the keyboard.

"No, wait!" I said. "Can you just explain it one more time?"

She pointed to her computer screen. "As I *said*, I can see in our records that three months of your rent were already paid at the new rate, so you don't owe anything right now. Is that clear enough for you?"

Had someone paid their own rent but accidentally paid mine instead?

"Who wrote the checks?"

She let out a deep sigh before tapping a few keys and pointing again, a long nail aimed right at a line on the screen. "Says in your file it was paid in cash."

Was the universe fucking with me? Or was it possible that I was actually having a moment of good luck?

I'd had so few moments of good luck over the past year that it felt wrong to question it. Maybe this was a sign that fate was finally moving in the right direction, that life was going to go my way from now on.

Nah, was I really naive enough to believe that?

I'd been so confused by my rent being paid that I somehow didn't pay attention to the fact that my apartment door was unlocked when I came in, that I hadn't used the glass I saw on my counter in weeks, and it could only mean one thing...

There was someone in my apartment.

I slowly walked to my purse and found my knife inside. I slipped it out of my bag and gripped it in my hand.

My apartment was tiny, only a main living area, one bedroom and one bathroom. There was no one other than me in the main room, which meant the other person must be in my bedroom. I could try calling the police, but I wasn't sure if they would even listen to a human or how long they would take to come out to this shitty apartment building. If it was Jae, back to wreak more havoc in my life, I wasn't sure if even a knife was enough since he'd have his own.

I took a deep breath and tiptoed toward my bedroom, trying to make as little noise as possible. The door was slightly ajar, and I could hear faint rustling sounds coming from inside. I tightened my grip on the knife and took a step forward, pushing the door open just enough to peek in. There I saw a figure rummaging through a big black bag on my bed. The intruder had their back to me, and I couldn't see their face. But I recognized their build—it was definitely not Jae.

"Charlee?"

My only human friend in Vestia turned around and waved. "I was wondering when you were coming back."

"I was only gone for a few minutes. How did you get in here?"

"*Anyway*, check out what I brought us for tonight."

"We're just glossing over the fact that you broke into my apartment?" I asked, putting the knife down on my dresser.

She stopped what she was doing and looked back at me, confused. "I didn't know when you were coming home. And nothing is broken. Check for yourself. *Anyway*, I think we're about the same size, so you have two options, and since I'm nice, I'll let you pick first."

Totally ignoring the fact that she had broken into my apartment and hadn't even bothered to explain why, Charlee pulled two dresses out of the bag and laid them out on my bed.

"Where did you get all this...? And what is it for?"

She ignored that question as well and dangled two small pieces of paper in front of me. "I also got us tickets to the ball at the Vestian palace. We're going."

I raised an eyebrow, skeptical but intrigued. "How did you manage that? And why should we go?"

"Let's just say a very generous demon left them unattended, and I couldn't resist."

In Charlee's book, if it wasn't tied down, it was fair game, and it was shocking how good she was at picking locks and hacking computers. Anything mechanical could and would be broken by her if it came into her line of sight and was left unattended.

Charlee simply smiled, not even bothering to hide her shamelessness. "You're seriously going to turn down free booze?"

"I feel deeply uncomfortable using stolen tickets and stolen clothes to go to the royal palace of all places. I think that's a very logical way to feel."

"Who said anything about logic? Wouldn't it be fun to pretend we're rich people just for one night?"

Hadn't I had a similar thought when I was standing on Max's terrace?

"If I say yes, there's still another problem." Slowly, I raised my sunglasses and watched Charlee's face fall when she saw the cut under my eye.

"Oh, Lilly."

"It's nothing. I'm handling it."

"But you don't have to." Charlee went back to rummaging around in the bag and finally held up two masquerade masks. "Because it's a masquerade!" One was black with whiskers and sharp ears like an angry cat, the other painted gray and white with big openings for the eyes to look like a mouse.

"It's perfect timing if I do say so myself. If there was ever a time to spend a night forgetting who we are, I think it's now. Agreed?"

I ran my hand over the masks, touching the bristles of the cat's whiskers. It was just one night. "Okay. I agree."

Charlee clapped her hands together, excitement radiating from her. "You won't regret it, Lilly. Now let's pick a dress."

No matter what I'd said, guilt continued to gnaw at me as I fingered the delicate fabric of a crimson gown adorned with silver embroidery. It was exquisite, much nicer than anything I had in my own closet, but wearing something stolen felt wrong. However, I knew Charlee meant well, and maybe wearing something this nice would help me forget my troubles for a few hours.

"Okay," I said, finally relenting. "I'll wear this one."

"Excellent choice!" Charlee beamed, handing me the black cat mask.

"Why do I have to be the grumpy cat?"

"Do you really have to ask?"

〜

CHARLEE WAS RIGHT; the free booze was worth it.

A server passed by with a tray of champagne flutes, and I grabbed one, the crisp liquid courage soothing my nerves.

As we entered the palace's grand ballroom with its vaulted ceilings and glittering chandeliers, the hum of conversation and laughter floated through the air, all of it swirling around me in a heady mixture of sights and sounds. The music of the orchestra and the rustling of expensive clothing, the idle small talk and clink of glassware. I was used to being in the crowded club, but this ballroom was something different altogether. The whole scene was oddly familiar in a way I hadn't felt in over a year, in a way I'd thought I would never feel again.

In Eden, elaborate affairs like this masquerade were typically reserved for the extremely wealthy, yet Charlee had told me that the king had invited all economic classes to this party, all to celebrate the kingdom's wealth. Still, the attendees were mostly demons, with a few humans here and there, though there was no way to know if any of the humans were actually shifters. A quick glance around the room told me that at least the wolf shifters weren't holding back, displaying traits they normally kept hidden until shifting, like fluffy tails or pointy canine ears. I assumed they didn't want to be mistaken for a human when in Vestia, at the Vestian palace no less. I didn't blame them.

Everyone's elaborate masks gave them an additional layer of anonymity, and I had to wonder: How many of the attendees at tonight's masquerade had come into my club at some point? How many of the men here had bought me drinks, told me their sob stories, and then tipped me well before going back home to their wives?

"Don't the knights look dashing?" Charlee squeezed my arm and nodded toward a pair of knights striding through the ballroom. Their steps were purposeful and confident, and demons and humans alike moved out of their way as they passed. It was hard not to look at them; not only were they both tall demons with large black wings, their masks—one shaped like a fox complete with pointy orange ears

and a brown snout, the other plain but made from a black metal—
were just as striking.

The Knights of the Flame, always dressed in their signature fire-
red jackets, stiff white shirts, and black pants, were known for their
uncompromising honor and dignity, and I would have believed that
description if I hadn't spent more than one evening with a few of
them.

One knight was bad enough, but two of them, together? The
worst.

When knights spent time with me at the club, they complained
about the training regimen, the pay, their fellow knights, just like
every other guest at the club who felt like bitching about their job.
More than anything, I could tell they felt powerless serving as a pawn
for the king and enjoyed spending a few hours getting to exert that
power over someone else for a change. A pretty human was an easy
target, and they never tipped enough at the end of the night to make
the excruciating hours with them worth it.

No, I knew better. When I saw the world-renowned demon
Knights of the Flame, I knew to stay far, far away.

My eyes stayed on this particular pair of knights until I saw they
were headed for a couch where another demon in a peacock mask
was being fawned over by half a dozen women. Then I turned away.
The whole scene made me think of Jae and his constant stream of
groupies. Apparently it didn't matter if you were a royal knight or a
nightclub owner; demon men were all the same.

Whatever. What those knights did was no matter to me.

"Relax," Charlee whispered as we sipped our drinks, her eyes
scanning the crowd for familiar faces. "You've earned this night off.
Just enjoy it."

I nodded, trying to push my worries about Max and my situation
to the back of my mind. She was right. For one night I would let
myself forget about the weight of my debt and the shadowy figure
that haunted my thoughts. Tonight was for me. There was no one
staring at me tonight, no one demanding my attention, no one I had
to hustle for money. Tonight I could just be me.

Charlee nudged me in the side. "You know, I bet we could make a killing here."

"What?"

Charlee shrugged. "The alcohol is flowing, people aren't paying attention. The last place you'd expect to lose your wallet is at the royal palace, right? All these partygoers, their guards lowered, thinking they're safe? Easy pickings."

"Charlee..."

"And no one will want to accuse the palace of having lax security, so even if a couple of credit cards went missing, it's unlikely that they'd say anything to the royal guard. And we're wearing masks."

"Charlee!"

"I'm just saying!"

"And I'm saying no."

"Fine, fine!" She held up her hands as if surrendering. "Geez, I was just talking. Simply making conversation."

"We cannot have that kind of conversation here."

"You're right, we should have had it before we left, then we could have come up with a solid strategy. I need to take notes on this ballroom now so that next time—"

I grabbed Charlee and yanked her behind a nearby column. I covered her mouth with my hand and looked around to make sure no one was watching us.

"We are here for drinking and dancing and not..." I gestured to her even as she stared at me from behind her mouse mask as if she was the most innocent creature to ever exist. "And not for any other reason, got it?"

Behind my hand, Charlee nodded.

"If I take my hand off your mouth, will you stop talking about... that stuff?"

She nodded again.

"Okay."

I stepped back, and Charlee smiled.

"To make it up to you, I'll go get us some food," she said. "Back there I saw a coatroom behind the buffet, and if that's where everyone stores their purses—"

I put my hand up to stop her. "I'll wait here."

"Are you sure?"

"Absolutely. Go. Just get food though. Okay? Food only."

She let her hand fly to her heart dramatically, pretending I'd wounded her. "Lilly. Do you really think that I, your dear sweet friend, would do anything else?"

"Honestly? Yes."

She flashed me a grin before running off, and just as I'd expected, Charlee did not return with food.

Charlee returned with a man. No, two men, humans, one on either side of her, her arms linked with theirs, a huge smile on her face.

"Charlee," I said behind clenched teeth as soon as she was close enough to hear.

"I brought friends!"

"I thought you were getting food."

"I did." She nodded to the two men. "I brought two snacks, didn't I?"

Why hadn't I picked a mask that covered my entire face so no one would see how badly I was cringing right then?

"To make it up to you, we'll go find some of those appetizers I saw." She let go of one man and patted the other on the chest. "Won't we?" she asked him, not that she was taking no for an answer.

From the way he swayed into her, I could tell the guy was obviously drunk, and I felt a small pang of sympathy for him; if the poor man had any kind of money in his wallet, he probably wouldn't by the end of the night.

As she dragged him away, leaving me alone with this complete stranger, Charlee looked back over her shoulder and waved.

I would have to murder her later.

At that moment, a server brought over a tray of champagne, and the human took two, handing me one, giving me a moment to take a good look at him. He was tall and slender, dashing in a classic black tuxedo. A tiger mask covered only the top half of his face and pushed his blond hair back from his forehead. Two deep brown eyes peered down at me as if he was studying me as well.

Brown eyes. A welcome change from the usual silver of demon eyes that I was used to having watch me each night.

Maybe I wouldn't murder Charlee after all.

20

MAX

The ballroom was a sea of masks and finery, a dizzying whirl of colors that rushed past me as my gaze scanned the room.

There. The hulking form leaning into the far corner of the room, somehow still managing to look sullen and annoyed even behind a black masquerade mask.

I chuckled and adjusted my own mask as I slipped through the crush of bodies toward Blaise.

"You're late," he said when I got close enough. Now that I was near him, I could tell the black mask that covered the upper half of his face wasn't made of fabric. It was metal. No surprise there; I didn't even need to ask whether he'd made it himself in his workshop because I knew he had. Whereas my fox mask was made of supple brown and black leather with a gold design around the eyes, Blaise's was entirely matte black, but with his skilled craftsmanship, the edges were smooth and even, somehow making the hard metal still look soft.

Blaise's jaw was tight and his stare was as cold and sharp as the knives he still owed me.

"Took me some time to dig around and find this uniform," I said as an excuse. Even though we were both wearing the same Knights of the Flame uniform, Blaise's red coat was pressed to perfection, and the fabric of Blaise's coat stretched taut over his huge shoulders.

"I'm not used to wearing it," I told him.

"Because we aren't meant to."

"We're both knights."

"You know what I mean."

I shrugged. "We protect the kingdom like everyone else. Let's find our friend, and he'll tell you the same."

"How are we supposed to find him?"

"He's right over there." I pointed to the side of the ballroom where several couches had been set up. "He must think the masks make him disappear into the crowd."

"How can you tell that's him?"

I draped an arm around Blaise's huge shoulders and grinned as we headed over. "That's why you make the weapons and I do all the work, friend."

"You wouldn't be able to do your work without my weapons."

"But where would you be without my money?" I asked.

"Probably at peace."

Rand was lounging on a red velvet sofa, a goblet of wine in one hand and a masked woman draped over his lap with several other ladies standing around him, laughing at what he must have just said. There was no sign of his normal regalia, no indication that this twentysomething demon was the ruler of an entire kingdom, yet he still commanded the attention of these ladies, his silver eyes gleaming behind a ridiculous peacock mask covered in blue-and-green feathers.

He caught my eye and placed his drink on a side table. "Uh-oh, ladies, looks like I'm in trouble. My sincerest apologies, everyone, but two Knights of the Flame seem to be here to speak with me. If they don't haul me off to the dungeons, I hope we can continue later where we left off?"

With promises to speak later, the women slowly got up off the couch to walk away. There was a soft rustling of fabric, the sound of shoes scuffing on the floor and hushed murmurs of disappointment.

Rand's smile dropped as soon as we were alone. "I was beginning to think you two weren't coming."

"It has been a while, Your Majesty." Blaise bowed deeply at the waist but stayed standing even as I sat down.

"For the love of the gods, don't do that!" Rand leaped to his feet as Blaise straightened up. "Why are you always so formal? This is the one night that I get to be normal, and I'll be damned if my friends are the ones who reveal my identity. I didn't decide to host a masquerade ball just to be immediately outed as the king, you know."

"My apologies, Your Majesty," Blaise intoned, no less formal but with only a slight bow of his head this time.

"Stop calling me that. That's a royal order."

"Of course, Your Majesty."

"Blaise. I don't know how else you want me to say this. I'm not the king tonight. For this party, I'm just a regular guy having a good time for once."

"You are always the king," Blaise said behind a clenched jaw. "You're responsible for the fate of this kingdom. You don't get to pretend like you're not the king just because you're bored."

"Bored? You think I'm bored?" Rand seethed, his black wings starting to spread out behind him. "I'm spending every waking minute dealing with the bullshit that bastard of a former king left behind, not to mention all the insanity that the prince barely addressed before he left too. You think I wanted to do any of this?"

"It doesn't matter what you want, Your Majesty."

"Obviously!"

I did a quick glance around but didn't see anyone watching us. Yet. If these two got any louder, we were going to draw more attention than we needed right now.

Standing between them, I clapped one hand on each of their shoulders. "So this is fun, guys. I'm having a blast. Great party."

Rand adjusted his mask, his fingertips tugging at the edges of the fabric and securing it firmly in place.

"That's right." Rand took a step back, his posture relaxing as he moved away from Blaise. "It *is* a party. You might not be familiar with the concept, Blaise, but a party is an event where people try to have fun and relax. You should try it sometime."

"I'm sorry that I'm normally too busy making weapons to protect your entire kingdom."

"Weapons you get paid a lot of money to make. That's what tonight is all about, isn't it?" Rand gestured out to the crowd of attendees, mostly demons but a few humans, one or two fae. "I called for this event to celebrate the thriving economy of Vestia. I've invited leaders from all the major businesses to thank them for contributing to Vestia's coffers. If you're making money, you're making me money, after all."

"Making *Vestia* money, you mean," Blaise said.

"That's what I said. And now look at them. Nobles and commoners, humans and demons, mingling on the dance floor, identities hidden behind these masks. Isn't it great? Aren't I magnanimous?"

"Do you even know what that word means?"

"You're going to talk to your king like that?"

"I thought you were just a regular guy tonight, Your Majesty."

"Oh, shut up."

"Rand, should your only true and loyal knight duel this rogue for besmirching your honor?" I asked, my grin only making Blaise frown.

Blaise huffed. "I'd like to see you try."

"I hate both of you. We need more wine." Rand snapped his fingers, and in an instant, servants were bringing trays of wine to us.

"Are you sure about that?"

"Completely." Rand scooped up a glass, the wine spilling over his fingers. "These days it takes a lot of alcohol for me to feel this sober."

"I have no desire to drink at the moment. If you'll excuse me, Your Majesty," Blaise said, bowing and earning a scowl from Rand.

"You're excused," Rand said through clenched teeth.

As soon as Blaise was gone, Rand downed the rest of his drink in one gulp. "That demon is insufferable and always has been."

"He thinks the same of you."

Rand's tail tapped against the floor as he seemed to consider that for a moment. "I won't deny it. But I'm the king, so I can do what I want and demons still have to kiss my ass."

This ballroom seemed safe and not in need of any knights or assassins. For the moment at least. Everyone danced and laughed, free of cares in their temporary escape from the real world.

Almost free of cares. A portly demon in a yellow cat mask was making his way through the crowd, heading straight for us with a determined waddle. I groaned. No rest for the wicked, it seemed.

From the graying hair and long wings, I recognized Count Roland, a minor noble in Vestia. The teenage girl with similarly long, drapey wings that he dragged behind him seemed to want to be as far away from her father as possible. Not that I could blame her.

The count stopped before Rand and bent over at his waist in an elaborate bow. "Your Majesty, what an honor to see you tonight. I am Count—"

"Is the king here?" Rand asked, making a big show of scanning the ballroom.

The count faltered. "Oh? Well... Your Majesty, if I could introduce you to my daughter, the Lady Everly, she is an excellent dancer and—"

"Where do you see the king?" asked Rand.

"Well, um..."

"Because I haven't seen him."

"Uh, Your... Your Majesty?"

"I am not sure who you mean, but surely you do not think I'm the king."

"Oh... Uh... No?"

Rand waved his wineglass around in the air as he spoke. "Because our amazing King Rand is so much more attractive, and with his charms he could never be confused with a regular demon like me, just a regular, average, normal demon who is—"

"I'll leave you to it," I whispered to Rand, not wanting to stick around for another second.

Rand gripped my sleeve. "Don't you dare leave me," he whispered back.

I sighed. It was my sworn duty to obey and protect the king after all.

"Oh my!" I suddenly shouted, the count and his daughter immediately turning to me as if they hadn't realized I was even there before. "You'll have to excuse us," I said, draping an arm around Rand's shoulders and tugging him against me, "but I'm afraid you're mistaken. I have to say that I am so flattered that you think my boyfriend is the king."

His eyes growing wide, the count stumbled over an apology while I reached around to squeeze Rand's cheeks.

"He's just so cute, isn't he?" I asked. I did my best to hold back a laugh as Rand's silver eyes flashed with anger. "I can see why you might confuse him for the king."

Pretending to hug him, I leaned in close to Rand and whispered in his ear. "You told me not to leave you."

"Yes, quite right," Rand muttered behind clenched teeth, his grip on his wineglass growing tighter. "But aren't you ready to go, my dear knight?" he said, louder this time. Rand tilted his head toward me with mock affection, the green-and-blue feathers of his peacock mask brushing against me. "You promised me a dance."

"How could I have forgotten? I must have been so enamored by the sight of you that I lost all sense of time. Please excuse us."

The count shuffled away with his daughter while I guided Rand out of the ballroom. We made our way toward a set of glass doors, which I opened for us, taking us out onto a stone balcony overlooking the palace gardens.

Rand immediately stepped away from me, downing the last bit of wine in his glass. "That was one way of making an exit."

"Would you have preferred me to whisk you out onto the dance floor for a waltz, Your Majesty?"

Rand barked a laugh. "No, thank you, but did you have to do all that? You're not at all my type, you know."

"You were the one who wanted my help." I shrugged. "I'm sure that girl is very nice."

"Then why don't you go dance with her? I'm not interested."

"Maybe you should be. An unmarried king with no heir sounds dangerous for Vestia, doesn't it?"

Rand leaned over the balcony and chuckled. "Like you can talk. Your father passed his title to you, but at this rate I don't see you with anyone to pass it on to yourself."

"What do you expect with all the work you give me? And can you imagine me on a first date? The second a girl asks me what I do for a living, I would either have to lie or tell her that I kill people."

"Awkward."

"You're telling me. I think about it sometimes though. What it would be like to be married, have some kids running around, to be... I don't know..."

"Normal?" Rand asked.

"I was going to say happy."

"You're asking for too much." Rand gestured out to the city, the skyscrapers of Vestia bright in the distance. "You and I exist so that everybody out there can be happy."

"Then don't we deserve at least a little bit ourselves?"

"I'd like to agree with you, but then we'd both be wrong. Face the facts, friend." Rand grabbed his drink and raised it to the night sky. "To the single life!"

"Your glass is empty."

"As is my toast." Rand's shoulders sagged and he sighed. "I really thought tonight would be more fun." He ran a hand through his black hair. "What if we ditched this whole thing and went flying?"

I smiled, imagining the freedom of the night sky. "I wouldn't mind sneaking you out. For old times' sake."

Rand laughed, a flash of his old mischief in his eyes. "It is tempting. But I have a feeling some of my guards would lose their shit if I disappeared." He shook his head. "Another time?"

"Anytime."

When we reentered the ballroom, I caught a glimpse of Blaise out of the corner of my eye. No matter what he said, he was still a Knight of the Flame, and I had no doubt he'd been watching the door to the balcony this entire time.

"Well, isn't this interesting?" Rand murmured beside me.

I followed Rand's line of sight to the main doors where a large group had just arrived.

In walked a crowd of demons, mostly women in vivid-colored gowns and masks covered in all kinds of feathers and ribbons. They were accompanied by a couple of men whose upper bodies were so muscular they seemed to strain under their tuxedo jackets. All of them laughed loudly, too loudly, loud enough to be heard over the orchestra on the other side of the room. They strolled in confidently, black wings spread behind them, each step purposeful, as if they knew that all eyes were on them.

"Entering the royal palace with their wings like that. Bold move."

"Mm-hmm. It takes all types to make our economy work, but I'll take some flashy demons over the scum that Eden sent tonight."

"What do you mean?"

Rand nodded to two men in the corner, chatting with two women, one woman in a mouse mask and the other a black cat.

"I didn't expect the trash to actually leave its trash cans, but I suppose I shouldn't be surprised," Rand said. "I didn't actually think the Thornfields would send anyone, but looks like I was wrong."

"You know those two guys?"

"You do too. The Thornfield family sharks. And here I thought they hated my guts for outlawing Dust. Really though, I thought you had better eyes than that, Max. Look closer."

So I did, focusing in on the human in the tiger mask, and he did look familiar with his shaggy blond hair, but I couldn't focus on him for long because he stood talking to a human woman with brown hair that hung down her back in soft waves.

As pleased as I was to see Lilly, I had to wonder.

Why the fuck was she talking to them?

21

———

LILLY

y companion clinked his glass against mine, and we both took a sip.

My instincts to fill the uncomfortable silence were starting to kick in, but what would a human man want to talk about? We weren't at the club; we were at the royal palace of all places. We should have a normal conversation about... normal things. *But what were normal things?* Oh gods, had I really forgotten how to make small talk?

"So...," he said after a moment.

"So...," I repeated.

Yep. I had totally forgotten.

"I'm Patrick."

"I'm Lilly."

"Lilly. Is that short for something?"

I flinched but forced a smile. "It's just my name."

"How long have you lived in Vestia?"

I let out a breath, thankful for something else to talk about. "A while. You?"

"Only a couple of weeks."

"For business or pleasure?" I asked.

"Well, business, but... now maybe both?"

I took a big gulp of champagne. This was so awkward, like neither of us knew how to talk to someone else. It felt forced on his part too, like he was making himself have a conversation with me, and that only increased the discomfort.

"I'm working on a couple of deals," he continued, "but hopefully I can wrap them up quickly. Demons aren't the easiest to work with."

I had to laugh at that. "That's an understatement. I'm surprised they're doing business with a human company at all."

"Yeah," he said. "It helps to have a bargaining chip."

"Must be a pretty good one."

"I think so. Can't be helped though. If I go back to Eden empty-handed, I'll have a whole new set of problems. Edenians are ruthless in their own ways."

I knew how true that was.

Thinking about the world back home made me pause.

"I'm sorry," he said in a rush. "We're here at the Vestian palace, and I'm boring you about Eden. I'm not very good at this."

"I'm not either," I admitted. "And I'm sorry about my friend earlier. She can be... a lot."

He nodded in agreement. "I noticed. But I should thank her really."

"Why is that?"

"Because if she hadn't tried to pick my pocket, I would never have followed her over to you."

Oh no.

Charlee...

I wanted to melt into the floor. Or disappear completely if that was an option. Did someone around here have magic that would allow my entire body to evaporate?

"I am so sorry. I can't believe she did that. I'd like to tell you that there's been a misunderstanding, but... I can't. If anything is missing, I'll replace it, I promise. I'm so, so sorry—"

"It's no problem," he said, smiling at me even as I felt like hiding in embarrassment. "Truly. No harm done."

He took our empty glasses and placed them on a tray as a server passed. Then he reached into his inner jacket pocket and took out two wallets, holding them up.

"I made sure to take my buddy's wallet from him before they walked off together, in case she tries something else."

"This is so embarrassing. I promise I'm not like that. I would never—"

"I know. I can tell. But the fact that you're friends with a thief makes me that much more curious about you since you seem like the honest type."

"I don't know about all that."

"Judging by the way you blushed earlier when I was flirting with you, I think I'm at least mostly right."

"I wasn't blushing! It was the champagne."

"So you *do* know how to lie." He grinned. "Either way, I was telling the truth when I said I was curious about you."

He glanced to the side where we could both see Charlee and the other man laughing and stumbling back toward the food. "I think our friends are going to be busy for a while, so... would you like to get out of here?"

"Oh. Um... I don't know."

"I hear there's a terrace off the ballroom that overlooks the south lawn. Does that sound okay?" When I didn't answer, he continued. "To go talk. What? Did you think I meant something else?"

Actually I had.

I had just assumed he meant leave the ball entirely since going home with a demon was the type of offer I was used to turning down at the club. But this man wasn't a demon, and he wasn't a guest at the club. This man didn't know I was a hostess at the Red Rose. He didn't even know what I looked like behind this cat mask. For once, I wasn't spending time with a man because I was wondering how much he was going to tip me later. This conversation wasn't transactional; I wasn't trying to hustle him for a few extra bucks, and I wasn't worried that he might stop talking to me and I'd earn nothing for my time.

And he was human, like me.

It was… refreshing.

I cleared my throat.

"There you are, darling. I've been looking everywhere for you," said a male voice, smooth as velvet. I flinched as arms wrapped around my waist from behind. What the hell? I was about to tell whoever this was to get his hands off me when I looked up to find the demon in a fox mask—one of the knights I'd seen earlier—gazing down at me, silver eyes glinting behind the brown leather.

That only made me want to get away that much more.

"I apologize for my tardiness," the knight continued, grinning even as I stared at him in confusion. "I know you were missing me desperately. Shall we dance?"

"I was… *What?*"

"Please excuse us," he said to the guy I'd been chatting with, and then, before I could say a single word, he spun us around and away from the alcove.

"Just keep walking," he whispered, one hand on the small of my back as he guided us toward the dance floor.

"No. Wait one second. I never agreed to—"

The knight pulled me flush against him, the hand on my back now circling around my waist completely. I stumbled briefly, but he held on to me, adjusting and keeping us in sync. When I looked up at him, he seemed perfectly content, softly humming along with the music.

For my own safety, I just needed to suffer through the next minute or so and then get far, far away. I forced myself to relax in his arms, letting him lead while I listened for the song to end. At least he was a good dancer, better than most of the men back home.

"Hey. Why did you do that?"

"Hmm?" He glanced down at me.

I tilted my head up toward him, and he was smiling widely back at me. Because of course he was. These knights walked around like they were sent by the gods to protect the kingdom, but when had they ever protected me? Or any human? It wouldn't be socially acceptable to take off my one of my heels and stab a knight in the eye, would it?

No, the couple hundred demons in the room probably wouldn't look kindly on a human who stabbed a knight.

"You looked like you could use rescuing."

"My hero," I said dryly. I hadn't needed rescuing, especially not by a Knight of the Flame.

His hand settled on the small of my back, hot even through the layers of silk and lace, guiding me effortlessly through the steps. This wasn't exactly the kind of dancing that I was used to, but he was comfortable guiding me through the movements. It wasn't entirely unfamiliar to me; it had just been a while since I'd danced like this in someone's arms. The last time I'd danced at all had been that night at the club when I'd danced for Max.

Max...

He leaned down, whispering in my ear. "You have to hold kittens close to keep them from running away."

Kittens, eh?

I peered up at him, seeing the supposed knight in a new light. I tipped my head back to meet his gaze, emboldened by the champagne and my new realization.

"What if this kitten doesn't want to be caught?"

He only chuckled before spinning me out and back into his arms, countering any effort I made to move away from him as if it had been part of the dance the whole time. If anything, he held me tighter now, right up against his chest.

"Once she sees how good life can be as a house cat, she might change her mind."

I could feel Max's eyes staring at me, and when I finally looked back up at him again, he was still watching me.

"Don't you have knightly duties to attend to other than dancing?"

"Actually, I was supposed to be off duty tonight."

"Are Knights of the Flame ever off duty?"

His smile vanished, and he was silent for a moment before speaking. "No, I suppose not."

"Then is this dance official business?"

"Saving a damsel in distress is always official business," he said, smile returning.

"I am not a damsel in distress."

"But you were," he insisted, taking my hand and holding it against his heart. "Before I rescued you."

"I didn't need rescuing."

"Yes, you did." He spun us around so that I could see where we'd been standing earlier. The blond man in the tiger mask was still there, drink in hand as he watched us. "Do you know who that man was that you were talking to just then?"

"No."

"That, my dear damsel, is not a man you should ever talk to."

"That guy? He seemed mostly harmless. Trust me, I've talked to worse."

His exhaled loudly, and then his hand squeezed mine. "I'm sorry about that. Sincerely."

The softness in his voice and the way he held my hand… it was all too much.

"Isn't it a crime to impersonate the royal knights, Max?"

For just a second, his steps seemed to falter, but he recovered almost instantly, that damned grin returning. "You don't think I'm actually a knight?"

"I know you're not. We both know you're not."

"Hmm." He spun the two of us across the floor before suddenly coming to a stop.

"Wait, why did we stop?"

"Because the music stopped, Lilly."

He was right. It had, and I'd missed it entirely.

"I'm not through with you," I told him.

"Oh?"

I grabbed his hand, fully expecting to drag him out of there if I had to in order to get some answers, but he followed behind me easily, both of us moving through the crowd of dancers and dresses until we were out of the ballroom.

"Turn left. Through that door," I heard him say behind me, so I did, taking us through a set of large glass doors that opened onto an empty terrace with stairs leading down to an expansive lawn. Even out here, I could still hear a hint of the music from the orchestra. I looked around, making sure no one else was out there with us.

"Now that we're alone," I said, "take off that ridiculous mask and start talking."

"Can we keep holding hands?"

"Can we... What?" I felt my face heating up as I realized that I was, in fact, still holding his hand. I dropped it immediately, crossing my arms over my chest.

"I didn't want you to get away, that's all," I said.

"I know the feeling."

"Max."

"My lady." He held up his arm at his side, indicating for me to take it. "Let's take a walk."

"And then you'll tell me what's going on?"

He raised his arm a little more. "For you, anything."

22

MAX

The moonlight filtered through the leafy vines overhead, the dots of light hitting Lilly's mask not at all hiding her furious expression.

"So are you stalking me now or what?"

I had to hold back a chuckle as she stood in front of me on the garden path, her hands on her hips, her pretty green eyes narrowed behind her mask. How was it possible for her to be so cute when she was so mad?

It was almost as if she was asking me to tease her.

"Lilly. Did you think that I came to this ball just to see you?"

"I... I... didn't say that."

"But you implied it. I am sorry to disappoint you, Lilly, but I am not stalking you."

"First you sent some of your subordinates to watch me at the bar. Yes, I knew about that. Then you came here dressed up as a knight and made me dance with you."

"Did I?"

"You did."

"Hmm. Was it really that bad?" I asked. "People tell me I'm a great dancer."

"That's not the point."

"So I am not a great dancer?"

"You know you are, so why do you need me to tell you?"

"Because it means more when you say it." I sighed, raking a hand through my hair. As much as I enjoyed teasing her, this was not at all going the way I'd hoped. I took a step forward slowly, my hands out in front of me, not wanting to scare away my favorite feral kitten.

"I'm not stalking you," I said. "I'm here for the ball, same as everyone else."

Judging by the way she kept her hands on her hips, she didn't seem convinced.

"For argument's sake," she said, "let's agree for a second that you actually are a Knight of the Flame. Although unlikely, knowing you, I will admit that your fellow knights have come into my club before, so it's not outside the realm of possibilities."

Other knights had been at the Red Rose? Other knights had spent time with... her? If any of them had touched even one hair on Lilly's head...

"What other knights?" I asked, trying to hold back the tension from my voice. "What were their names? Tell me."

I knew I was doing a shitty job of controlling my tail, which was currently thumping against the ground behind me, but I couldn't help it. I had trouble controlling anything around her.

"How should I know? If you don't know what your supposed coworkers are doing, maybe ask that friend you came with."

I froze. My tail froze. This was a new development. This was... interesting.

"You saw the other knight with me tonight?" I asked her.

"Of course I did. That dude's shoulder muscles practically made their own entrance, and you were right beside him, peacocking your way through the crowd."

"You were watching me," I said, unable to stop the smile spreading across my face. "Now who's the stalker?"

"I didn't know it was you at the time!"

"You were just checking out two hot knights."

She threw her head back, her dark hair tumbling back over her shoulders. "That's not it at all. I wasn't... I mean, how could I *not* look? You two are all..." She gestured wildly into the air. "You know what I mean! What are we even doing right now?"

I knew what I was doing. I was staring at a beautiful woman in a dark red dress that clung to her body in a way that made me want to never look at anything else.

"If you're not going to give me any real answers, I'm going back inside and finding my friend."

"That human?"

"Yes."

"I thought I told you to stay away from that man."

"I didn't mean him. I don't even know his name."

"Good." I took a step closer, unable to stop myself. Her scent flooded my senses, something sweet and floral that made my blood burn. "Let's keep it that way. He works for Thornfield Enterprises, a trading company in Eden. They're shady as fuck."

I didn't need or want to tell her more than that. I didn't want to think about work for one second longer than I had to. Not when she was right here, in my arms.

Even so, Lilly was quiet. Too quiet. Was it because I mentioned Eden?

"He works for them," she said quietly.

"Did you know about them in Eden?" She nodded, and I reached out to tuck a stray hair behind her ear, thrilled by the softness of her hair against my fingertips.

Silence fell between us. The strains of music and laughter drifted from the palace, a stark contrast to the tension in the garden.

I gazed down at her, at the stubborn set of her jaw and the challenge in her beautiful green eyes. Here was a woman who had been dealt a bad hand and was distrustful of everyone, but I couldn't give up on this challenge. Not yet. Not ever.

"Do you remember when I flew you up to your apartment?"

"Yes..."

"Good, then hold on like that again."

"What? Wait!"

But I wasn't waiting. We could have stood in that garden all night and Lilly would never have believed a word I told her. I didn't want to wait around for all that, but I also couldn't be honest with her when we were so close to the party and the prying eyes and ears of Vestia.

Scooping Lilly into my arms, we flew into the night sky, up and over the palace gardens.

After the initial shock wore off, I watched her eyes move from me to the expansive gardens below. I knew exactly what she was looking at and why she was so surprised to see it; I'd come to the palace many times as a child with my father, and I knew the place like the back of my hand. This much greenery was a rarity in Vestia, and the palace was the only place that boasted a lawn or garden of any size. Almost everything else in the city was wall-to-wall concrete and asphalt, the buildings taller than any tree you could find, if you could find a tree at all.

This high up, we had a view of the entire back gardens and the terrace, both of which were lit with small lights that allowed us to see just the outline of a few partygoers who must have followed us out. We were too far away to hear more than a murmur of their conversations, and only the barest trace of music floated up this high. It was a miracle the previous king hadn't paved over the gardens in the name of progress, but thankfully he hadn't.

I didn't care about any of that. The only thing I wanted to look at was right in front of me, against my chest, with her two adorable arms still latched around my neck. Lilly craned her head to see out over the edge of the balcony. Had she even noticed how close we still were? Not that I was going to tell her.

"I knew the palace was beautiful," she said, her voice quiet with awe, "but I had no idea the property stretched out this far or that it was so..."

"Pretty?"

She turned her head to me sharply at the sound of my voice, as if suddenly remembering I was there.

"Are we allowed up here?" she asked. I shrugged, and Lilly's eyes widened. "Maybe you should put me down."

"I don't want you to fall."

Lilly batted her eyelashes. "You wouldn't save me if I did, brave knight?"

Damn, this girl knew how to play me.

I let go of her legs, placing her on the balcony in front of me. Instead of continuing to look out into the gardens, however, Lilly turned around to face me.

"Oh, that's right," she continued. "You aren't a knight at all. You just like to pretend that you're one."

"I'm not the only one pretending, Lilly."

"What is that supposed to mean?"

"I mean that there's more to your story. Things you haven't told me about how you ended up in Vestia."

"There's nothing worth telling, I promise."

"That's not true. I want to listen. I'll hear everything you want to say."

She shifted away, her back turned to me. Missing our closeness, I let my hand trail gently down her back, marveling as I always did at the smoothness of her skin and the absence of wings.

"You okay?" I asked her.

"Max... there's something I need to tell you."

"You can tell me anything."

"What do you know about the Thornfields?"

Did she want me to tell her how I knew the owners were notorious fae slave owners? That they were suspected of smuggling Dust into Vestia? Should I tell her that I knew they were connected to Jae and his clubs? I sat up behind her, wrapping my arms around her waist and hooking my head over her shoulder. Instead of leaning into me, Lilly stared at her hands, her focus obviously elsewhere, all of it making me uneasy.

"They're bad news," I said.

"That's my family's company."

I froze. "What?"

"My father is Richard Thornfield. He died before I came to Vestia. My stepmother took over the company, and she…" Lilly's voice trailed off, leaving an unspoken heaviness in the air. "I can't even escape her here," she murmured.

"Lilly." At the sound of her name, she turned slightly to face me, my heart sinking at the sight of the sadness in those beautiful green eyes. I didn't know what had happened with her family, and Lilly had only dropped the smallest pieces of information about her past, but if those bastards were able to make her look this sad, I'd burn all of them off the face of the planet.

"Can I… Can I talk out loud for a while, and you just listen? No questions?"

I nodded.

"It's a long story."

"I don't care."

"Once I tell you… will you promise to still look at me like this?"

"Lilly, I'll look at you like this forever."

That seemed to satisfy her. I stood behind her and busied myself with touching her long hair, feeling the strands slip through my fingers. I pulled all of it back, gathering it at the nape of her neck.

"If you're familiar with Thornfield Enterprises, you know that their main headquarters is in the city, but I grew up near the Caspian Mountains with my father and stepmother. Marion, my stepmother, and I lived at my family's northern residence. We did not get along, but the house was big enough that we could avoid each other. Most of the time." Lilly stared off into the sky. "It was like a winter paradise. Fresh snow year-round, frozen lakes perfect for skating… I would take food coloring from the kitchen and draw pictures in the snow. She hated when I did that because it would end up all over my clothes.

"My father would visit every few months when the snow receded, but most of the time it was just the two of us. One winter years ago, he came home for a holiday party we were hosting, and he brought several demons with him. Business acquaintances, he said.

"We were all out on the lake. It stayed frozen most of the year, and everyone was ice-skating. My stepmother was never very good at skating, but she was making a big show of it since we had company. She was always like that. She wasn't paying attention and slipped, hitting her head hard on the ice. I was the first one to her, yelling her name, and I put my hand on her forehead to stop the bleeding. That's when it happened. That's when I felt... something."

I stood up straighter. I don't know what I'd been expecting from Lilly's story, but it certainly hadn't been this. "Lilly. Are you telling me that...?"

"No questions. Not yet. It felt like a jolt of caffeine, like an electric pulse." Lilly let go of my hand and stared down at her own again. "Right underneath my fingers, the wound grew smaller. It stopped bleeding completely. I couldn't even process what was happening or why or how or any of it. I was so shocked that I didn't even notice that the ice below us had cracked. When I did finally realize we were in danger, I shoved her away and..."

Lilly's voice grew quieter, and I took her hand again, squeezing it.

"I remember the cold. I remember the weight of the water. I remember waking up in my bed, a roaring fire in the fireplace warming the room. The wound on Marion's head had healed, and she was fine, but it took me weeks to fully recover. I had healed her, but I couldn't even figure out how to heal myself. A demon had seen it happen and had pulled me from the water, saving my life."

"When I was finally able to walk on my own, my father brought me into his study. He locked the door. It was just the two of us and Marion. That's when he told me the truth. That I was his daughter, but my mother had been a slave. A fae." Lilly let out a breath and hung her head.

No. I wouldn't let her do that.

I reached for Lilly's face, taking her cheeks in my hands and tilting her head up toward me.

Was it shocking to hear she was part fae? Sure, but who cared? Lilly could have been half unicorn and I wouldn't have given a shit. What I cared about right then was hearing her out, and I could tell she wasn't done.

She looked up at me, her green eyes searching mine. Then she seemed to relax.

"I've never told anyone this before." She moved back a little, my hands leaving her face, and she held out one arm, several small scars dotting her otherwise perfect skin. "I can't heal myself, but I can heal small wounds on other people pretty easily."

I reached up, tracing my hand along her soft skin. "That's amazing. You're amazing."

She shook her head. "Since full-blooded fae don't usually manifest their wings and powers until they're twenty-one, my father must have thought he had more time before he had to tell me. He seemed at least a little apologetic for not telling me, but Marion... I'll never forget the look of disgust in her eyes. In the days that came after, he stayed with us in the mountains, and I was grateful for the buffer... until my father died. In Eden, the children of slaves are—"

"Property." I finished the sentence for her.

"There was a meeting to go over my father's will, and the night before the meeting, one of my father's business acquaintances came to me. He'd been there that day at the lake the year before. He'd seen it all happen and had figured it out on his own when he heard about the will. I was barely old enough to know what was happening, but he told me he had heard that Marion was going to sell me. *Sell me.* That it was allowed in the will. Like we hadn't lived together for most of my life. Like I was nothing, like I wasn't even a person. This demon had money, he offered me a way out, and... I took it."

The pieces all seemed to fall into place as I listened to her story.

"And now you work for him."

Lilly spun around to face me. "I'm paying Jae back," she insisted. "For all of it. Once the debt is paid, I'm done. It isn't like I haven't thought of strangling him in his sleep," she said, and my stomach churned at the idea that she was ever around that monster when he slept, "or cutting off his ugly wings bit by bit, but I want a clean escape. I don't want to be chased by the ghosts of my past any longer. I want to leave on my own terms, not as a fugitive. I'm going to move to the coast, find something there. Or at least that's always been my plan, but now..." Her eyes dropped.

With each new word from Lilly, I had to bite back the anger that was simmering right at the surface, threatening to escape. I had to consciously make my tail stop flicking against the ground in hopes that she wouldn't notice. Finally I couldn't take it anymore; I had to walk to the railing, grip the edge so she wouldn't see my face and the expression of murderous rage I was desperately trying to hold back.

"Max?"

I took a deep breath, attempting to channel the fury that was bubbling to the surface into something calmer. Kinder. Less murderous if possible. Composing my expression, I went and stood beside her, taking her hands in mine.

"You're with me now. Okay?"

As I held Lilly in my arms, as she cried on my shoulder, I only had one thought.

Those fuckers were going to pay.

All of them.

With the tip of my finger, I tilted her mask up and slid it back into her hair, uncovering those beautiful green eyes, eyes so different from my own, so different from everyone else's in Vestia, so that I could wipe away the tears.

It wasn't just her eyes; Lilly herself was different, unlike any woman I'd ever known. She was fierce, sure, but there was this softness hidden just below the surface, a part of her that she was fighting tooth and nail to keep secret, only making me want to see it that much more.

Softness, like the feeling of her skin as I moved my hand to cup her cheek, but—

Everything inside me tensed as my thumb grazed a cut just below her left eye.

"What the fuck is this?"

Lilly's hand flew up, knocking mine away.

"Lilly." I grabbed her cat mask before she had a chance to pull it back on again, tossing it onto the floor.

"Was it Jae?"

"I want you to fly me back down now."

"No."

"Max."

"Was it Jae?"

"Max. I can handle this."

"You keep saying that. Is this what you call handling things?"

"You don't understand. If I run away, he'll find me. If I try to kill him, he'll kill me first. Even if I have to suffer now, I will eventually make a clean break without anyone else's help, and then no one can hold anything over my head ever again."

I could see it in the tension of her shoulders, her frustration, her irritation, all of it. She was right—I'd been keeping her shut out while still trying to protect her. Using her inside knowledge when it suited my own purposes. But now that I knew her story, should I reciprocate with my own? She'd just shared her past trauma, and here I was, still too much of a coward to say anything?

There was so much I could say, but the words seemed to stick in my throat, choked back by my training. If I told her, would she look at me differently? Would she trust me more or would she feel disgusted by the monster in front of her? I wasn't sure I could stand that, not from her.

But if I didn't say anything at all, there was always going to be this barrier between us. If I wanted to know more about her and learn her secrets, I'd have to be the one to start tearing that wall down first. Until I did that, I was never going to be able to truly take care of her. And how could I protect Vestia if I couldn't even protect Lilly?

I stepped back, putting some space between us, and folded my wings behind me. For a long moment, the silence hung in the air, thick and heavy.

It was now or never.

"Lilly. I kill people."

23

———————

LILLY

I blinked. "What?"

"I mean"—he shrugged a little—"I don't really do the whole killing thing that often. Only when I have to. Or when I'm ordered to. Or when someone deserves it."

"I'm sorry." I shook my head. "Can you say that again? Does that mean that, like... you're... you're..." I shook my head again, trying to make sense of this. "You're a... hit man? An assassin?"

"I guess."

My jaw dropped. "You can't say 'I guess' to something like that. Either you're a hit man or you aren't."

Max was watching me, waiting to see my reaction.

"Okay, then yeah, I am. That's not my official title or anything though. I really am a Knight of the Flame."

"An illegal one?"

"It's not illegal to be a knight."

"It is if the knight is doing illegal things!"

"It's not illegal if it's my job. It's my business, how I make my money. I pay taxes," he insisted, but then he wrinkled his brow. "Or at least I think I do. I have an accountant."

"You... what?"

The world felt like it was spinning, and everything I thought I knew about Max vanished in an instant. Instead of the demon I'd known, now he was something else.

An assassin.

That also meant that I was alone with an assassin. I couldn't even comprehend the kinds of things he must have done in his past. What exactly *had* he done? Who had he killed? My heart ached at the realization that the last thing I needed was to be involved with someone like this, and I certainly did not need to be alone with him.

Fuck. I'd been such an idiot.

How quickly could I get away from him? With his wings, he was faster than me, no doubt, but could I distract him somehow and make a run for it? Now that I knew what he did for a living, was he going to have to kill me?

No. That was crazy. This was Max, not some psycho killer. He wouldn't kill me.

Right?

I started to back up. One step at a time. Slow enough that maybe he wouldn't notice.

"Why are you backing up?"

So much for that.

"I'm not backing up. I just took a couple of steps... backward."

"That's the same thing."

"Is it?" I asked, scooting back a little more. There were probably only five steps to the door of the balcony. Seven or eight at most.

Max sighed and rolled his eyes. Then suddenly he was airborne, swiftly flying around me and placing himself between me and the door, his black wings spread out, blocking my ability to see around him.

"Lilly. I didn't tell you that to scare you. You really think I would have flown you up here, confessed that I'm an assassin, and then tried to hurt you? After everything you just told me?"

I didn't know how to answer that. "How do I know you're not lying about that too?"

"Why would I lie? I have no reason to want to hurt you. That's not what I do. I'm not a liar."

"Sounds like something a liar would say."

"Lilly. I am telling you about myself because I want to be honest with you."

"Have you, like, killed a lot of people? No, wait, don't tell me. I don't—"

"Yes."

"*Fuck*," I groaned, covering my face with both my hands.

"Only if I had to. I'm paid nicely for it, and I do a damned good job. If it means making Vestia safer for everyone, I do what I have to do. I'm not apologizing for that."

"How did you even get started doing this?"

"I guess it runs in the family? My father was a soldier in the Blood War, one of the best actually. The old king realized my father's potential, so he hired him to do some private work for him on the side. Investigating threats and various illegal activities, trusting my father and his crew to handle them discreetly."

"Your father was a hit man."

"A soldier for the king."

"A royal hit man."

Max waved a hand in the air. "Sure. As his connections grew, more people wanted my father's help, so he expanded the business and grew it into an empire. After he died, that role fell to me."

"What happened to your father?" I asked, unsure if I even wanted to know how lives ended in this career.

"A job went wrong. Intel was bad, and that was that."

"I'm sorry to hear that."

"It happens."

"And your mother? Is she involved in your family business too?"

"My mother? Never knew her. She died when I was born. Death is part of life, and this life isn't easy for families." He kept staring out at the gardens and huffed a laugh. "It's not easy for anyone. Don't get me wrong, financially it's great. I have never wanted for anything. The old king made sure my dad was very well paid for his silence, and that on top of the business on the side, it hasn't been a bad life. I just have to keep in mind that each job could be my last."

"That's depressing."

"Not really. It means that every day I need to have the best day ever. Right?"

"And you chose to come to my shitty club as part of your 'best day ever'?"

"I did. I wasn't there for the ambiance, Lilly."

"Then why were you there?"

He sighed. "I didn't bring you here to tell you this."

"Then why *did* you bring me here?"

"Because I wanted to kiss you again."

"You... wanted..."

"To kiss you," he repeated.

"You can't confess that you kill people and then try to kiss me."

"I think I just did."

"That isn't how it works."

"Why not? I want..." Max took a step toward me, and then when I didn't move, he took another. "To kiss." Another step. "You." Until he was right in front of me. "I want to kiss you, Lilly. I want to kiss you every day of my life if you'll let me."

Despite what he'd just told me, even though I now knew what he did for a living, I wanted to kiss him too. But if I did, did it mean that there was no turning back? That this was it? Slowly he reached out, cupping my face in one of his hands.

"So can I?" he asked.

"No."

His hand dropped from my face and he frowned.

This time I took a step toward him, my lips curling up in a small smirk. "I thought you liked it when I told you no." And before he could respond, I reached up and wrapped a hand behind his head, pulling him down to my level. I hardly had time to gasp before his lips crashed against mine.

Instantly his arms were around my waist, pulling me against him. His hold was firm, as if he was scared that I might back away even though he should have known from the way I melted against him that running away was the last thing I wanted to do right then.

It felt so good to lean into him and let him hold me, feeling weightless in his hold as I wrapped my arms around his neck and held on.

"I will protect you, Lilly," he murmured against my lips. "No one will ever hurt you again. I swear it."

I kissed him harder, hoping, dreaming, wishing that he was right. I let my fingers wander to his shirt, unbuttoning it slowly, but his hand stopped me.

"Not here."

He punched through the glass door before reaching through the jagged glass, unlocking it from the inside. The door flung open and he grabbed my hand, pulling me behind him into the room. His wings pushed him forward, and I had to rush to keep up.

"Whose room is this?" I asked.

"It's mine. Or at least it is whenever I need it. And I need it right now."

Max spun me in his arms with a breathy laugh, and we fell onto the bed in the middle of the room in a tangle of limbs and lips, touches and tastes, both of us unable to get our clothes off fast enough. His kisses were intoxicating; the weight of his body on mine was intoxicating. The way his hands slid up my sides felt like fire on my skin.

Until that fire was gone.

I opened my eyes to see Max hovering over me, the few inches between our faces suddenly feeling much too far. His chest rose and fell rapidly as he caught his breath.

I reached up to pull him back to me, but he resisted. "Is something wrong?"

A grin spread across his face and he shook his head, his eyes trailing over my body beneath him. "Not at all."

"Then why'd you stop?"

"Because I need you to know that if you tell me to stop, I will."

"Max..." I smiled up at him and reached up to tangle my hands in his unruly black hair. His lips were swollen from our kisses, but that only made them look that much more kissable.

As if he'd read my mind, Max leaned down, dotting a kiss on my forehead. "If you tell me to wait, I will." Another kiss, this time pressed gently on my cheek. "But"—he came closer, so close that our lips brushed against each other's—"if you tell me to leave you alone, I don't think I can."

"Don't," I insisted. "Don't stop, don't wait, and don't... Please don't leave me alone."

"Never." Max smiled. "Lilly, I'm in love with you."

My heart swelled at the words, yet a small voice of doubt held me back from saying them in return. I'd never felt this way for anyone else, but could I love someone who ended lives for a living? Someone who could be torn away from me forever at any moment on a mission gone wrong? I wasn't sure if my heart could handle the fear and anxiety, and the thought of losing him was too painful to fathom.

But if losing him was my biggest worry, didn't I already know my answer?

"I think...," I said quietly. "I think I'm falling in love with you too."

Max's entire face lit up, and he dove back in. If I'd thought his kisses were hot before, now they were downright feral. I gave it right back to him, matching his intensity and forgetting about whatever self-control I'd had before, instead giving in to the pleasure of his mouth on mine.

Our bodies moved together, the heat between us growing with each moment. I moaned as Max's palms traveled everywhere—my breasts, my hips, my thighs—leaving a trail of heat wherever they touched. I arched into him, needing to feel him everywhere all at once.

"You feel so good," I mumbled between touches.

"And you're so beautiful." His mouth moved over the soft skin at the base of my neck, his teeth biting gently. "I want to have all of it, all of you."

"Then take it. Take me."

"Are you sure? You... Your beauty... It doesn't exist just for me or anyone else. Your beauty is yours. Yours alone. You don't have to give me anything if you don't want to."

"What if I choose to give it to you?"

His breath hitched. "Now that... That is... That is something I would like very much. *Fuck.* I need you," he groaned, his voice thick with desire. "Now.

"I know." I let out a soft breath. "I need you too."

If I'd thought my body was already in overdrive, I'd been wrong. Because as soon as he was inside me, filling me completely with the most delicious stretch, all my senses seemed to blink off and there was only him and me, his silver eyes staring into mine. He was watching me, carefully observing my reactions.

So I decided to give it to him.

There was an urgency in the way our bodies moved, a furtive energy like we were both trying to prove something, showing each other just how much we wanted this, how much we wanted each other.

When my fingers found the soft leather of his wings, his whole body shivered.

"Keep doing that and I won't last long," he huffed against my ear.

"Is that a challenge?"

"If you want it to be."

Max continued to thrust his hips harder, pushing himself farther into me. I gasped at the sensation of his cock pounding against my walls, and I could feel my orgasm building quickly.

He reached down and grabbed my wrist, pulling it up to his lips. His rhythm didn't falter, and his eyes never left mine as he kissed my fingertips, each one, and then each knuckle in turn.

This contrast between the softness of his kisses and the intensity of his thrusts had my head spinning. I was close—so close—and Max seemed to sense it too.

"Can I?" he moaned against my mouth. "Inside?"

With a nod from me, Max groaned, throwing his head back, his thrusts becoming more urgent, faster and deeper. His mouth found mine again, our tongues twisting together, all semblance of gentleness gone and only a burning heat remaining.

My own orgasm crashed over me, and he was close to follow, burying himself deep inside me with a throaty groan. But he didn't stop; he continued to work me through my aftershocks, taking his time to relish those last minutes together before finally pulling out.

We stayed like that for a few minutes, both of us enjoying the beauty of what we'd just done, our bodies damp with sweat and flushed. When our breathing finally managed to steady itself and the two of us came back to reality, I finally was able to see beyond the demon in front of me to take in the room around us. A large bedroom with tall ceilings and only a few pieces of furniture. Simple by palace standards.

I rolled over on my side, wrapping my arms around his chest. I felt his tail curl softly around my ankle, connecting us, keeping us close.

"I never want to leave this room," he said.

A thought flashed through my mind before I had time to bury it away.

I could get used to this.

We had hardly walked back into the ballroom when a red-haired demon took long, menacing strides toward the two of us. Another knight, the one I'd seen with Max earlier, dressed in the same uniform. He didn't seem to notice me, instead yanking Max violently toward him.

"Where the hell have you been, huh? Don't you ever check your fucking messages?" he spat out, his face twisted with fury.

"What's going on?" Max asked, pushing back against him.

"What's going on?" the redhead snarled, releasing Max so suddenly that he staggered back. "You fool, while you were off doing whatever the fuck you wanted, there's been an attempt on the king's life."

24

LILLY

"**I**s Rand—" Max's mouth hung open as if he couldn't bring himself to finish that sentence.

"He's alive. He's with a doctor, so you better get your ass in there fast."

"Shit."

"Shit is right. That's exactly what you're in for, disappearing like that. Who is this?" The red-haired demon gestured to me. "No, it doesn't matter. Come on."

Max took a step to follow the other knight but then turned back to me, grabbing my hand and pulling me along with him. I didn't even have time to protest; they were both moving so fast that I had to run to catch up with their long strides.

We turned the corner and were confronted with more guards than I'd ever seen in one place. "Where were all these guards when this was happening?" Max asked.

"Who the fuck knows?"

"Where were you?"

"Right by his fucking side when he started coughing up blood, that's where. One moment we were talking to some demons, and then the next thing I knew, he was coughing up blood and passing out."

"He was coughing up blood? Are you sure?"

"Yes, I'm sure."

With servants running everywhere, I stayed close behind Max and kept my hand in his, and one look from Max was enough to allow me to slip right behind him into the king's chambers. The room itself was huge, yet it seemed smaller with the team of servants and doctors swarming around the young king. The rustling of the doctors' black wings as they flitted about the room and the tapping of tails against the stone floor combined with the aroma of strange medicines to permeate the room with a sense of anxiety and fear.

Max and his friend were not the only Knights of the Flame present; a few more milled in the corner, their voices hushed. One or two of them looked familiar; it was possible they'd been guests at the Red Rose at some point and that's why I recognized them. Max didn't pay them any attention, immediately rushing to the king's side, seeming to forget that I was there. It was better like that. I didn't want to get in anyone's way, and I probably wasn't even supposed to be there. So I stayed near the door, lingering like an intruder in this intimate and desperate scene, listening and trying to piece together what they were talking about.

The lights were being kept dim, and the heavy velvet drapes surrounding the large canopy bed were hastily drawn back, so I could only catch glimpses of King Rand lying there, his black wings limp against the mattress, his skin pale. Dots of blood decorated his pillow.

That's when it hit me. He really might die.

The king that we'd seen celebrated in the streets, this king that was Max's friend, this demon who was not much older than me. He could die from some coward's poison in his own palace. From what Max had told me, the king was barely holding the kingdom together now that Dust and fae slavery was illegal, yet someone had the gall to try to kill him? Tonight?

Then I had a second realization. I was the only person in the room who wasn't a demon. Demons didn't have healing magic... but I did.

When I saw the king cough up blood again, I knew I had to do something. Or at least try.

I swallowed hard, my throat dry. No, what was I thinking? Surely these demons had access to the best medicine and technology available in Vestia. When I thought about it, what could a half-fae woman with barely any healing magic do that the king's royal doctors couldn't?

...but if I didn't try?

With a shaky breath, I stepped forward. It was now or never. Swallowing my fear, I inhaled deeply and walked over to Max, my steps firm but my hands trembling slightly.

Max was going to seriously owe me later.

"Max," I said, my voice barely above a whisper as I tugged on his sleeve. He turned to look at me, his eyes clouded with worry. "I want to help."

He seemed to understand immediately what I meant, and I saw something akin to hope flicker in his silver eyes. Max nodded and stepped aside, his faith in me a tangible thing that made my heart swell.

"I have... I might have a way to help him." I could feel the weight of every eye in the room, every black wing and tail suddenly still. "Please let me try."

Some of the king's doctors started to object, their voices rising in protest, but Max silenced them with a look.

"Let her try," he said firmly, his voice allowing no argument.

The skepticism in the eyes of the king's doctors was unmistakable as I approached the bed. One of them, a severe-looking older woman with a sharp expression, turned to Max, her voice trembling with outrage.

"What is this human doing here?" She pointed an accusing finger at me. "You can't seriously be thinking of allowing this stranger near the king."

"She's not a stranger," Max said. "And she might be able to help."

"Help?" Another doctor scoffed, his eyes narrowing. "She has no place here. Knights? Can you please escort this young lady out of the king's chambers?"

Max's face flushed with anger, and he took a step forward, his fists clenched as he stepped between me and two approaching knights. "You're wrong," he growled. "You need to trust me on this."

One of the knights, a tall demon with a sneer on his face, looked me over, his eyes lingering in a way that made my skin crawl. "Oh, I recognize her." He smirked. "She's one of the girls from the Red Rose, isn't she? Max, I knew you were a dog, but you're seriously letting some whore near the king?"

I was no stranger to this kind of treatment, but Max's face turned crimson with rage. The insult was clear, not just to me but to Max's judgment. The room seemed to hold its breath, the tension growing palpable.

"Watch your tongue." Max's voice was a low and dangerous growl, his wings spreading at his sides. "She has healing abilities."

"Healing abilities?" the older woman spat out, her voice dripping with disdain. "You expect us to believe that a human has such a gift?"

Max's eyes met mine, and I could see the internal struggle in them. He was on the verge of revealing my secret, that I was half-fae. But he held back, his jaw tightening as he turned back to the doctors.

"She's not just any human," he said carefully, his voice laced with a warning. "I will vouch for her."

The room was filled with tense silence as the doctors exchanged wary glances. Their distrust was evident, but Max's conviction was unwavering.

Finally I took a deep breath, knowing that the truth had to come from me. "I'm not fully human," I said, my tone soft but firm. "I'm half-fae. I have the gift of healing, and I want to use it to help the king."

It was the first time I'd ever admitted that out loud to a group of strangers.

The room went still, the doctors' eyes wide with shock.

Surprisingly, it was Max's friend's voice that I heard next. The tall, red-haired demon pushed through the team of doctors, his huge form looming over all of them. "It's not like you idiots have any better ideas. Move out of the way and let the woman try."

The older woman scowled but didn't protest. I met her gaze, my heart pounding, knowing this was my moment to show them all what I was capable of. With a determined nod, I moved closer to the king's bed, ready to do whatever it took to save him.

The eyes of the king's court were on me, expectant, confused. The doctors exchanged uneasy glances, but Max's reassuring presence behind me gave me the courage to continue. My palms were sweaty, my thoughts a whirlpool of doubt. But beneath it all was a deep, resonating truth: I could save him. I *had* to save him.

After a tense moment that felt like an eternity, the head doctor reluctantly stepped aside, skepticism in his eyes but desperation winning over.

I approached the king's bedside, my heart in my throat. His eyes were closed, his face ashen, his breath shallow. My hand trembled as I reached out to him, but then I felt Max take my other hand in his, and that small gesture gave me all the confidence I needed.

The room held its breath as I placed my hand on the king's chest, and for a moment, everything else fell away. It was just me, the king, and the power I'd kept hidden for so long.

My secret was out. There was no turning back now.

25

———

MAX

When Rand sat up in bed, he pointed right at me.

"You. Where the hell were you?"

"Your Majesty—"

"Cut all that bullshit and tell me you caught whoever fucking tried to kill me in my own palace." Rand threw up his hands in frustration, making even the doctors back up. "Can everyone just give me some room to breathe? Damn."

"Rand." I kept my voice steady, my eyes darting over to where Lilly was standing with several of the doctors. "Let me fill you in on what's happened."

"You fucking better. Everyone out! Except you two," he said, pointing at Blaise and me.

"This is Lilly," I said, gesturing toward her.

"The girl you were using to get info about Jae? Looks like you didn't work fast enough. You're not scoping out a club for me anymore, Max, this is my life we're talking about. I gave an order. Obey it."

I'd never seen him this angry. I started to say something, but the look on Lilly's face stopped me.

Shock, betrayal, and pain twisted her features, her eyes wide with disbelief as she stared at me. The words Rand had just spoken—*the girl you were using*—they hung in the air between us like a dark cloud.

"Lilly, wait, let me explain—" I stammered, reaching out for her, but she was already heading for the door. I followed her out, not letting her run away from me.

"I have never lied to you about how I feel about you. Jae Balakir is someone we're keeping an eye on. He's dangerous, Lilly, you know that. Part of my job is to rid Vestia of dangerous demons like him."

"By using a gullible human? Like me? Then the dance we shared, our first conversations, were they all just to get closer to Jae?"

"Lilly."

"Was tonight also part of your investigation?"

"Lilly, it wasn't like that."

"If you slept with me, maybe I'd spill secrets about Jae, is that it?"

"No. That wasn't what happened. I already know he's a Dust dealer—we're trying to find out who his financial backers are. It's not what it sounds like, Lilly, please." I took a step toward her, but she turned down one of the hallways, determined to go without me.

"Max!" Rand's voice was sharp, carrying all the way down the hallway to where I stood, his tone pulling me back to the situation at hand. "I said get everyone out. That includes her. Now come back here and tell me what the hell is going on."

I cast one glance at the hall, at Lilly walking farther away, torn between my duty to Rand and the need to explain myself to Lilly. But I knew Rand was in no mood to be kept waiting. Swallowing the lump in my throat, I turned back to go to the king, my mind racing as I tried to figure out how to make things right with Lilly while dealing with the immediate crisis.

"Your Majesty," I began once I was back with him, forcing myself to focus on Rand. "I assure you, we are doing everything in our power to find the one responsible for this attempt on your life."

"Don't give me assurances, Max. Give me results. I've been patient as hell, but now I'm pissed. I've been relying on you to find out who's trying to assassinate me, and tonight they tried it under your fucking nose."

"To be fair, you didn't die."

"But I could have!"

"We'll find out who did this," Blaise said.

"Damn right you will. One second I was at the party talking to someone..." Rand held his head in his hands. "And then... I don't remember. My brain feels like it's going to explode."

There was a knock at the door, and a timid guard poked his head into the room.

"I told everyone to get out!" Rand shouted at the guard.

"Please excuse me, but there's a young lady here. She believes she has information about what has happened to Your Majesty."

"At least someone does." Rand swung his feet over the side of the bed and stood up, gathering his coat and buttoning his shirt. "Let her in."

The three of us were standing at the end of the bed when the door swung open and the guard escorted in a young woman with a gray mouse mask pushed back over her black hair. Charlee, I remembered.

The guard nudged her forward. "This is Charlotte Pembroke. Miss Charlotte, please tell His Majesty what you know."

Her blue eyes looked at each of us in turn before she leaned over to the guard, whispering loudly. "That one is the king?" The guard gestured to Rand, but instead she turned to me. "Hey, fox, where's your girl?"

"You didn't pass her on the way here?"

"Nope."

"Hello?" Rand stepped forward to interrupt us. "King here. Kind of the one in charge. Did I mention that I got poisoned? Hurry up and tell me what you came to say."

She looked incredulous. "It's not like you died."

I nodded. "That's what I said!"

Blaise crossed his arms over his chest and frowned. "Max, do you know this annoying human?"

"She's friends with Lilly."

"I live in the same building as her." She eyed Blaise up and down.

"Who is this ray of sunshine?"

"It doesn't matter," Rand said. "Get on with it. What do you know?"

"Okay. So I was chatting with a gentleman, and you know, one thing led to another, and I happened to reach into his pocket."

The room was silent.

"Anyway, that's when I felt something hard."

"Is she for real?" Rand asked me. "Are we being pranked?"

"Listen," she said. "I'm not kidding. But something wasn't right. It was too small."

I heard Blaise curse under his breath.

"Then a few moments ago, I heard people talking about a syringe," she continued, "and that's when I knew. It had been a syringe all along. It all made more sense then, because I saw how big his feet were, and there was just no way—"

"Who was this man?" Rand asked.

"I think his first name was Patrick. Human guy, blond hair, super proud of whatever business he worked for. I'd tried setting him up with Lilly, but she suspiciously disappeared in the middle of a dance, so I stepped in."

Rand and I exchanged a look. Patrick Samuelson, one of the two men sent from Thornfield Enterprises. It all kept going back to them.

"A tiger?" Rand asked.

"Yes, a tiger mask."

"Thank you, Miss Charlotte," Rand said. "I appreciate your help."

"If you have no further information, you are dismissed." Blaise walked toward her, and she took a step back.

"Whoa. Okay, big guy," she said, holding up her hands. "I'm leaving. Hey, fox, tell Lilly to call me when you see her."

"I'm not sure when that will be. We had an argument..."

"Oh. So you fucked up. Good luck with that. I'll see if I can find her before I head out. See you guys later!"

As soon as the door closed and Charlotte was gone, Rand turned to both of us. "Find these bastards from Thornfield. Find your human. And get me some answers. Now."

26

LILLY

Lost. Again.

The palace hallways twisted and turned like a serpent, and even when I finally found a staircase, it had led me to another hallway, none of which looked familiar.

I should have forced Max to fly me back instead of stomping away like a child throwing a tantrum. Going into the building itself had seemed like a good idea at the time, and the fastest way to get away from him, but now I was lost, in the palace no less, one of the largest buildings in the entire kingdom.

Not my smartest decision.

I wasn't making a lot of smart decisions lately.

Like admitting to Max that I was in love with him.

What had I been thinking?

I made it to the ground floor and found a window to look out, hoping I could at least orient myself once I had a view of where I was in relation to the palace gardens.

"Lost, are we?"

I jumped at the sound of a familiar voice and spun around to find the man I'd been talking to earlier, the blond guy in the tiger mask, the man Max had whisked me away from so quickly. The man who worked for Thornfield.

"Seems that way," I said.

He smiled behind the mask and gestured down the hallway. "I can lead you out. Did you lose your mask?"

I remembered Max taking it off and throwing it down on the balcony. Who knows where it ended up. I hadn't much cared when he was telling me that he killed people for a living and confessing his love.

"I'll find my own way."

"I'm leaving anyway," he said. "Looks like everyone is heading out the front entrance."

Another glance out the window told me he was right; there was a steady stream of partygoers leaving the palace. Had Charlee already left too?

"I saw your friend," he said as if reading my mind. "She left with my friend already."

"Seriously?" But then again, hadn't I basically done the same thing when I'd vanished with Max? I'd have to apologize to Charlee later. "Did you say everyone is on the palace's front lawn?"

I saw several Knights of the Flame organizing the people as they left. Would Max eventually be out there too? The last thing I needed was to run into Max again tonight, not until I'd had a chance to sort through my thoughts. If he was looking for me, he was probably there with everyone else.

"That's where they were moving people. If you want to try a different exit, I saw one around the corner."

I followed right behind him, eager to escape the palace at this point. The sooner I left the palace, the sooner I could clear my head and decide what to do about Max. But I didn't want anything to do with someone who worked for Thornfield.

As I was thinking about how I could lose this guy, I felt a hand on my arm. I tried to spin around, but his grip on me was unrelenting.

"What are you doing?"

Patrick's fingers were like vises around my arm as he forced me down a dimly lit corridor. His grip was strong, unyielding, and every time I tried to pull away, he only tightened his hold. The way he guided me felt mechanical, almost practiced, and I couldn't shake the feeling that he had done this before.

"Lady Thornfield already briefed me on your background," he said. "She said all you can do is heal little scrapes. Seems pretty worthless."

"Fuck you."

When I looked over my shoulder at him, his face was a mask of indifference, but his eyes were cold and calculating. I could feel them on me, watching my every move, waiting for any sign of resistance.

He didn't speak anymore as he forced me to walk in front of him, his silence a weight that settled heavily in the air. I kept hoping I would see someone, anyone, but the hall was empty. Every step was calculated, every movement deliberate, as he led me closer and closer to a set of stairs. The only sound was our footsteps, a constant rhythm that echoed off the walls, a drumbeat that matched the pounding of my heart.

I tried to look for signs of escape, for anything that could offer me a way out, but Patrick's grip was unbreakable.

"Just wait until I tell your owner what you've done. Then he'll get to decide what to do with you."

"You're working with Jae? You can both fuck right off."

His eyes raked over me, making my skin crawl. "You didn't know? He's owned you since your sweet stepmother sold you to him years ago."

"No. That's not true. I owe him a debt, but it wasn't like that."

He laughed cruelly and reached into his jacket, pulling out a syringe like the one I'd used before. An almost empty syringe. My blood turned to ice. Had that been used on the king?

"Silly girl. Jae gets to decide if he wants to keep you or sell you to someone else. I hope you've had fun pretending to be a human," he said, "because that all ends now."

"Let me go," I said, trying to wrench myself away from him.

"Shut up," he said, "or else I'll use what's left in my syringe on you."

"What?"

"It won't be enough to kill you. Just like it wasn't enough to kill that idiot king. I was just told to create a distraction."

"It was you. You injected Rand with that drug?"

"That's enough talking," he snarled. "I'll carry you the rest of the way."

"Wait, what?"

Then I felt a sharp pain in my neck. I stumbled forward, but he held me in front of him, and from the corner of my eye, I could see that he'd stabbed me with that same syringe. My vision started to swim as the drug began to take effect, my head spinning.

"You thought you could run away from your family, didn't you, Elizabeth?"

No one had called me that in years. Not since I left Eden.

And I didn't plan on anyone ever calling me that again.

Without warning, I mustered all the strength I could, lifted my foot, and stomped down hard on his with my heel. He let out a shout of pain, his grip loosening for just a moment.

That was all I needed.

With a swift movement, I pulled away from him, breaking free of his hold. My heart was in my throat as I sprinted down the stairs, my legs like jelly, but I forced myself to go on. The clatter of the syringe on the stone stairs, the echo of his curses, and the pounding of his footsteps chased behind me. I screamed, hoping the noise would draw someone's attention, anyone's attention at this point.

Reaching the bottom of the stairs, I spotted the exit. My legs ached and I could hardly see, but I pushed myself harder, desperate to reach the outside. As I burst through the door, the humid night air hit me like a physical force, but before I could take a breath, I ran straight into something—or someone—solid.

I looked up, my eyes widening in horror as I realized who it was. Jae, his face twisted into a sinister snarl, eyes gleaming with malice.

"Going somewhere, pet?"

I tried to back away, but he was too fast and I was too slow. His hand shot out, gripping my arm with a strength that left no room for escape. Panic surged through me, and I lashed out, clawing at his face, kicking at his legs, anything to get away.

"Feisty, aren't you?" He chuckled.

With a sudden, terrifying strength, he scooped me up, his arms like steel bands around me. I struggled wildly, my screams echoing in the night, but he only tightened his grip, laughing at my feeble attempts to break free.

He slapped a hand over my mouth to muffle my screams, but I saw Jae's eyes flick to Patrick, who was limping out of the palace, his face twisted in anger and confusion. Jae's lips curled into a cold smile.

"He's all yours, guys," Jae called out.

Almost immediately, the sound of footsteps approached, and a group of guards, faces stern and weapons drawn, rounded the corner. Their eyes were fixed on Patrick, and it was clear they were under Jae's command.

"That man there," Jae said, his voice dripping with authority as he pointed at Patrick. "He is the one who attempted to murder the king. Seize him."

The guards didn't hesitate. They surged forward and grabbed Patrick, who let out a cry of protest and disbelief. But his words were drowned out by Jae's laughter as he watched the man who'd once been his ally being dragged away.

"It's a cruel world, Patrick," Jae called out, his voice filled with mock sympathy. "But then you should have known that."

27

MAX

The stone walls of the palace dungeon oozed with decay. Blood stained the floor, and my boot heels kept sticking to the floor in gods knew what as I strode toward the human slumped over and chained to a chair. The guards had done their job locking down the ballroom, and only a few guests had managed to leave before all the doors were sealed. One guest, Mr. Patrick Samuelson, a human from Eden, had not managed to escape at all.

And I doubted he ever would.

Kal signaled for me to join him at the door to the cell where he waited with Sam. I'd filled the two of them in on what was happening, and they'd arrived in an instant, just in time for the guards to have detained the very man we were looking for. Sam knew a couple of the guards from when he was a kid living on the street, and thanks to him, I now had some alone time with the prisoner.

"He's confessed to having the syringe used on His Majesty," Kal told me. "The guards are essentially done with their interrogation, so take your time. They'll handle any cleanup later."

"If he hurt Miss Lilly, I'll kill him myself," Sam added.

"We will await your instructions, sir," Kal said, bowing slightly.

"Perfect."

I shrugged off my red jacket. I wasn't a Knight of the Flame right now.

I was the flame.

While I chose a weapon from the table Kal had so neatly prepared for me, the blond man's head lolled to the side, his eye swollen, his cheek marred by a jagged gash. His hair was already matted with sweat, his chest heaving with panicked breaths.

Wrapping my tail around one leg of the chair, I yanked it forward and the man fell out onto the hard ground with a thud. I crouched down in front of him, scanning his face. "I'm going to bet this isn't where you thought your night was going, is it?"

Patrick's eyes fluttered open, his gaze glassy with pain and fear. Good. Fear I could work with.

"Who... Who are you?"

"Someone very interested in a woman named Lilly," I said. "Does that name sound familiar?"

He mumbled something I couldn't understand.

"Tell me where she is and I'll kill you quickly."

Patrick swallowed hard. "That fucking... bastard."

I curled my fingers around the hilt of my dagger, unsheathing the blade in a whisper of metal on metal.

"Who?"

"Jae."

"He has Lilly?" The tip of the knife caressed his throat, and as soon as it cut into his flesh, a small flame appeared. Patrick yelped as the fiery blade singed his skin.

His eyes snapped up to look at me, and I took away the blade. It was still hot in my hand, but I ignored it.

"...fucking bastard. I'll talk... I'll tell you... Just... please."

"Hurry up."

"The daughter." Patrick panted, his eyes wide as he stared at the dagger. "I was supposed to get the daughter. Then no one could help... the king."

"Who told you to do that? Jae?"

"No. The old lady. Thornfield. She wants her... She wants her back home. Said if we caused a distraction and took her, we could use her."

I pressed the dagger tip under his chin again, and now that the blade had grown hotter, blisters instantly bubbled up on his skin. Patrick writhed, desperate to get away. I grabbed him by the collar of his shirt and yanked him up so he was inches away from me.

"I want names, details, locations—everything you've still got in here." I pressed my blade against his forehead, and a thin line of blood ran down from where it had cut into his skin. "You already know you're not walking out of here, but if you lie to me again, I will make sure your death is not quick or painless."

Patrick sobbed under my grasp as he gave me every detail he knew, including who sent him on the mission to kidnap her, Lady Thornfield's current whereabouts, and even where her estate was located. The ultimate goal was to assassinate the king if Rand wouldn't cave to their demands to make Dust legal again.

These humans were working with a demon here, funneling drugs through his nightclubs. I didn't need to torture this pathetic human to know exactly which demon that was.

I touched my earpiece. "Blaise, did you hear all this?"

"I'm already on it."

"Find him. Find her. Now."

28

MAX

The Red Rose's front door splintered under my kick, shards of wood raining onto the floor.

"Jae!" I roared into the darkness. "Show yourself, you coward!"

That weasel had taken Lilly, I was certain of it. And I would tear this place apart if that's what it took to find her.

I overturned tables, shattered liquor bottles, ripped down curtains. The debris did nothing to abate my rage over Lilly going missing from the palace tonight. And Jae's smug face swam before me, taunting.

Finally a figure emerged from the back rooms. Jae held up his hands with a slimy grin. "We're closed tonight since most of our guests would be at the palace."

I clenched my jaw so hard it ached. "Where is she?"

Jae examined his nails, his expensive rings shining. "You'll have to be more specific. I know so many lovely ladies."

"I swear, if you've hurt her…" My voice was a venomous hiss.

"You'll what? Really, Max, what are you pretending to be now?" he drawled. "The hero, here to rescue the girl? I'm supposed to send her back home, but if you want to make me an offer instead, I'm listening. You'd be surprised at what she can do. Or maybe you already know."

In two strides I had his throat in my grip and slammed him back against the wall. His silver eyes bulged as he choked for breath.

Jae clawed at my hand. "She... left... willingly," he rasped.

Jae's face purpled. His heels drummed against the wall as he fought for air.

"Enough!" he wheezed. "Let me... explain..."

Reluctantly I loosened my hold. Jae collapsed, coughing violently. As he struggled to regain his breath, hatred simmered in my gut.

"Talk," I snarled.

Jae massaged his bruised throat. "Your pretty pet agreed to entertain a client tonight. Left here smiling, eager for her payday." He smirked. "Can't blame a girl for chasing a big tipper. Especially one so... desperate."

Lies. I tightened my hold, rage coursing through me like fire. If Lilly was gone, this bastard was to blame. And I would see him suffer for it.

My fist cracked across Jae's jaw, sending him sprawling. I stood over him, trembling with rage.

"You're lying. Lilly would never—"

"Wouldn't she?" Jae dabbed at his split lip. "Face it, she's no innocent. Do you even know what she's capable of doing? I did her a favor by letting her work here and pretend to live a normal life. If she'd been sold to someone else, who even knows—"

"Sold?"

"The girl has fae blood. I thought you must already know that or you wouldn't be so mad. Not much of it apparently since she can only do a little pathetic healing, but who's counting? Her family sold her to me years ago."

That wasn't at all the story Lilly had told me. She'd said that she left her family with Jae to prevent being sold. Yet all along, she'd already been owned?

With a guttural cry, I launched myself at him. We crashed into a table, smashing it beneath us. Glass shattered. Jae clawed at my face; I drove an elbow into his ribs. We rolled across the floor, trading blows.

Jae was slick as oil, but the haze of fury gave me strength. I pinned him beneath me, fingers tightening on his windpipe once more. As the life drained from his eyes, my lips peeled back in a savage grin.

"Where... is... she?" Each word was a snarl.

Jae just laughed, the sound rough and grating. "Wouldn't you like to know?"

With a howl, I seized him by the collar and hurled him across the room. He crashed through a doorway into the back storeroom, collapsing in a heap amid shattered crates and boxes.

I stalked after him, grabbing a bottle of liquor from the wreckage. Jae's eyes widened as I lifted it high.

"Wait, I'll tell you!" he cried, throwing up his hands. "I told the client about you and her! He wasn't too happy his favorite plaything had a lover on the side. They want her back in Eden so they can sell her to someone else."

The bottle came down hard, exploding in a spray of glass and alcohol. Jae slumped bonelessly to the floor.

I stared down at his motionless form, chest heaving. Then I reached into my pocket, pulling out a few of Blaise's new knives.

Four should be more than enough.

Twirling them in my hand, I contemplated my options. I threw the first one across the room—the flame started instantly. So Blaise had made improvements.

I hurled another knife across the deserted club, its blade bursting into flames midair. It sank into the velvet curtains, igniting them the second it touched. Orange tongues licked up the fabric, adding to the fires already raging around me. The empty liquor bottles exploded one by one as the heat intensified.

I let the third knife fly, using my rage to fuel my flames. It spun end over end, trailing embers before slamming into a wooden beam. Timbers creaked and groaned as fire spread through them. The club was becoming an inferno, but my wrath demanded more fuel.

Sweat poured down my face from the oppressive heat. I tore off my shirt and threw it into the flames. Everything would burn tonight, just as Jae deserved to burn.

My last knife struck the DJ booth, exploding into a fireball that consumed the equipment and melted records into bubbling plastic. Flaming debris rained down as part of the ceiling collapsed with an earsplitting crack.

The fire now raged fully out of control, surrounding me in a vortex of heat and blinding smoke. But I had eyes only for the fiery destruction, vengeance coursing through my veins. Tonight Jae would pay the price for everything he had ever done to Lilly. And this club would burn to ash around him.

I was about to leave it all behind me when I heard a noise upstairs.

29

LILLY

The acrid smoke stung my eyes before I even opened them. I coughed and gagged, my lungs burning as I tried to suck in fresh air that wasn't there. I was still woozy from the small amount of the drug that had been injected into me, but with each passing minute, I seemed to come back to my senses.

It was so hot.

I tried moving my arms, but my wrists chafed against the coarse rope that tied me to a chair. Jae's office. At the Red Rose. That's where I was. Like hell I was going to die in this miserable place. I couldn't remember how I'd gotten there, but I could tell from the abnormal heat that I needed to get the fuck out immediately, if not sooner.

Smoke trickled under the closed door, an ominous orange glow seeping into the room.

Shit. This was bad. Very bad.

I thrashed against my bonds, but the ropes only pulled tighter. "Help!" I screamed. I tried yelling a few more times, but my cries were lost in the roar of the inferno. Sweat dripped down my back as the sweltering office filled with oily smoke. I couldn't breathe. My head spun, my vision blurring. The Red Rose was burning, and if I didn't figure this out, I was going to burn right along with it.

No. I wouldn't let that bastard and his club win, not when I'd survived here this long. With a burst of adrenaline, I lunged against the ropes, ignoring the pain as they scraped my wrists raw. The chair creaked but held firm. I was sobbing now, choking on the black smoke that poured under the door. The fire was almost to me, and if I didn't pull off a miracle quickly, I was going to be out of time.

The flames were at the door, ready to consume me. I sagged back, defeated.

Was that it? Was I going to die here, tied up like an animal while Jae's empire burned down around me? After everything I'd survived, this was how it ended?

The door exploded inward with a deafening bang, torn from its hinges. A dark figure stood silhouetted in the doorway, backlit by the raging fire. Shirtless, his massive black wings spread wide.

It was Max.

He strode through the doorway, eyes glowing silver in the smoke. I was so stunned I could barely speak as he hurried over and sliced through my bonds with a flick of a knife.

"You came for me."

"Of course I did." His voice was gruff as he hauled me from the chair. The fire raged closer, surrounding us. "Now let's get the hell out of here."

Max wrapped an arm around my waist, shielding me with his body and wings as flames licked at our feet. The entire building seemed to tremble, beams crashing down around us. We had seconds to escape before the ceiling gave way.

But it didn't matter. Max held me close, muscles taut, and I clung to him, my face pressed against his bare, smoke-scented chest. His arms encircled me tightly, and I could feel his rapid heartbeat, but there was something else. I leaned back to look at him, gasping at the sight.

"You..."

Angry red burns covered his chest and neck, blistering the skin. His arms, usually so strong, were mottled with charred patches where the flames had licked his flesh. Even the tops of his wings were singed, the edges crumbling away.

He must have sensed my thoughts, because he held me tighter against him. I looked up at him, and even though everything was crashing around us, the entire building in flames, Max smiled.

He smiled.

"Good thing I'm in love with a healer."

His wings flared out, and with inhuman strength, he leaped through the wall of fire. I buried my face in his chest as we burst through flames and smoke, the inferno raging all around us. But Max didn't falter. He kept going until finally we erupted from the burning building and tumbled to the ground.

We lay in a gasping, coughing heap on the pavement. In the distance, sirens wailed. Max's wings were charred, his body and hair smelling of smoke. But his arms stayed wrapped protectively around me.

Max's thumb brushed over my cheek, and I realized I was still crying. Everything we'd been through hit me in a rush—the terror of the fire, the relief of his rescue. I pressed my palms to his chest, needing to feel his solid strength.

"Lilly..." Max's voice was a strained rasp. His eyes searched mine with an intensity that stole my breath.

In answer, I leaned forward and crushed my mouth to his. The kiss was desperate, hungry, saying everything I couldn't put into words. How much I needed him. How he meant everything to me now.

Our lips moved together slowly, exploring each other with a gentle tenderness. I ran my hands over his bare skin, feeling the burns and cuts the fire had left behind. I wanted to heal him, to make it all better. Max's hand cupped the back of my head as he deepened the kiss, and I felt myself melting into his embrace. The flames were forgotten—there was only us now.

Max groaned softly as I pulled away, my lips still tingling. He reached out and touched my face, his eyes burning. "Do it."

I smiled and nodded, then placed my hands over his chest. I

closed my eyes, focusing on the warmth of his skin beneath me. Gently I drew out the heat from his burns, calming the angry red marks on his skin. I moved lower to his neck and arms, feeling every inch of him as I worked to heal him with my magic. My palms glided over the contours of his body as if memorizing him for eternity—his broad shoulders, strong back, tight stomach muscles... Even beneath the scars from battle and fire, Max was beautiful in every way.

I let the warmth of my healing magic flow through me, stronger than I'd ever felt before, marveling at how it spread across Max's body. I touched every inch of his skin, tracing patterns on his arms, neck, and torso with my fingertips. I could feel him tensing beneath my touch, his wings shuddering in pleasure. His chest vibrated against mine in a gentle purr as the heat of my magic soothed away the pain and replaced it with a pleasant tingle.

The burns on his skin slowly disappeared as I worked, though some left behind faint pinkish scars that would probably remain forever. My fingertips grazed his chest, feeling the lingering traces of heat from where the fire had burned him. But as I continued to heal him, even those disappeared, and soon there was no sign that Max had been injured at all.

Max made a rough sound, clutching me tighter. Our lips moved together until finally we broke apart, both breathing hard.

"I thought I'd lost you," Max murmured.

"I'm here." I smoothed back his hair. "We're together. That's all that matters now."

He nodded, the tension leaving his body. The sirens neared, but for now it was just us. The demon who came through fire to save me. And me, the human who now knew she could not live without him.

30

MAX

My footsteps echoed on the stone floor as I made my way through the palace. All I could hope was that my crisp uniform hid how tired I felt. A smug grin crept across my face as I thought of Lilly these past few nights, safe in my penthouse, safe in my bed.

It was worth every yawn.

In the weeks after the fire, my life had become delightfully domestic, and I wouldn't have it any other way. The sight of Lilly's bare thighs peeking out from under my oversized shirts as she made us coffee, kisses when I somehow managed to tear myself away from her—she had changed my world in the best way possible.

I found Rand's study and slipped inside. Not surprisingly, Rand wasn't there yet, but our guests were.

"Am I late? What'd I miss?" I asked as I flopped down in Rand's chair behind his desk.

The woman sitting on the other side of the desk stared at me wide-eyed. Marion Thornfield was in her late sixties, but her appearance spoke of someone who had gone to great lengths to retain the illusion of youth. Her blond hair, streaked with artificial gold, was rigidly styled in a way that matched the severe expression etched onto her face. Her skin was stretched taut, no doubt the result of countless treatments and procedures, giving her a doll-like but unnatural look.

This was the woman who had once planned to sell Lilly, her own stepdaughter, as a fae slave.

"Who are you?" she asked. "Where is the king?"

She stayed completely still. Her eyes, cold and calculating were the eyes of someone who was used to getting her way, someone who would stop at nothing to achieve her goals. Those eyes narrowed as they met mine, as if trying to dissect and analyze what lay beneath the surface.

I shrugged and leaned back in the chair, kicking my feet up onto Rand's desk. "Who knows? Probably doing king things."

"I'm sure he is very busy, of course." Marion Thornfield smiled, but there was no warmth in her smile, no genuine emotion in her voice. Everything about her seemed rehearsed and insincere, from the way she held her teacup to the polite but empty words that flowed from her lips.

She was dressed in a tailored suit of the finest silk, its dark hue contrasting sharply with the pearls that adorned her throat. The earrings and matching bracelets sparkled along with the rings on her fingers. They seemed almost garish in their opulence. Every movement she made was accentuated by the glitter of diamonds, the clinking of expensive jewelry.

"Will he be available soon?"

I laced my hands behind my head. "Unfortunately, you're stuck with me at the moment."

Marion looked taken aback by my words. She stared at me for a few moments before finally nodding. I could tell she was trying to make sense of this new development; no doubt she'd expected Rand himself would be present for their conversation.

"Very well," she said finally. She cleared her throat and began to speak again. Her voice was strong and assertive with a commanding edge. "I have recently had several of my company's deliveries to Vestia returned. It appears that customs is now refusing all Thornfield's shipments, citing unspecified errors in the paperwork as the reason for their refusal. I want to know," Marion continued, her voice becoming more forceful with each word, "why our shipments are being refused and who is responsible." Her eyes narrowed as she looked at me expectantly. "I demand an answer from Rand immediately."

"*King* Rand," I said.

"Yes?" All eyes in the room suddenly focused on the doorway as I heard my friend, our king's, voice resonate through the air. Marion and I both stood as Rand entered the room, tall and imposing in his full regal robes, crown on his head, his long cloak draping on the floor behind him. The king stepped farther into the room, moving slowly but surely with an air of confidence that radiated from his every gesture.

He only spared a brief glance at Marion, taking in details with a single glance; Marion's imperious demeanor, her expensive clothing, and my own relaxed posture. His brow furrowed as he looked directly at me, and I gave him a small nod to acknowledge his presence. I moved out from behind his desk to give him space but stayed standing, not wanting to get closer to Marion than I had to.

"You two were talking about me?" Rand asked, taking a seat.

Marion sat back down in her chair, immediately launching into her complaints again, her attention firmly fixed on Rand in a way that showed she did not expect to be challenged. "Yes. Everything we are trying to sell has been turned away by Vestia, and I demand an answer as to why."

Demand, huh? I tried to hide a smirk. This was going to get interesting.

Rand simply nodded, his golden crown dipping slightly. "I understand your concern, Lady Thornfield." He leaned forward, placing his elbows on his desk. "All my information tells me that Thornfield Enterprises has always kept selling at the top of its priorities."

"Certainly," she said, as if relieved that Rand was finally understanding. "Thornfield Enterprises has always been one of Vestia's closest trading partners."

"Indeed. Then why the fuck did you decide it would be a good idea to kill me?"

The question startled Marion, and she jumped back in her seat as if she had been struck. Her face drained of color, and I saw her hands start to tremble.

"What?" She sprang from her chair, looking between the two of us with fear clearly etched on her features. "What is the meaning of this? How dare you... I mean, Your Majesty, how can you accuse me... Your Majesty, I..."

"Max." Rand gestured to the entrance, and in an instant I was there, leaning against the heavy wooden doors in case she tried to leave the room.

Rand stayed in his seat at his desk, his face hard and solemn. For one of the first times, I realized how well he had taken on the role of king, how here in this moment, he really did exude an aura of authority. "Let's be frank here, shall we? You conspired with Jae Balakir to financially back an assassination attempt, and you had him kidnap your stepdaughter and attempt to bring her back to Eden where she would officially be his slave."

Rand's accusation was met with nothing but silence as Marion stared wide-eyed at Rand and then back at me. She opened her mouth to speak, but no words came out.

"I don't know what you think you know," Marion said eventually, and I could tell she was trying her best to sound offended. "I won't stand for this. You have no proof."

"That's where you're wrong, Lady Thornfield. My informants have confirmed your involvement in Balakir's plot from start to finish. Isn't that right, Max?"

It gave me great pleasure to watch the look on her face. "The ugly bastard admitted to all of it before he died."

Marion's composure crumbled instantly, her legs shaking as if she might break down at any moment. Tears welled up in her eyes, and the color drained from her face. She sank slowly into her chair, unable to look either of us in the eye. After a few moments of silence, she finally spoke up.

"I... You're right," she admitted in a small voice, tears streaming down her cheeks now. "Your Majesty... please forgive me..."

"Save the dramatics," Rand said, waving a hand in the air. "I really don't give a shit if you apologize to me or not, because it won't change anything. But there's someone else you need to apologize to. Max, will you?" Rand signaled to me to open the doors, and I did, letting in several guards who walked straight to Marion Thornfield, cuffing her before she could protest.

"Max, will you bring in my guest?"

"It would be my pleasure."

31

LILLY

Could I do this?

Could I really go in there and face her?

I clenched and unclenched my hands for the thousandth time as I waited in the hallway with three of Rand's guards. In the days since the fire, I'd grown more and more used to being around them; Max dragged me to the palace with him frequently under the guise of going to "meet with the king," which I was pretty sure was just a chance to parade me in front of his friend since none of those meetings were more than casual conversations.

But not today.

Today *she* was in a meeting with him. The woman I'd hated for years was on the other side of those heavy wooden doors, and even the thought of her filled me with a mix of dread and anger.

The door opened, and Max stepped out, his face calm and reassuring. He took my hand, giving it a gentle squeeze.

"Are you ready?" he asked, his eyes filled with concern.

I looked up at him, feeling a surge of strength and confidence. With Max at my side, I could do this. I could face her.

"Yes," I said, my voice steady. "I'm ready."

He led me into the room, and my breath caught in my throat at the sight of Marion. She was just as I remembered her, her face taut and unnatural, her eyes cold and calculating. But now there was something else in her eyes, something desperate and wild.

"You!" she screamed, lunging at me. "You ruined everything! This is your fault, Elizabeth."

Max pulled me behind him, and the guards grabbed Marion, restraining her.

Her face twisted with rage as a steady stream of hate spewed from her lips. "You little witch! You did this, didn't you? You and your filthy fae blood! I should have sold you when I had the chance!"

I could feel the bile rising in my throat at her words, the memories of the years of abuse and cruelty flooding back. But I wasn't that scared little girl anymore. I was strong. I was powerful. And I was not alone.

"Marion," I said, my voice firm as I moved away from Max and closer to her. "You did this to yourself. Whatever you got yourself involved in, you did this, not me."

Her eyes narrowed, her face contorting with hate. "You ungrateful brat! After everything I've done for you! I raised you, and this is how you repay me? Your father would be ashamed of you."

Something inside me snapped, and I stepped forward, slapping her across the face. Her head snapped to the side, and the room fell silent.

Damn.

That had felt great.

"You could always do that again," Max offered. "I'm not stopping you."

"I won't either," Rand added. "But since she brought up your father..." Rand got up from his desk and came around the front of it, taking out two sets of paper from his pocket and unfolding it. "Do you know what these are?"

Marion shook her head. Rand gestured for me to come over, and as I skimmed over both, a lump formed in the pit of my stomach.

"That one is... a bill of sale." I felt sick. "With my name on it. And... Jae's."

I wasn't sure if I could keep standing. I wasn't sure if I could keep breathing. It was all too much...

She'd really tried to sell me. Technically she had, like her own stepdaughter was a piece of property, an object to be traded and owned. The idea was so abhorrent, so unthinkable, that it made me physically ill. A wave of nausea rolled over me, my stomach twisting into painful knots.

But then, out of the corner of my eye, I saw Max stride over and yank the document from Rand's hands before ripping it into pieces.

"It never existed," he said, his voice hard and unrelenting. He held the pieces in his hands and touched his wrist, the paper catching fire and burning in his hands.

It crumbled to ash, and Max let the black specks fall onto the carpet.

Max's eyes then met mine, filled with a fiery determination and an unspoken promise. Without hesitation, he closed the distance between us and enveloped me in a strong, comforting hug. His arms were warm and secure, a stark contrast to the cold reality of what had just been revealed. My body was trembling, a mixture of anger, betrayal, and shock threatening to overwhelm me, but Max's embrace anchored me.

"Perfect." Rand's voice brought us back to reality. "Now that that's out of the way, we have one more. What is this one?" He handed me the rest of the papers.

Did I even want to know? I wasn't sure.

Forcing my hands to stop shaking, I took the papers from him. "My father's will."

"You got it."

"That's probably a fake," Marion hissed.

"I'll add accusing the king of lying to your crimes. Lilly, would you read this part right here?" Rand pointed to the bottom of the first page.

"By virtue of the last will and testament of Lord Edward Thorn-field," I read aloud, my voice growing stronger as I continued, "I hereby bequeath Thornfield Enterprises and all its associated holdings, properties, and assets to my lawful heirs."

I paused for a moment, glancing at Marion's face. Her eyes were wide, and her complexion had gone from pale to white as a sheet. She knew what that meant as well as I did.

"Lilly, do you have any brothers or sisters?"

"No, Your Majesty."

"So you are the sole heir of Thornfield Enterprises now." Rand paused for a moment, giving us all time to take it in. I could hardly believe it was true, and my heart began to race with anticipation.

"Marion Thornfield," Rand said slowly, his voice now heavy with authority. "If you haven't guessed it by the handcuffs on your wrists, your stewardship of Thornfield Enterprises is hereby terminated. We'll put the company under the governance of Vestia since it's such an important trading partner for our kingdom." His words dripped with venom. "I'll give Lilly some time to consider what she wants to do. Although I will hate to lose the newest royal doctor if she chooses to go into business instead."

"Your..." Had I heard him right? "Your what?"

"This is outrageous." Marion was still arguing, even with the guards pulling her out of the room. "She is a slave!"

"You're still here?" Rand asked her. "I thought you realized we were done with you."

The guards dragged Marion out of the room, her protests growing fainter as the doors closed behind her. The room was filled with a heavy silence, a mixture of shock and relief. I turned to look at Rand, still trying to process what he had just said.

"Your Majesty," I stammered, "did you just say 'royal doctor'?"

Rand's face broke into a smile, and he came over and placed a reassuring hand on my shoulder. "I did."

"But I don't understand," I said, feeling a whirlwind of emotions. "Why would you want me as the royal doctor? I'm not trained or anything..."

"You have a gift, Lilly," Rand said, his voice sincere. He glanced at Max. "I'm not one to waste gifts. You have skills and knowledge that would benefit not only me but the entire kingdom. We'll get you some training, you'll take a few classes, it will be great."

I looked at Max, searching for support, and he smiled, giving me a nod of encouragement.

"Lilly," Max said softly, "you deserve this opportunity. And I believe in you."

Rand chuckled. "And I'll look good for having someone other than a demon in my cabinet."

I felt a lump in my throat, overwhelmed by their faith in me. All my years living in Vestia, I'd been made to feel worthless, weak, and incapable. Now there were people who saw something in me, who believed in me.

"Your Majesty," I finally said, tears welling in my eyes.

"I've told you a hundred times that when it's just us, you can call me Rand."

I shook my head. "Not when I'm accepting a job."

Rand's silver eyes lit up. "So you're accepting?"

"It would be an honor to serve as a royal doctor, Your Majesty."

Rand's smile widened, and he pulled me into a warm embrace, his black wings wrapping around me. "Welcome to the royal family then."

"Um, excuse me? Hello?" Max's voice broke through.

When I broke away from Rand, there was Max, his arms crossed, a look of mock indignation on his face. "What about me? Don't I get a hug?"

"A Knight of the Flame complaining about not getting a hug." Rand shook his head and held out his arms as if to hug Max. "Come here, you big baby."

"I don't want one from you." Max ignored him and scooped me into his arms, twirling me around before setting me down.

As Rand and Max escorted me out of the room, I glanced back at the heavy wooden doors, reflecting on everything that had just happened.

The door to the past had closed, and the path to the future lay wide open.

32

LILLY

Max's hands covered my eyes as he led me down a deserted road. His familiar scent, one I'd grown used to in the months since the fire, enveloped me—smoke and spice, earthy and comforting even though I couldn't see where we were going. He'd had my eyes covered the entire time he'd flown us here; we were out of the city, but that was as much as I knew.

The crunch of gravel underneath our shoes was the only sound in the silent night.

"Your hands feel soft against my face," I said.

"Because you spoil me now that I have someone who can heal me whenever I want. Maybe I should be more reckless. Train extra hard. Learn some new weapons."

"Sounds like you're just making more work for me. Plus I don't think Blaise will be happy about more work either."

Max chuckled. "You're right. I think he has his hands full lately with a new human assistant I found for him. If he can keep her from stealing his toys."

"Wait... do you mean Charlee? She's working for Blaise? She hasn't told me that."

But then again, I rarely saw her now that I was living with Max.

"We're here," he said instead of answering, his lips brushing against my ear, the vibration from his voice sending a delicious shiver down my spine.

He removed his hands, and I blinked at the dimly lit warehouse looming in front of us.

"What is this?"

"Your surprise." Max grinned, eyes full of mischief. He nudged me forward and pulled open one of the metal doors.

I stepped inside, my heart pounding. The huge warehouse was empty except for—

"Why is there an airplane?" When I looked closer at the sleek private jet in the middle of the building, I had even more questions. "That's not just any airplane, is it? That's the royal seal."

"Rand owed me." Max turned toward me and took both my hands in his. "It's for you." Max's voice was soft beside me. "I had Charlee pack some bags for you, and they're on the plane. I've already told the pilot you'll be flying to Cambria tonight, the port town you've always wanted to see. You can stay as long as you'd like; Rand knows and he'll deal with it."

Cambria. I stared at the plane, stunned into silence. He'd remembered. After all these months, he still remembered the postcard I'd kept and the place I wanted to see.

"Or if you don't like that, you can go anywhere you want. You just have to tell the pilot."

Warmth flooded my chest, and I turned to Max. But before I could say a word, he captured my lips in a searing kiss that left me breathless. I searched his silver eyes, looking for any hint that there was some catch here. But there wasn't.

Max shifted on his feet, his tail swinging behind him. "I'm not asking anything of you," he said. "I... Lilly, just want you to do something... for yourself."

I swallowed the lump in my throat and forced a teasing smile. "And what will you be doing while I sightsee? If I really like it there, I might never come back."

Max's wings drooped behind him. "I'm not sure actually. Rand granted me the use of this plane, but there was actually something much larger that I asked for."

"Oh really? What?"

"Lilly, I quit."

"What!"

Max shrugged. "Sam and Kal are going to work for Blaise instead. That grumpy bastard will do fine. I closed up shop officially; closed all my accounts and transferred money into a new bank account that isn't in my name. I'm going to make a fresh start. Who knows? I'll have to find a boring, normal job, I guess. A boring, normal job where I can do what I want with who I want."

I didn't even know what to say.

I held up a hand. "Wait. Did you say you transferred it into a new bank account in someone else's name?"

"Yeah."

"Are you crazy? What if they spend it all? Or keep it for themselves? Have you lost your mind? Who on earth do you trust enough to have access to all of your money?"

His silver eyes searched mine for a moment before he spoke. "You."

"I'm sorry— What?"

"It's all yours. This isn't a threat or something I'm holding over you. There are no strings attached to it. I don't even want the money anymore. It's yours. I love you, but you can leave me and go do whatever you want. If that's what you want. All I want is for you to be happy, Lilly. I hope that means you're with me, but—"

"You're ridiculous, you know that?"

"I do try my best." Max pretended to examine his nails modestly. Then he glanced up at me through his lashes, silver eyes gleaming. "So? Do you like your present?"

I rose up on my toes and brushed my lips over his. "Thank you," I whispered. "And I love you too. But..."

"But? No, you're not allowed to say 'but' after that."

I chuckled. "*But* it's a shame that first thing I'm going to have to spend all my money on is new clothes for you, because I'm pretty sure my clothes won't fit you."

Max's tail thumped against the ground, and I knew I'd said the right thing.

His arms came around me, drawing me close against his chest. I could feel his heart beating in time with my own. "You're welcome, darling. But the night's still young—we have a whole trip ahead of us yet." He grinned down at me, eyes glinting with promise. "Ready for the adventure of a lifetime?"

Arm in arm, we walked up the stairs into the lavish cabin. Plush leather seats and polished wood gleamed in the low lights. It looked more like a luxury lounge than an airplane interior.

As the engines rumbled to life, Max and I settled on the couch by the window. My skin tingled with the knowledge that soon I would finally fulfill my dream of seeing that fabled port town perched on the cliffs above the sea.

I snuggled against Max's shoulder as the plane accelerated down the runway. Together we gazed out at the receding lights of Vestia. Though there were bittersweet memories here, our future lay ahead.

When we touched down again, it would be in Cambria. A chance to explore a new place, our bond now stronger than ever. This plane would carry us toward the next chapter in our life together, full of hope and possibility.

Wherever Max was, I had found home.

THE STORY DOESN'T END HERE! We can't let Max and Lilly have all the fun, not when their friends Charlee and Blaise still need to find love. To find out what happens next for our little thief and big blacksmith, be sure to read *Desired by Fire*, Book Two in the Claimed by Flames series.

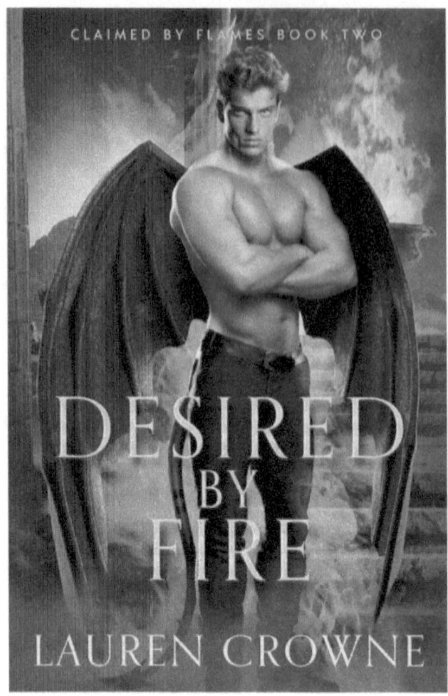

I also have a completed three-book series that starts with *Sold to the Demon Prince*, now available wherever you get your books. Check it out!

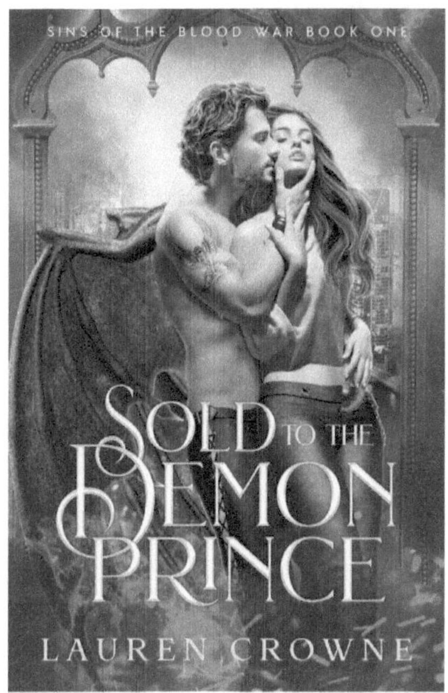

If you enjoyed this book, please leave a review. These reviews help new readers find my stories.

Want to receive updates on new books and sneak peeks? Sign up for my newsletter at http://www.laurencrowne.com.

THE END

ACKNOWLEDGMENTS

THANK YOU, readers! All the hugs, kisses, and high fives are owed to you, my amazing readers. You're the reason why I keep writing, and I can't thank you enough for picking up this book. Please reach out on my socials to let me know what you thought of Max and Lilly's story. I can't wait to hear.

As always, I want to thank my husband for his support during the process of working on this book. He makes me coffee, keeps me fed, and tries his best to keep the kids from driving me crazy while I'm tapping away on my laptop. He's my sounding board and brainstormer, and I would be lost without him.

Finally, this book would not have been possible without Anne and Crystalle at Victory Editing, Heather at Book Cover Artistry, and Tori at Cruel Ink Editing. They're an amazing team, and I couldn't have done this without them.

ABOUT THE AUTHOR

Lauren Crowne writes sexy, funny, action-packed fantasy and paranormal romance, transporting readers into a world of fae, demons, wolf shifters, and more. She always dreamed of being an author, and she is delighted and honored to share the stories that have been bouncing around in her head for years. When she isn't writing, Lauren is addicted to drinking iced coffee and traveling with her husband and kids. You can find out more about her on Facebook, Instagram, and TikTok.